MW01714315

Dedicated to my mother, Dora; my father, Les; my sister, Marina; and my brother, Michael. For all the times that I made you listen to all my crazy ideas, I couldn't wish for a better family than the one that I have. Thank you for all your love and support.

- Dorothea Sawatzky

Mascot Books
560 Herndon Parkway #120
Herndon, VA 20170
info@mascotbooks.com

ISBN-10: 1620863448
ISBN-13: 9781620863442
CPSIA Code: PRW0613A

Printed in the United States

www.mascotbooks.com

Canvas of Dreams

Dorothea Sawatzky

MASCOT BOOKS

"There is no telling how many miles you will have to run while chasing a dream."

-Unknown

Chapter 1

Promise

Dear Journal, *July 5, 1902*

I sometimes question why the world works in the mysterious ways that it does, and why such terrible things happen to great people. On this day God has taken my wife, Cecilia, from me and rejoiced her with her beloved family in heaven. Despite the fact that she is in a better place, she has also left me to fend for myself along with our ten-year-old daughter, Evangeline. I blame myself for her death because I was unable to provide my family with all our needs. I'm a man of little money, I did not inherit into wealth, and instead, I work with machinery on Dawson's Farm. I make little income and therefore my family is constantly on the move, we are considered lucky if we find shelter for the night. It kills me inside to see us live this life especially my sweet Evangeline. Cecilia died from cholera due to our lack of shelter. Cholera is an infectious disease that is caused from consuming water from contaminated water resources. I began to notice something was terribly wrong with her when her skin started to turn purple. It is said that cholera causes the blood circulation to slow which is the cause of the skins colour turning purple. My wife died from consuming water. I wasn't able to provide her with clean drinking water and therefore I am suffering for my poverty and my lack of success. I owe my daughter a chance at life and therefore I have written my very first journal entry to promise myself that I will introduce my daughter to success and provide her with clean water so she may live the life that Cecilia wasn't able to. There is a difference between a poor man and a rich man: When you have everything, losing one thing doesn't affect you entirely. However, when you have nothing, losing one thing can change your entire world. I'm a broken man but I will not give up now, my daughter needs me and I will give her what I can.

Sincerely,
Charles Welsh

Chapter 2

Shire Dale Academy

"Dad, how come we don't live in a house like everyone else?"

Sweet Evangeline's question cut him like a million knives stabbing at his heart. His daughter was still young and didn't understand why life worked the mysterious way that it did and sometimes, neither did Charles. The question remained unanswered as he struggled to find the proper answer for his daughter. He stopped walking and knelt down in front of her and placed her small hands in his palms. Cecilia had only passed away a few months ago and Evangeline had taken her death much better than Charles had expected her to. She was a strong little girl and with every passing day, she grew more courageous and more beautiful. Charles looked in her dazzling green eyes and answered her question, "People that live in big fancy houses make a lot more money than I do, sweetie. That is another reason why you're going to school today, because I want you to be able to live in a big fancy house one day, too. All of my income is going towards your education because I want nothing but the best for my little girl."

Evangeline gave a weary smile as she looked into his sad eyes. She was only ten years old but she already knew life better than the majority of Knaresborough. Knaresborough, North Yorkshire, England, is where

Charles and his daughter were living.

Evangeline grabbed her father's hand and continued their journey to her new school, Shire Dale Academy. Charles spent the last few months working two jobs so he would be able to place his daughter into Shire Dale. He was never given the opportunity to study and therefore he didn't want his daughter to miss it, too. Shire Dale was a boarding school for girls where they taught them all the essentials of life and advanced knowledge of English literature, mathematics, geography, and history. Evangeline was considered to be too old to enter at this time of the year but they made an exception because they saw potential in her. She was roomed with six other girls of the same age group. Evangeline was different than all of the other girls and could feel them glaring at her and whispering about her appearance.

"I threw those rags out a month ago; maybe I should tell my father to put a lock on our garbage to keep people from picking our trash," said Frances Scott.

Frances Scott's father owned a machinery company and was a wealthy person in Knaresborough. She had blonde curls that reached her elbows, skin pale as snow, and piercing brown eyes. People adored her beauty and therefore they failed to see the cruel remarks that she had for the poor. It was certain that she would never like Evangeline and that they would remain enemies. Evangeline didn't feel wanted at Shire Dale and missed her father already; she wondered what he was doing and if he missed her, too. It was times like these that a mother would have been really nice to have.

On the first day of school, all the girls did was get settled into their dorms and have one of the nuns show them around the school. The school was located in an old church and therefore every dorm had a nun that watched over the girls and taught them. In this case, they were located in dorm twelve and Sister Nelly was in charge of the girls. Class began at eight am; all the girls were given uniforms that they were required to wear. The uniform was a long sleeve shirt with a skirt that hung just below the knees. Evangeline had never owned proper clothing before and thought that it was strange how there was not a single rip or tear in the fabric. She pressed her hands over the polyester material and admired how it fit her so perfectly. She was mesmerized by the fluorescent blue colour of the uniform and it was the first time she ever owned a pair of shoes that wouldn't get her feet wet. All the girls had already made their way to class but Evangeline stayed behind for a few minutes unable to grasp the reality she was living. She sat on her bed and wondered how hard her father must have worked in order to get her into this school. Sadness swept over her and tears formed in her eyes. She held it back and remembered that she told herself she would not cry anymore, the last time she cried was when her mother had passed away.

"Excuse me, miss, but you must go to class now otherwise you will be late and will get punished."

Evangeline peered to the door where a little black girl stood. She wore dirty clothes and over it hung what once was a white apron. "Thank you," said Evangeline as she rose from her bed to make her way to mathematics.

When Evangeline entered the classroom, everyone had already seated themselves. She sat at the back of the classroom near the garbage.

"She must feel like she's at home with the aroma of the garbage right beside her." Frances spoke her words loud enough for Evangeline to hear but quiet enough for Sister Nelly not to hear.

The girls all giggled but refused to look to where she sat. Sister Nelly started the class off with simple fractions and worked her way to trigonometry. All the girls finished their assignments and spent the remainder of the class reading their independent reading novels. Everyone was done expect for Evangeline, she sat at her desk staring at the calculations she had written down on her notes. When everyone was dismissed from class, Evangeline remained seated in her chair as she was still struggling to figure out what the equations were.

Sister Nelly took a seat beside her and asked to see her papers. “Evangeline, you have never gone to school before, is that correct?” She nodded her head ashamed of her assignment. Sister Nelly sighed and continued to speak. “I can’t imagine what your assignments would look like if you had gone to school because you got every single question correct, my dear.”

Evangeline looked up in shock and smiled in relief. The entire class she thought she was doing something wrong but every time she re-did the equation she still ended up with the same answer. “I’m going to enjoy teaching you. Now go on before you are late for English.”

As she rose from her seat, Frances quickly went to class, too. She waited outside of the classroom and overheard the conversation. She snarled under her breath, “Two can play at that game, I’ll show her that garbage is meant to stay outside.” Frances was a very competitive young lady and she would stop at nothing to demolish any objects that stood in her way. She had been attending Shire Dale Academy for four years and this was the first time that anyone had scored a higher grade than her.

The second class of the day was English literature where the girls’ main focus was creative writing. Sister Nelly assigned the girls to create a writing piece which would describe who they are. Evangeline took interest in the subject but was uncertain how she would tell her story. Her life was rough and although they had little money, she still loved her life. It was a struggle sometimes to find shelter or proper meals but she was shown love like no other and that is what kept her on her feet. Her new life still felt so unreal; she was waiting for someone to wake her up and bring her back to reality. She considered writing a piece about herself being trapped in this make-believe world, this dream world, and how even in the most perfect places, things can still fall apart. In this case, her problem was Frances Scott, whose goal was to get rid of Evangeline no matter what the circumstances may be.

Chapter 3

Cecilia Welsh

Dear Journal, *November 8th 1902*

I enrolled my sweet Evangeline into Shire Dale approximately two months ago and I have not seen her since. I have the authority to go and see her but I cannot bring myself to it. I feel that I must do more for myself so that I may be able to provide her with all her necessities. It tore at my heart when she asked me about our living situation and why we could not stay at one place for more than just one night. I have made it my goal to give my daughter a reliable future and give her a place called "home." When my dear Cecilia died, I considered the extremes of joining her in the afterlife, I even made an attempt to jump off Shire Dale Academy's rooftop and that was when I had the brilliant idea of enrolling my daughter into the school. As I stood on the roof seeing all these young girls roaming around the school grounds, laughing and learning, it made me realize that just because my life has ended, my daughter's was just beginning. I grew up in a poor family and I suffered terribly throughout my life and then I married my true love and then I lost her along with my pride.

Cecilia grew up from a middle class family and I worked on their farm as their mechanic. She was three years younger than me and she was the most gorgeous woman I had ever seen. Although her life seemed perfect considering her family had money and she had beauty like no other, there was sadness in her eyes. I caught a glimpse of her one day as she was yelling at her father and stormed out of the house. He ordered me to go after her and as his employee, I followed his orders. At first, she fled amongst the field and slowed into a power walk. I found it hard to keep up with her but I managed. For a long time, I did not say a word to her or even try to call out to her, I was curious where her feet would take her, so instead I kept my distance but continued to follow her. She was well aware of my presence and for the longest time she did not say a word to me either. We were five miles away from her country home when finally she stopped walking and turned to face me. She walked towards me and grabbed my hand and said, "We don't have to go back; it can be just you and me from this moment on." She was so stunning; her smile took my breath away and left me speechless. My lips remained sealed as I was unable to respond to her out outrageous but yet wonderful plan. She tightened her grip and spoke again, "If we go back, you will just be my father's employee again and I will be engaged to Henry Beckem. I would rather die than marry that prick."

I stood motionless for a brief moment taking in the information that she was telling me. I searched her eyes for lies but only found sadness and bravery and it made me adore her even more. "I'm a poor man, Cecilia. I could not give you everything that Henry can. Running away with me would not be the smartest decision to make, as much as I adore you and care for you, I advise you to stay where you have a future."

She released my hands from her grip and turned away from me, "I envy those who are not born of money because when I see them all I see is the love that holds them together and their faith that keeps them going. If I shall turn back now, then my future shall consist of a false love and sadness on my part. If your first thought was money when I mentioned running away with me then in truth you are the greedy one, my dear."

I smiled in relief to hear her speak those words. I then approached her and took her hand in mine. "We shall get a move on then before he decides to capture you himself." Her eyes lifted off the ground and met mine, for a moment we stared at one another as we were looking at our future. I saw happiness in her eyes for the first time from that moment on and realized that she spoke no lies. For her safety and mine we decided that it was for the best that we leave Scotland and move somewhere that her father would never find us and that's when we decided to move to Knaresborough, North Yorkshire, England. It was a small town and I was able to find employment on Dawson's farm where I still work up to this day.

Cecilia and I had a love so strong that it was hard to depart from her for moments at a time. Shortly after we had arrived in Knaresborough, we decided to wed. Due to our minimum income, we weren't able to afford a proper wedding so instead we just signed our marriage papers and said our vows in front of Father Black. She was the light of my life and although love doesn't always last, ours would have. The night of our marriage we treated ourselves with the little money we had and rented a hotel room to consummate our marriage. I will never forget how soft her touch was and how warm her body felt pressed against mine. If perfection existed, then she would be the definition.

Shortly after our marriage, we were blessed with a beautiful, healthy baby girl whom we named Evangeline. Our life was a constant struggle for shelter and food, especially now that it was no longer just the two of us but we also had our sweet baby girl. Evangeline became our main priority and if all we were able to afford that day was a slice of bread, then I would give it to my wife and child. Sometimes I went days on end without food but told Cecilia that I had already eaten my portion. Sadness befell her for the first time when she realized that I was starving myself so that my wife and child could live rather than myself. From that moment on, she never let me go without food for a maximum of two days and she began to find her own beverages and food so that we would all have enough to eat.

Cecilia never heard from her father and I had often suggested that we go back to visit but she always refused and said to me, "I cannot risk losing you and you know as well as I do that if we went back to Scotland, my father would have you murdered. I will not stand for that, Charles!"

She was my inspiration and sometimes I think that if I would not have run away with her that I would have given up on my life, but instead, she was the blood that ran through my heart and kept it beating. When Cecilia died so did my heart, therefore I have made it my objective to stay around a while longer so I may please my daughter before I rejoice with my wife.

Sincerely,
Charles Welsh

Chapter 4

Into the Horizon

It has been four years since Evangeline started attending Shire Dale Academy and in those four years, her father had only seen her three times. There were days where she believed that her father had given up on her and didn't want her anymore and that's why she was placed in the boarding school. Then she thought back on those few days that he had visited her and knew that he would never abandon her like that. Her father was the kindest man around and if there was one thing about Charles that people knew, it was that he never gave up.

The last time Charles visited Evangeline was on her fourteenth birthday which he had promised to take her out. Despite the fact that Evangeline was growing fond of her new living style, she still remembered how her old life was and knew her father could not afford very much and therefore she protested when he said he would take her somewhere special. Charles showed up at Shire Dale at approximately quarter to twelve to pick up his daughter. She froze at the bottom of the staircase when she saw her father wearing brand new clothes that had not a single rip in them.

She smiled at him and acknowledged him with a warm hug hello. "You look very dashing but I must ask, how did you afford your garments?"

He smiled at his daughter and examined her for she had grown another three inches since the last time that he had seen her. "My boss gave me a raise so I decided to purchase some new garments for this special occasion; it isn't very often that my little girl turns fourteen."

Evangeline did not bother to question him any further for she knew that he would not tell her anything else. Instead they walked side by side to a small diner that was located in the heart of the city. It was a family-owned business where they served mainly pasta dishes which was no issue for the Welshs because they both loved pasta. It was seldom that they had the meal because they usually did not have very much money and only ate whatever they could afford.

A waitress seated them to a table that was located outside of the diner where they would be able to enjoy the sunshine and have privacy to talk amongst themselves. Evangeline looked around the diner and wondered what kind of raise her father had gotten that he was able to afford lunch at Sally's Pasta.

Evangeline browsed through her menu and couldn't help but notice how extreme the prices were. "Father, you didn't have to take me here, I honestly wouldn't mind just sharing a sandwich with you. In fact, I'm not even that hungry. Maybe we should just leave."

He looked up at his daughter and smiled for he knew exactly why she was behaving this way. "That is nonsense, Evangeline! It is lunchtime and I know for a fact that you haven't eaten anything yet because as we were walking, I couldn't help but notice the rumbles coming from your stomach. Money is not an issue if that is your concern. Do not look at the prices, my dear. Instead choose your favourite dish."

Evangeline raised her eyebrows at her father in confusion, had she missed something here?

They ate their meals in silence but Evangeline couldn't help but to sneak glances at the man seated in front of her and wondered what happened to her father. He walked her back to Shire Dale after they had finished their meals although Evangeline had hoped that his visit would be longer than just two short hours.

They were close to the school before either of them spoke a word, her father said, "I wish that I could stay with you longer but I must return to work, it is very busy there at the moment and they need as many men as possible in order to finish the job as quickly as we can."

Evangeline stopped walking and stared at her father, "Why are you keeping secrets from me, Father? It does not take a genius to know that something is going on and I am your daughter. I think that I would deserve an answer or an explanation as to why you are able to afford nice clothes and fancy meals all of a sudden."

Charles stared into the horizon; there was a twinkle of happiness in his eyes and it shown off like the sun's rays. "Some things are better left unsaid, my dear, but believe me when I say that you ought not to worry about a thing."

She didn't like the fact that they felt more like strangers than family and how she only saw him once a year if she was lucky. Charles walked his daughter back to the school and gave her a hug. "You are so beautiful, Evangeline, and I hope that you will forgive me for my eccentric behaviour but I promise you that you will understand soon." She felt a sadness befall her for she knew that it would be another year before she would see her father again.

That night Evangeline dreamt the most bizarre but surreal dream ever. Evangeline opened her green eyes to find herself located in a small house that was made entirely of wood. She was beyond confused and frightened how she had gotten here and most of all she wondered where she was to begin with. She peered out the window and quickly grabbed hold of the bed frame in which she sat on. The house was located in a rather large tree and she was terrified of the possibility of the house collapsing at any moment and most of all she wondered how the house found its way up a tree. She proceeded to the exit which was a small opening on the floor which was followed by steps that had been built into the tree's trunk. Evangeline took each step with caution in fear of falling, she sighed in relief when she finally placed her feet on the ground. She took a few steps away from the tree to examine it and whispered to herself, "How bizarre to place a house in a tree. The craftsmen must not have considered the fact that it could possibly fall."

Evangeline turned to face the direction where laughter was coming from but saw nothing but nature's beauty. "It will not fall off the tree. That house was built many years ago and it is still standing strong like all the others in the village." Evangeline heard a high pitched voice but she could not spot the woman who spoke the words.

Evangeline turned around when she felt a soft tap on her shoulder, "My name's Sparkle. Who may you be?"

Evangeline screamed in sight of a small floating girl and turned to run in the opposite direction. Before she could escape, Sparkle flew in front of her and put out her hand to stop her, "Now wait a minute, girlie. I'm not that frightening that you must scream at the sight of me. If you want to see something terrifying then wait until you meet the others!"

Evangeline calmed down and examined the small levitating girl in front of her and wondered how it was possible to be so tiny. "What are you exactly, if I may ask?"

Sparkle giggled at her silly question but proceeded to answer, "I am Sparkle the fairy! All the other fairies and I are in charge of keeping balance here in Somnia Viveret, and I am the craftsman of that house that stands behind you."

Evangeline glanced at the house once more and asked, "Why did you place it in a tree?"

Sparkle giggled, "If you take a closer look, you can see many other homes that are also placed in trees. A few years ago, there was an invasion here in Somnia Viveret and all of our homes were destroyed. We rebuilt our homes that following year but Sahara's evil minions struck us again and destroyed everything we had rebuilt. Remember I mentioned earlier how we keep nature in balance here in Somnia? Well they discovered our location and tried to vanquish our existence so that they could control Somnia Viveret and try to take Mathias' place in thrown. That is when I came up with the idea to build our homes in trees because one usually does not think to look up while in search for a city." Evangeline looked up into the tall oak trees and saw hundreds of houses and, like Sparkle had said, it really did look like a city built in the trees.

Evangeline was stunned at the sight of the city and took into realization that this was only one small part of Somnia Viveret. She turned to face Sparkle again and asked, "What exactly is Somnia Viveret?"

Sparkle flew to the nearest tree branch and took a seat before she spoke again, "Oh my, girlie, you certainly do have a lot of questions. Somnia Viveret is a planet where anything fictional, any creation or imagination from a human comes alive. Each human will encounter different experiences and each individual has their own path to follow. Why Somnia Viveret, you ask? Somnia Viveret is Latin for 'dreams alive' and Latin is actually the main language here, if you didn't already guess that."

"So I'm in a dream?" Sparkle was so small it made Evangeline wonder how all the knowledge she knew fit into her tiny brain.

"Technically yes, but you must be careful because our worlds are connected and if something terrible were to ever happen here then something terrible may happen to you. It is a dream that you cannot control but it is a dream that you may guide into the right direction. Do not worry, child. For the time being, I have everything under control, I am your guardian and won't let you down."

Evangeline looked at Sparkle and examined her. "You are my guardian? You are nearly six inches tall!"

Sparkle stood up and flew in front of Evangeline's face, "The rabbit does not always win the race, girlie. Size, speed, appearance, they do not have anything to do with success or strength, the power to lead or guide."

It was silent for a moment. Evangeline knew that Sparkle was right and she felt terrible for sounding so rude. "I apologize for my terrible manners. After all, you are my superior."

Sparkle smiled at Evangeline. "In time, you will be my superior. But for now you are just a child."

Sparkle guided Evangeline around and showed her all the houses she had put up and where she was living. To Evangeline's surprise, Sparkle's house was the smallest of them all, it made her question it. "If you are the craftsman of these homes, then how come you have chosen the smallest one of the bunch?" Not only was her house the smallest but Sparkle was also the smallest fairy in the city.

"Do you not remember what I said earlier?" Evangeline thought about it for a moment but could not recall or even knew what she was referring to. Sparkle shook her head in disappointment, "Size does not matter and if you have everything you need. Why do you need to upsize just because you can?" Evangeline thought about it for a moment but could not come up with the answer to her question. "Has Shire Dale Academy corrupted your mind to think like a wealthy individual? Have you forgotten that your father is still living in the sewers and working just so he can afford to place you in that school? Have you forgotten what life is truly about and that others are still suffering and dying each day because they don't even have a tiny house to go home to?" Evangeline felt like she was getting a lecture from Sister Nelly but the only difference was that Sparkle was educating her to view life from different angles. Sister Nelly only did what she was paid to do and that was to teach young girls to become successful.

Sparkle spent nearly an hour showing Evangeline around her neighbourhood and this was only a small part of Somnia Viveret.

"You mentioned earlier about how they invaded your city. May I ask who Mathias is and why did Sahara want to take over his thrown?"

Sparkle looked around her to make sure no one was in sight; she didn't want to get anyone worried about another possible attack. She took a deep breath and began to talk, "Years ago, Sahara's father worked for Mathias' father, William. He was the commander of William's army. Sahara's father began to disobey William behind his back and started to form his own army using Williams' recruits. Not only did Lance, Sahara's father, being to form his own army, but he also wanted to get to the king himself and by doing so, he had his daughter enchant him with her beauty to be the perfect bride for his son, Mathias. His plan worked because Sahara truly is beautiful and she has taken it to her advantage. However, no one knows what Sahara's story really is but she used to be the sweetest little girl and everyone adored her charm, that is, until her father began to betray King William. She gained powers and was able to transform people into different creatures or objects, she would erase people's memories, blind them and paralyze them, and the list goes on. Anyhow, Lance and Sahara had William hypnotized into believing that she should marry his son, Mathias. Mathias was mesmerized by Sahara's beauty and charm and agreed to the marriage but was in no hurry to proceed with the wedding. This turned out to be a wise decision but everyone ended up suffering from his decision. Mathias found Lance hypnotizing his father but kept silent for the time being and held the wedding off even longer. He soon discovered that Lance was forming his own army and knew that he needed to stop him before his kingdom would be in serious danger. At nightfall, Mathias and a few of his guards snuck up on Lance at his chamber and cornered him and forced him to confess the truth. However, Lance did not confess to any of it. Instead he grabbed Mathias' sword and struck himself in the chest and said, 'In time, you will thank me for what I have created.' They were unsure of what he was referring to until they woke up the following morning and found Sahara weeping over her father's dead body. Mathias never saw any evil in Sahara's alluring green eyes until the day she held her father's body in her arms. She knelt beside his body, her long black hair reaching the ground; she gazed up at Mathias and smiled, 'You will pay for this, Prince, for I am the creation that you should fear.' He stepped closer to her to comfort her but instead, he froze standing before her as he watched Lance's body turn into black ashes and the wind take it away. Mathias realized that this was the work of Sahara, the work of black magic. She rose from the ground, and by now, the whole town was surrounding the scene; she stood motionless for a few minutes as she watched the wind take her father away. Then she began to smile and ashes were circling her body, Mathias stepped back a couple feet, she looked up at Mathias as her glamorous green eyes had turned into a blazing red. She slowly walked closer to him and spoke, 'Pain, loss, fear, betrayal, and hatred will all favour you for what you have just done to my father. I will seek my revenge on you, Prince, and you will be sorry because the darkness is rising and I am its leader. Do not waste your time trying to hunt for me for I will be impossible to find and your father will never see the light of day again, his end is my beginning to salvation.' Sahara turned around and began to walk away and as Mathias and his guards tried to grab hold of her arm they could not, instead she disappeared into the distance. She disappeared three years ago and so did King William, some believe that King William is still alive but others think he was murdered by Sahara to get revenge on Mathias for murdering Lance. Every now and then Sahara's army strikes us or strikes other parts of the forest but she never strikes the kingdom. I think that she is waiting for the perfect time to strike or when he is weakest."

Evangeline was silent for the longest time thinking everything over that she had just been told but still she wasn't sure how to respond to it. Then suddenly she asked, "You said that our worlds are connected, right?"

Sparkle looked at her and answered, "Yes."

"So basically from what you have just told me, there was lots of betrayal in the kingdom as well as death. How does this reflect to my life?"

Sparkle sighed. "Although this did happen three years ago it does not necessarily mean that it happened three years ago in your life. I'm not sure what your father has all told you but betrayal falls in place when he ran away with your mother and betrayed her father and his boss. Death favoured your mother and left you and your father broken-hearted and as Mathias and Sahara seek revenge, you and your father seek success to prevent the reoccurrence of another death."

Evangeline saw the connection and couldn't help but ask, "Did my mother die because of this world then? Is Sahara and Mathias' actions the cause for the madness in my life?"

Sparkle knew that Evangeline was turning things around now because Evangeline was still grieving and needed someone to blame for her mother's death. "Sorry, girlie, but you created this world when your mother died. You may not have noticed it or been aware of it but this is your creation and although we are worlds apart, we still live everyday as you do. You gave us a starting point and from here on it is our mess to resolve."

"How do I leave this world?" Evangeline was eager to leave because she felt that her life was causing harm to another world and as bizarre as it sounded she knew it was true.

"You leave when your tasks are completed."

"What was my task today?"

Sparkle smiled and responded, "To understand the importance of your life." Sparkle disappeared into the distance and soon everything was black. Evangeline opened her eyes and found herself back at Shire Dale lying in her bed.

She lay in her bed and stared at the ceiling as she was trying to remember everything that Sparkle had told her. Evangeline felt exhausted, like she had not slept all night. As much as she wanted to believe that Somnia Viveret really existed she could not help but to think on it as just a very bizarre but very real dream.

"Look at her, she has no life. I bet her father was glad to get rid of her when he did."

Evangeline sat up and gave Frances Scott an evil stare as they laughed at Evangeline and walked away. Evangeline wanted to scare them just as Sahara had scared the people of Somnia Viveret with her blazing red eyes.

"What a freak!"

It has been four years that Evangeline has been attending Shire Dale and Frances Scott still held a grudge on her and because of her hatred towards Evangeline, she has the majority of Shire Dale Academy hating her , too. Frances had brainwashed the girls to believe that Evangeline has not earned the privilege to be here and most certainly does not deserve to be here, whereas she should be out in the sewers alongside her father. The main reason for Frances' hatred towards Evangeline is because Frances does not like competition and as far as she's concerned, Evangeline is an issue. Every year Evangeline grows more mature and more beautiful than ever which is the exact image of her dead mother, Cecilia.

Chapter 5

Professor Luther

Dear Journal, *April 15, 1906*

Over the past five years, I have been taking private lessons in mechanics and basic mathematics from a retired professor. His name is Professor Luther and I found out about him through a newspaper ad. He told me that being retired is a wonderful life but at times it gets lonely and boring, especially if your wife has passed away. I knew how he felt when he told me all about his wife's passing and therefore we were getting along very well.

I feel like I have been a terrible father to my sweet Evangeline but I have been so busy these past few years working on creating a new life for us so that we may both have a future. The last time I saw my daughter was on her fourteenth birthday and that was over a year ago. This is the longest that I haven't seen my daughter and I miss her terribly. She was right; I have been keeping secrets from her along with the rest of Knaresborough. There are so many things that I would like to do before I face my daughter again and I am so near to reaching my goal and I have promised myself that I will not see her until I have. I feel like a terrible father though because I do not know how long this may take me. It has already been five years since my wife has died and I still have nothing to show for my hard and dedicated work.

I will be at Shire Dale Academy soon, Evangeline. I will take you home with me the next time that I do come.

Sincerely,
Charles Welsh

Chapter 6

Old Friend

Professor Luther has been teaching Charles for three years and today was their last lesson together. "If you don't mind me asking, what was your reason to take these lessons?"

Charles thought on it for a moment. He wasn't sure if he wanted to share his idea because he feared someone else would steal his idea from him. He hesitated for a moment before he began to speak. "I want to create something that people will never forget but before I was able to do that, I needed the knowledge to understand how machinery works."

Luther nodded his head. "So I take it that you are going to be creating some sort of machine?"

Charles smiled. "Indeed I plan to but I apologize that I cannot inform you of what exactly that is. I would much rather keep it a secret for now because I fear someone may take credit for my invention."

"Of course, I understand exactly what you mean. I don't mean to be such a bother to you but I am curious, have you started it yet?"

Charles thought about it for a moment because he didn't want to give out too much information. "As a matter of fact, I have."

Luther did not ask any more questions because he knew that he wasn't going to get anything else out of Charles. Instead the two men shook hands and went their own ways.

Charles had built himself a small shack where he had been living the past few years. It was located in the middle of a small forest just outside of Knaresborough. He wasn't able to afford his own piece of land so therefore he illegally built his home in a forest where people would not think to look. It was a nice place though because he had plenty of fire wood around him and was able to hunt for his food whenever he wasn't able to afford food.

That evening, Charles built himself a fire and took out all his blueprints he had been working on. He examined them one last time because once dawn breaks he was planning on introducing his invention to the world, or try to that was. He wasn't sure whether people would like his creation or if they would just laugh or turn their backs on him. If that was the case then he would continue to work his two fulltime jobs but he would take his daughter home and confess to her that he was a failure and can't give her what she needs.

Dreams only die when you give up.

Charles was awake before the sun had even risen. He had gathered all his blueprints and put them neatly into his knapsack and began his journey back to the heart of Knaresborough. It took him nearly three hours till he got there and by then, the sun had finally risen completely. Charles thought, *Well this shall be an interesting adventure*. He was planning on striking the wealthiest people in Knaresborough to see who would take interest in his invention without giving out his idea entirely. If he had the money, he would have started it already but he wasn't able to afford it so instead he needed to have a partner even if it meant giving the other some credit for it. Sometimes one must lose a little in order to gain a little.

The first place that Charles visited was a company named Wilson's Architectural Design which was owned by a wealthy man named Thomas Wilson. The majority of the buildings in Knaresborough were designed and built by him and his workers. Charles thought that this was the best place to go to because they were very well known and have helped to build the town.

Charles wore his best and only suit that he owned. It was a grey suit which he had purchased a year ago for special occasions such as these. He opened one of the large brown doors of the entrance to Wilson's Architectural Design and walked towards the reception desk where an elderly woman sat. "Can I help you, sir?" She was a cranky old lady and Charles knew she didn't like his presence there.

"Yes, actually, you may. I do not have an appointment but I would like to see Thomas Wilson if that is possible."

The elderly woman sighed at him. "One moment, please. I will try and call Mr. Wilson and see if he has time for you. What is your reason for seeing him?"

Charles said, "I have some designs that I need to share with him."

She picked up the telephone and made a short phone call to Wilson's office which was located on the fifth floor. "Alright, he will be down shortly but until then, you may go have a seat in the waiting room."

Charles sat waiting patiently for an hour before Wilson finally came to meet him. "Thomas Wilson, and who are you?" Wilson stuck his hand out at Charles for a hand shake.

"Hello, Mr. Wilson. I am Charles Welsh."

Wilson examined Charles for a moment and noticed that his shoes were dirty and did not match his suit at all and also noticed how Charles carried a knapsack rather than a briefcase. "Well then, let us go to my office and speak in private."

Charles followed Wilson up the five cases of stairs before they finally reached his office. The building was huge and Wilson's office was ten times the size of Charles' shack that he had built in the forest. "This is a really nice building that you have here, Mr. Wilson."

Wilson sat down on a large black chair that was located behind his desk. “Thank you, I designed it.”

Charles glanced around the room. “I figured that you might have. It is nice work.”

Wilson nodded his head and changed topic. “So what brings you here today, Charles?”

Charles placed his bag on the ground beside his feet and began to speak. “Well you see, Mr. Wilson, I am not a man of money and I know that you noticed that the moment you laid eyes on me. However, I am not here today to beg for your money nor am I here to beg for a job at your company but instead, I am here to ask you if you would be interested in a partnership and help me create something that no one else has ever made.”

Wilson took interest in his idea but at the same time he also did not like the idea of working with a lower class man. “So then you are asking for my money, Mr. Welsh.”

Charles thought on it for a moment and nodded his head. “I suppose I am in a way but the thing is that I have no money to start building and therefore I figured that a man like yourself would take interest in my design because well, you are a craftsman.”

Wilson raised his eyebrows and nodded his head, “Yes, you are correct on that matter but I do not just partner up with anyone, Mr. Welsh. I prefer to work as an individual and I do not share my profits that I make. Sure I pay my workers, but all the other money that I make off those buildings belongs to me and I’m not sure if I would like the idea of sharing my success with another.”

Charles was shocked at how greedy Wilson was being even if the design was not his own. “Alright, I understand that but, sir, you will not regret working with me.”

“Why is that, Mr. Welsh? What sort of design have you created?”

Charles hesitated for a moment, “I will not give away my idea just so easily, Mr. Wilson. However, I will tell you that my creation is a machine not a building."

Wilson slammed his fists on his desk. "Excuse me? So you come into my office and harass me with your brilliant idea but won't share it with me? Machines are a waste of time. One cannot live inside of a machine."

Charles knew that it would take him a few tries before he would find a partner. "My idea is brilliant, sir, and therefore I will only share it with someone who actually takes interest in me and my idea. I knew the moment you started talking about money that you would not take up my offer in being partners. Sorry to have wasted your time today, Mr. Wilson." Charles rose from the chair and began to make his way to the door.

Wilson was very confused and followed him to the door. "Never in my life has anyone ever turned me down before and yet you were the one that came here to ask me for my part in your idea. Maybe your idea isn't as brilliant as you think since you can just walk away from someone so easily."

Charles turned to face Wilson and said, "You could be right on that, sir, but at least money has not consumed my soul and turned me into a sour man like yourself." Wilson opened his mouth but no words came out. "Goodbye, Mr. Wilson." Charles walked himself out of the building and knew that he still had many other places where he could go.

The sun was already starting to set by the time he had talked to the fifth person and yet no one took interest in Charles or even gave him the chance to discuss his idea. One man didn't even want to hear what Charles had to say, instead, he had his security escort him out of the building before he could even say hello to the man. Charles wasn't exactly upper class material and the majority of the town didn't even make eye contact with him.

Charles was exhausted from walking around the town all day and tired of being a failure to his daughter. There were days where he wanted to give up and join his wife in heaven but then he remembered that he still had so much to do on earth.

"Good evening, Charles. I haven't seen you here in a long time. What brings you to town?" Lawrence Scott sat next to Charles on a bench that was located just outside of Lulu's Bakery.

"Hello, Lawrence."

Lawrence was a wealthy man of Knaresborough and owned the largest machinery company in town. It would be a wise decision for Charles to share his idea with Lawrence considering the fact that Lawrence works with machines as a living and creates different types of machines all the time. Despite the obvious, Lawrence and Charles have a reputation in Knaresborough and everyone knows that the two men have never gotten along since the day Charles and Cecilia moved here.

The night that Cecilia and Charles arrived in Knaresborough, Lawrence spotted them creeping through the forest almost frozen to death. He offered the couple a blanket and warm clothes, and shortly after, he invited them into his home. Lawrence had a place of his own at the time and was not married nor did he have any children so therefore it was no issue for him to invite the couple into his home. Charles and Cecilia were grateful for his generosity but felt terrible that they had nothing to give him as a token of their appreciation.

"I will make a deal with you folks: I will let you stay in my home until you can find a place of your own but you must help take care of the household chores and seek your own source of income. Until you have found yourselves employment, I will allow you to stay under my roof." Lawrence smiled at the couple and glanced at Cecilia's hand to see if he could spot a wedding band. "I noticed that you do not wear a wedding band so I assume that you folks are not married?"

Charles glanced at his fiancée then back and Lawrence. "For the time being, she remains my fiancée but as soon as we get the opportunity, we want to marry one another."

Lawrence smiled as he adored the couple's everlasting love for one another and wished that he had someone in his life like Cecilia.

Weeks passed and the couple still lived at Lawrence's home but Lawrence never rushed the couple out. Instead he insisted that they wait until they had saved more money so they could purchase their own home. Charles found a job at Dawson's farm whereas Lawrence hired Cecilia to take care of his house. Charles worked long hours and sometimes only got home around eight o'clock at night. Since Charles always worked long hours, Lawrence would show Cecilia around town and they got very well acquainted with one another and soon became very good friends.

One hot summer day, Cecilia decided to clean Lawrence's book shelves and dust them off. It was extremely hot that day and no one was home besides Cecilia so she decided to lose layers of her clothing. She only wore her long underwear and her corset as she sang to herself in the large house. She wondered to herself if this is how her maids back in Scotland felt when they had to clean her parents' house.

Lawrence got off work early that day and as he walked up his drive way and stood outside of the house, he heard a sweet voice singing the most beautiful song. He did not want to interrupt so instead he peeked through the living room window and saw Cecilia half naked cleaning his house. His jaw dropped as he examined her from head to toe and wondered how Charles won over her heart. He felt shivers go up his spine as he imagined himself pleasing Cecilia in ways that Charles was probably not capable of. Lawrence quietly entered through the front door and locked it behind him. Slowly he removed his dirty shoes and began to unbutton his blouse. He walked quietly towards Cecilia and began to lose more clothes every step he took. By the time he had finally reached Cecilia, the only piece of clothing he wore was his long underwear. She felt someone's presence in the room and felt his warm breathing on her neck but she did not turn around for she thought it was Charles. Lawrence leaned towards her and as he began to kiss her neck he untied her corset and let it fall to the floor. She bit her lip for she knew that they should not be doing this until after their marriage but it was arousing and exciting. She still had her back facing him when he slowly removed her drawers and let them hit the ground as well.

She gasped, "Charles, as much as I want you, we must wait until we have married."

Lawrence was stung when she said Charles' name but he continued to kiss her neck and groped at her bosoms. "I want you, Cecilia. You should marry me, not Charles."

Cecilia froze when she heard Lawrence's voice and screamed in his face, "What are you doing?!"

He leaned in towards her and spoke, "You are such a beautiful woman. The only reason I allowed you and Charles to stay in my home was so that I could have a chance to win your heart over so that maybe you would decide to be my bride instead."

Cecilia was bewildered and began to grab her clothes off the floor. "That is the craziest thing you could ever say, Lawrence! I love Charles and if I would have known that were you standing behind me, I would never have let that happen. This only stays between you and me; promise me that you will not tell Charles about this!"

Lawrence thought about it for a moment and smiled at her as he examined her fully naked body, "Cecilia, my dear, I cannot keep something like this from my good friend, Charles."

She was terrified and didn't want Charles to know about the horrible thing that had just happened between Lawrence and herself. She walked closer to Lawrence and said in a desperate voice, "Please, Lawrence, I will do anything but please do not tell my fiancé about our actions."

Lawrence smiled at Cecilia and wrapped his arm around her waist and pulled her up against his warm naked body. "Then you must make love to me right now if you want my lips to remain sealed." He began to kiss her neck once again and then picked her up and carried her in his arms as he brought her to his bedroom. A tear rolled down her cheek but her lips remained shut for she knew that she had to do what he wanted and what he wanted was her.

That evening when Charles got home he sensed the tension between Cecilia and Lawrence and asked, "Did something happen that I should be aware of or concerned about?"

Cecilia did not say anything instead Lawrence shook his head and said, "Not at all, Charles. Why do you ask such a question?"

Charles looked between the two of them and then knelt beside Cecilia. "Please look me in the eyes and tell me that everything is alright."

She turned to look at sweet Charles and wondered how she could let Lawrence trick her into betraying her love. She smiled at her fiancé. "Everything is fine, sweetheart, and you mustn't worry so much. It will only stress you out more, my darling. It was just an extremely hot day and it has drained me completely."

He looked her in the eyes and knew that she would never lie to him. He then removed a small box from his pocket and held it out to her, "I know that I don't have very much money and that I cannot afford to give you everything that you deserve but I met a man on Dawson's farm who makes fine jewelry and I asked him if he could make you a real wedding band."

She opened the small box and inside was a gold wedding band and on it was one single diamond. Cecilia smiled, "Thank you, Charles. It is so lovely just like your heart." She kissed him. "I'm so grateful that you are in my life. Maybe we could find a pastor who will marry us now."

Charles stood on his feet and picked his fiancée up and swung her around in excitement. Lawrence was still in the room and said, "If she was my bride I would give her more than just one diamond on her ring because she is worth more than just that."

Charles stopped and looked at Lawrence, "I agree with you, Lawrence, but when you have little money, one diamond equals a million diamonds put into one solitary ring. If the woman knows that, then that is all that matters." Lawrence rolled his eyes at Charles and walked away.

A week later Charles and Cecilia got married in a small church. It was a very small wedding, their only guests were the pastor and as a witness, Lawrence. As the pastor announced them as husband and wife, Lawrence stood in the corner of the church with his arms folded across his chest and wished that it was him up there rather than Charles. He snarled under his breath, "He will throw her to the streets when he finds out the sin that his new bride is guilty of."

When the couple returned to the house Lawrence asked them to meet him in the sitting room so they could discuss a few things. When Cecilia heard Lawrence request a meeting with them, she began to sweat in fear of him revealing their secret. Once Charles was out of sight, she grabbed Lawrence by his arm and said, "You swore that you would not tell Charles about what happened!"

Lawrence gazed at her grip on his arm and tugged his arm out of her grasp only to place his around her waist. "Don't worry, Cecilia. I never break a promise. However, he will discover the truth soon enough that you are just an ungrateful whore." He bent down and stole a quick kiss.

"Stop it, Lawrence!" Cecilia freed herself from his grasp and smoothed out her dress as she made her way to the sitting room.

Before Cecilia fully entered the room, she stopped by the doorway for a brief moment as she stared at her new husband and wondered why she deserved someone as wonderful as Charles. "Cecilia, my wife, come sit with me." He smiled at his wife and gestured her to sit beside him. She made her way towards her husband and kissed him softly on his lips before she sat down. Soon after, Lawrence made his way into the sitting room and sat on a red sofa that was located beside a large bookshelf. The blinds were shut thus making the brown room darker.

Lawrence stirred his tea and took a sip before he spoke, "I have gathered the two of you here today to discuss your living situation." Cecilia sighed in relief that it wasn't about their secret.

Charles looked concerned for a moment but kept his mouth shut because he knew that Lawrence was not done speaking. "A few months ago I invited you two into my home because I was feeling generous and wanted to help out someone in need. However, I am not feeling generous anymore and I have decided to start my own business. With the two of you in my home, it is rather distracting and therefore I am not asking but I am telling you that you are no longer welcome here." The couple were stunned by Lawrence and for a moment were speechless. Lawrence continued, "I know that this is short notice but you must be out of my home before the sun rises tomorrow morning."

Charles wasn't thrilled about how things were being handled but understood that they couldn't live there forever. "We understand, Lawrence; however is it too much to ask if you could give us a week so that I may find shelter elsewhere for my wife and me?"

Lawrence rose from his chair and said, "This is not a hotel, Charles! By sunrise tomorrow I want you and your whore out of my house!"

Charles rose from his chair as well and was bewildered by Lawrence. "Do not speak about my wife in that manner!" Lawrence smirked at Cecilia and made his way to his office. "Lawrence! I am not finished speaking with you."

Lawrence turned his head to glance back at Charles. "Well I am, Charles, and unlike you, I have a career to start."

Cecilia sat silently beside Charles and could feel the tension between the two men. Lawrence could not help but notice the knapsack that was placed between Charles' legs. "May I ask why you carry that bag around with you everywhere you go?"

Charles looked down at his knapsack and smirked as he peered up at Lawrence's dark brown eyes. "Indeed you may, Lawrence; however I cannot guarantee that you will get the answer that you hope to seek."

There was a moment of silence as Lawrence patiently waited for Charles to continue speaking. That was when Charles had a brilliant idea. "What I carry with me is my career in the making, as you once clearly said to me that you had a career to start and now it is my turn to start mine. However, I cannot tell you what it is."

Lawrence was puzzled by Charles and began to laugh, "Then you are lying! If you cannot tell me then you are only ashamed because in reality, you know that you do not have a future nor do you have a career."

Charles shifted his body so that he was facing Lawrence, "My future lies in this bag and in the hands of another lucky fellow."

"Do women not interest you anymore, Charles?"

Charles continued, "I am not speaking about my love life, Lawrence. I will graciously share my idea with you but only under one condition."

Lawrence waited for a moment for Charles to continue but it was silent. "What is your condition then?!" Lawrence was getting frustrated with Charles and felt like he was playing a game with him.

"You must pay for the construction of it and be my partner."

Lawrence laughed at Charles because at first he thought that it was a joke until he realized that Charles was serious as ever. "What sort of structure is it, Charles?"

The two men were very serious now and were all business. Charles spoke in a whisper, "Before I say more, let us find a more private place to discuss this matter."

Chapter 7

My Wife's Killer

It had been four months since Evangeline last dreamt about Somnia Viveret and she began to wonder whether it truly was just her mind playing tricks on her or if it was as real as Sparkle had told her it was. She didn't want to forget anything about Somnia Viveret or Sparkle so therefore when she woke up the following morning she took out her journal and wrote down everything that had happened and everything that Sparkle told her. Evangeline sat in her bed and whispered to herself, "My life is important."

"Did you just say that your life is important?"

Evangeline turned around and saw Frances standing at the edge of her bed frame. Frances began to laugh hysterically when she saw Evangeline nod her head.

"I believe that everyone is important and is here for a purpose. God did not create us just to walk on his earth to look pretty, Frances."

Frances stopped laughing and looked into Evangeline's fierce green eyes. "You are strange, Evangeline Welsh, and perhaps God's plan for you is to lie next to your mother's tombstone."

Evangeline sat motionless for a moment and let the hurtful words sink in. Without thinking Evangeline sprung over to where Frances stood and extended her fist towards Frances. She hit Frances so hard in the nose that blood was running down her face. Evangeline stood over Frances and said, "Don't you ever speak about my mother again!"

Frances was bewildered at what Evangeline had just done. Tears began to form in her eyes as she covered her nose with her hands to stop the bleeding. Due to the loud ruckus that the girls were making, Sister Nelly came rushing in the room. "What is going on in here!?"

Evangeline backed away from Frances so that Sister Nelly could see what all the commotion was. She was stunned at the two girls. "Oh dear, are you alright!?" Sister Nelly bent over to where Frances sat and helped her rise from the ground. "Let us bring you to the doctor and Evangeline, you will walk with us and help Miss Scott because I take it this is your doing, is it not?"

Evangeline lowered her head and whispered, "Yes, Sister Nelly."

The three ladies made their way to the doctor's office and on the walk there Sister Nelly said, "Evangeline, apologize to Frances."

Evangeline's jaw dropped as she was about to protest. "I'm sorry for hitting you in the nose and making you cry. Please forgive me."

Frances was raging in anger. "Apology not accepted." She folded her arms across her chest as she was expecting Sister Nelly to make Evangeline give her a better apology. "Now, now, Frances. Evangeline has said she was sorry so be a lady and accept it."

Frances pouted her lips and refused to look at Evangeline.

Knock, knock.

"Good morning, Sister Nelly!" A middle aged man dressed in a white lab coat answered the door. "Oh my goodness, what happened to you, young lady!?" He gestured them into the room and immediately began to examine Frances' nose.

Sister Nelly spoke. "It seems that the two young ladies were arguing and Evangeline punched her in the face."

He couldn't help but giggle when Sister Nelly told him this; he had never come across fighting from Shire Dale Academy before. "I apologize for laughing; may I ask why you hit her?"

Sister Nelly and Dr. Wesley both turned to face Evangeline as they patiently waited for an answer. Frances interrupted before Evangeline even began to speak, "Alright, I understand you both want to know what happened but could you please focus on fixing my nose?" Dr. Wesley turned towards Frances and continued to bandage up her nose and felt like he understood exactly why Evangeline had punched her in the nose. She was snobby and a stuck up bitch.

Evangeline smiled as she watched Dr. Wesley bandage her up and enjoyed watching Frances be in pain. "You have a big mouth, Frances Scott, and talking about my dead mother in that manner was beyond rude and ignorant of you. You put this all upon yourself and you knew that sooner or later it would come to bite you in the ass."

Dr. Wesley tried to hide his laughter from Sister Nelly and Frances because he admired her courage to stand up for herself. Sister Nelly frowned at Dr. Wesley and said, "Evangeline! Watch your tone and sit up straight. We taught you better than that. I don't know what has gotten into you." She sighed in disapproval and ignored Evangeline for the time being.

It took Dr. Wesley nearly an hour to bandage up Frances' nose. "Unfortunately your nose is broken and you must wear these bandages for six weeks before it will be entirely healed."

Frances' jaw dropped as she looked at Dr. Wesley. "Six weeks!? Is there not another way to make it heal faster so I do not have to wear this hideous bandage on my face?"

Dr. Wesley shook his head and said, "I'm sorry but no. You must wear the bandage if you want it to heal properly. I'm sure that you don't want your nose to be crooked and ruin your pretty face, do you?"

Frances smiled and felt flattered that he called her pretty. "Yes, you are correct on that, Doctor. Thank you for fixing my nose."

He nodded at her and opened the door as they were making their way out of his office said, “You’re welcome. You ladies have a nice day now.”

Sister Nelly and Frances bolted out of his office to continue on with their day whereas Evangeline slowly made her way towards the door. Dr. Wesley placed his arm in the door frame and said, “Evangeline, if you ever want to talk to someone about anything you are always welcome to come to my office. I quite frankly thought it was hilarious and courageous of you to stick up for yourself in that way. You are quite the lady, indeed.”

Evangeline smiled at Dr. Wesley and said, “Thank you, Dr. Wesley. I will keep that in mind before I decide to strike her again.”

-Four months later-

Evangeline wrote in her journal every day. Sometimes she wished that her father would come and see her and other days, she wanted to return to Somnia Viveret and reunite with her new friend, Sparkle. However, she felt like the more she wished for it the more it didn’t happen. On this day, she wrote: *I have given up hoping for things to happen to me because I have discovered that the more I hope for something to happen, the more it doesn’t come true. While one’s perspective on life has gotten brighter, mine has fallen in the shadows and turned me into an angry person.*

Classes ended early that day and Evangeline decided to return to her dorm and write in her journal some more. When she returned to her room, she froze in the doorway as she saw Frances sitting on her bed reading her journal.

She sprinted towards her and snatched it from her hands. “What on earth do you think you are doing?!”

Frances remained seated on her bed and crossed her legs as she looked up at Evangeline. "I always knew that you were strange and now I have proof!"

Evangeline was furious and pushed Frances off of her bed. "How dare you go and invade in someone else's privacy like that." Evangeline was speechless because she knew that she had some very secretive things written in her journal. Sometimes she even wrote about how rude Frances was but instead of hating her she pitied her, especially because everyone knew that Frances' mother left her and her father shortly after she was born to marry another man. Evangeline on the other hand wasn't as rude as Frances to constantly bring up the topic of her mother as well. Not to mention, she also wrote about Somnia Viveret in her journal and knew that Frances would think she was crazy for thinking something so incredibly bizarre.

"How do you pronounce that, Somnia Viv—Viv..."

Evangeline was annoyed because she knew that Frances was mocking her, "The t is silent, Viveret."

Frances nodded her head to notify her that she understood. "You have an interesting imagination, Evangeline. It is rather bizarre if you asked me but I also found it amusing." Evangeline was puzzled by how Frances was responding to her. "You mentioned in your journal that any fictional creation or imagination that a human thinks lives in Somnia Viveret, is that correct?"

Evangeline pulled her eyebrows together in confusion and replied, "Yes, why do you take such interest in this?"

Frances smiled and simply said, "I was just curious." She turned her back to Evangeline and headed towards the door. "Sweet dreams, Evangeline."

Evangeline stared blankly at the door and wondered what Frances was up to because she knew for a fact that Frances hated her and was never nice to her. She opened her journal and found her photograph of her father and mother was gone. She was so furious she went to seek for

Frances.

Frances was nowhere in sight and as she wondered the halls of Shire Dale Academy, she ran into Dr. Wesley. "Good evening, Evangeline!"

Evangeline turned and faced Dr. Wesley; it had been four months since they were in his office due to Frances' broken nose. "I would like to stay and chat with you, Dr. Wesley, but I am on a hunt for Frances. Be prepared for another possible broken bone because once I get hold of her, she will regret taking that photograph from me!"

Dr. Wesley laughed at how silly Evangeline was being and said, "I'm sorry to hear that, Evangeline, but Frances has gone to stay with her grandparents for the remainder of the week so you won't find her lurking around the school until next week."

Evangeline's eyes widened in shock as she fell to the ground, "Are you serious?"

Dr. Wesley bent down beside her. "Indeed I am. Perhaps you'd like to come in my office and we could discuss this hatred between you girls and we could have some tea and biscuits?"

Evangeline looked up at his baby blue eyes and imagined him to be the father she never had, someone that she could easily talk to. "That sounds wonderful."

She rose from the ground and they walked to his office together. She felt like she had a wound and was on her way to get it fixed. When they reached the door, he fumbled in his lab coat to find his keys and unlocked his office door. He escorted her into his office and offered her a seat on the red couch that was located by the far wall near a small bookshelf. As he prepared the tea and biscuits, she browsed through his office and looked through the books that were displayed on his bookshelf. One in particular interested her and it was titled *A Tragic Journey* which was written by a woman named Yolanda Wesley. Evangeline flipped through the book and noticed that it was not a novel but rather a book filled with poetry.

"What do you have there?" Dr. Wesley came in the room carrying a tray with hot herbal tea and a bowl filled with steaming hot biscuits.

"It looks like a poetry book and I've read the first two poems and they are amazing."

Dr. Wesley took the book from her hands and sighed. "My wife wrote this book but she is long gone now. She was murdered a few years ago but we never did find her killer."

Evangeline stared at Dr. Wesley and felt sorry for him. She sat beside him and spoke in a very apologetic voice. "I'm so sorry, Dr. Wesley. I wasn't aware that you were married before."

He looked into Evangeline green eyes and smiled, "Don't worry, sweetheart. I have done my grieving and am ready to move on with my life."

Evangeline felt relieved and couldn't help but ask, "If you don't mind me asking, what happened to her?"

Dr. Wesley poured their tea and placed a glass in front of her and in front of him. He stirred in two cubes of sugar and took a sip of his tea. Evangeline patiently waited for him to proceed with his story. "I married Yolanda seven years ago and she was just so beautiful. If angels existed, then she was definitely one of God's angels. I'm sorry if I rant on about her but she was just so beautiful, Evangeline. She had blonde ringlets that reached to the end of her spine and she had beautiful blue eyes. Every time I looked into her eyes, I felt like I was looking into the ocean because she had a mixture of three different shades of blue in her eyes and it was so amazing I couldn't help but fall in love with her. I met her when I was going to college to study my degree in medicine to become a doctor. She happened to be the daughter of my professor and came into class one day to bring him his briefcase which he had forgotten at home that day. She examined his classroom and we locked eyes on one another instantly and after class that day, she stood outside of the classroom. I introduced myself to her, 'Hi, my name is Darren Wesley and I am a student of your father's.' She smiled at me and shook my hand, 'It's a pleasure to meet you, Darren. I am Yolanda Lu.' I stood there for a moment before I spoke again. 'Did you want to attend the spring festival with me, Miss Lu?' She smiled at me and responded, 'I would be honoured to go with you, Dr. Wesley.' She winked at me as she called me doctor." Dr. Wesley stopped speaking for a moment as he took a bite of his biscuit. "Is it alright that I am telling you how we meet or were you more curious about her death?"

Evangeline stared at him and giggled, "I was actually enjoying the story very much, Dr. Wesley, and would like to hear the entire thing if you don't mind sharing it with me." She could sense that he felt a rush of memories return to him as he told her the story and it made her happy to see him happy in another form other than healing people.

"I picked up Yolanda from her rather large house on the day of the spring festival. Professor Lu answered the door and was surprised to see me. 'Mr. Wesley! What a surprise to see you here this afternoon. What can I do for you?' I was speechless when I found out that Yolanda didn't tell her parents that she had a date with me. 'I guess she didn't tell you but I am here to pick up Yolanda. I've asked her to attend the annual spring festival with me and she accepted my invitation.' Professor Lu looked at me with puzzled eyes and then called his daughters name. 'Yolanda!' She hurried down the stairs and met us by the front entrance of their mansion. She looked back and forth at her father and me and seemed concerned. 'Is it true that you have a date with this young man here?' She peeked at me and looked back at her father. 'Yes, he asked me if I would like to attend it with him but he did not say it was a date.' I stared at her in disbelief as her father turned to face me. 'You hear that, Darren? You are not taking my daughter out on a date. It is only two friends spending time together.' I nodded my head and spoke. 'Yes, sir.' I whispered under my breath, 'And secret lovers.' 'What was that you said, Mr. Wesley?' he asked loudly. I straightened up my posture and smiled at him, 'I said it's getting late perhaps we should go to the festival now.' Professor Lu grabbed his jacket and said, 'Indeed. Let's all go to the festival.' I was very annoyed because he followed us like a shadow everywhere we went. I did not get a single moment alone with her. She did however tell me that her father was very protective of her and doesn't allow her to go on dates with men. I figured that much out already but found it rather ridiculous that he wouldn't allow his twenty-five-year-old daughter live her own life. Therefore the following day, I stayed after class and planned to have a word with him. Once the class was empty, he looked up at me as I still remained seated in my chair and he asked, 'Is there something that I can do for you, Mr. Wesley?' I got out of my chair and walked closer to where he stood. 'Indeed there is, Professor. I would like to talk to you about your daughter.' He stared at me and frowned. 'My daughter is off limits, Mr. Wesley.' I got really close to his face and was angry now. 'Why?! Do you love your daughter like you love your wife? Are you keeping her for yourself, Professor? Because I think that I am falling in love with Yolanda and would really like to ask for her hand in marriage.' He didn't appreciate my attitude and at the time being I didn't care whatsoever. 'Excuse me? You expect me to give my blessing after that outburst you just pulled?' I wasn't aware that Yolanda was standing by the door when she spoke. 'Yes, you should, Father, because I think I'm falling in love with him, too.' He stood motionless for a couple seconds as he looked between us then grabbed hold of Yolanda's hands. 'Are you sure that is what you want?' She nodded her head and looked up at me and smiled. He turned to face me again and said, 'Alright, Mr. Wesley, you have my blessing but you better take good care of my baby girl.' I shook his hand and smiled. 'I promise you won't be disappointed sir.'

"We got married a few weeks later and had the most wonderful couple years being newlyweds. Unfortunately I am unable to have children and she really wanted to have children. She always talked about how she wanted to have two boys and two girls and live on a farm and when she found out I wasn't able to give her that, she was heartbroken. That is when she began to write those poems, to let out her feelings without hurting me but I found her poems and turned it into a book for her. I never did show her what I did with it; instead I kept it for myself.

"In that last year that we were together, she grew apart from me and didn't treat me like her husband. She never wanted to make love to me or even be around me. She was constantly out elsewhere so one day I decided to follow her and see where she was always going."

Dr. Wesley stopped speaking and stared at his empty cup and slammed it onto the table. Evangeline was startled and jumped, "Are you alright, Doctor? You don't have to continue if it makes you upset."

He took a deep breath and looked at Evangeline through his honey brown hair. "I cannot just stop telling the story. I have started so therefore I will tell you how it ended and then I will show you the new beginning."

Evangeline looked at Dr. Wesley and said, "I don't want you to get upset about it though, perhaps I should come back another time."

Dr. Wesley grabbed Evangeline by the arm and whispered, "Please let me finish the story." She sat back down in her seat and waited for him to continue. "She wore a black cocktail dress and told me she was going to play bridge with her mother and some of her girlfriends. I followed her and hid behind objects so that she would not see me. She kept looking around her to see if someone was following her and that is when I noticed that she wasn't going to her mother's house because her mother lived on the other side of town. Then she stopped walking and once again she looked around her before she knocked on the door. A middle aged man answered the door; it was one of my former classmates from Professor Lu's class. He put his arm around her waist and let her into his house but before he shut the door he kissed my wife passionately." He stopped speaking for a moment and took another deep breath before he continued. "Once the door was shut, I walked towards the house and peeked through the living room window. I watched him, Benjamin, as he had his hands all over my wife's body and kissed her lips and then kissed her neck. He unzipped her cocktail dress and let it fall to the floor as she unbuttoned his shirt. I was shocked beyond belief and froze and just watched as they touched one another. He groped at her bosoms and brushed her hair with his fingers. He led her into another room, the bedroom, I presumed, but I still continued to stand there frozen in shock. I knew that on the other side of that door another man was making love to my wife and I could do nothing to stop it. I waited nearly two hours outside of his house before she opened the front door of his house and made her way back home. I followed her again and when there was no one in sight I snuck up behind her and covered her mouth with my hands. She tried to scream under my hands but no one was around to hear her. She struggled to fight me off but failed to do so. I pushed her to the ground in anger; she was unaware that it was me because her back was towards me. I lifted her dress and lowered my voice so she would not recognize it was me, 'Since you love the feel of a man so much I will give you one last memorable touch to take to hell with you.' I was so angry with her that I raped my wife from behind. As far as she was aware, she didn't know that it was me. I pushed her head against the concrete as she was constantly struggling to free herself. She started to become very irritable so I smashed her head onto the concrete ground. I didn't hit her very hard so she took her free hand and grabbed hold of my hair and began to pull at it. I then pushed my hand forward and smashed her head onto the ground once again, but this time, it was really hard and I heard a loud crack as she hit the ground. Her body twitched for a few seconds before it became paralyzed. I put her dress back down and turned her body around, she was dead. I stared at her and couldn't believe what I had just done, but at the same time, I felt victory. I cleaned up her body to make it look like Benjamin was the one who killed my wife. They believe that it was him because she carried his unborn child. I got my revenge because he was put on death row for the murder of Yolanda Wesley. Perhaps someday I will join them in hell for the sins I have committed."

Evangeline's eyes were wide as she stared blankly at Dr. Wesley. She remembered that he had locked the door earlier so she knew that running for the door was no option so instead she tried to remain calm and whispered, "You murdered your wife?"

Dr. Wesley snapped out of his daydream and stared at Evangeline as he ran the question threw his mind over and over. He smiled widely and said, "Not on purpose of course."

Evangeline pulled her legs onto the couch and crossed her arms on top of one another. "But you had them believing that Benjamin was her killer…"

He smirked at her and walked towards where she was sitting. He knelt beside her and said, "They betrayed me, Evangeline. I couldn't live with myself knowing that they were having a life of their own while I sat at home waiting for her to return to my bed." He sat only inches away from her and it made her nervous and scared. He noticed her begin to shake and grabbed her arms to stop her from shaking, "You asked me about my wife and I told you about her so do not be nervous. You are the one who has questioned it and the only one who I have ever told that to."

She stopped shaking and asked, "How come you decided to tell me?"

He got up from the ground and walked behind her and began to play with her hair. "You are my beginning."

Evangeline was puzzled for a moment and asked, "What do you mean I am your beginning?"

He moved her hair to one side and whispered in her ear, "I told you that I would show you the new beginning. Don't you love me anymore, Yolanda?"

Evangeline got off the sofa and faced Dr. Wesley. "I am not Yolanda, Dr. Wesley, you murdered her, remember?"

His smile vanished in the blink of an eye. "Evangeline, come back here." She refused to return to her seat and remained standing by his desk and looked around her for an emergency exit. He approached her, "I'm sorry, Evangeline. It's just that your personality reminds me so much of her and you are so beautiful. I really miss her and you can be her replacement."

Evangeline was scared of Dr. Wesley and feared that he would try to harm her as well. "I cannot replace your dead wife, Dr. Wesley, nor do I want to."

He slowly began to walk towards her and examined Evangeline's small figure. He stood only inches away from her as he put his arm around her waist and pulled her up against him, "I didn't say you had a choice." He bent down and pressed his lips against Evangeline's and kissed her aggressively.

She tried to push him off of her but he was much stronger and larger than she was. He started to tear at her blouse and reached under it as he felt for her breasts. She tried to scream but found it rather difficult with his tongue in her mouth so instead she clenched her teeth together and bit his tongue till she could taste blood. He pulled away from her and saw blood trails left on Evangeline's lips. He was furious and without thinking he smacked Evangeline across the face and pushed her onto the ground. She pressed the palm of her hand against her cheek and realized that this is exactly what he had done to Yolanda before he murdered her.

She was whimpering and whispered, "Please don't do this."

He sat on top of her looking at her as he covered his face and said, "Yolanda, why don't you want to make love to me anymore? Can't you see that I love you? I'm sorry that I cannot give you children but that doesn't mean that you have to stop treating me like I am your husband!"

Evangeline lay motionless on the ground beneath him and examined his face and knew that Dr. Wesley was not well; he was a mentally disturbed man. Considering his condition she figured that if she pretended to be Yolanda then perhaps she could get herself out of this situation.

"I do love you, Darren, but I do not feel like making love to you right now. It is not because you cannot bear children either it is because I think that I might be getting a fever."

He pressed his hand against her face and said, "You feel slightly warm but I don't think it is a fever."

Evangeline pressed her own hand against her forehead and said, "I feel one coming on and I don't want to get you sick, too."

Darren was still sitting on top of Evangeline and searched her eyes for the truth, "I understand but we do not need to use our lips anyways we can still make love."

Evangeline tried to sit up and push him off of her but he was much too strong for her. She stared into his baby blue eyes and said, "No, Darren, not today." His eyes fell to her breasts and he once again reached out to her chest and touched her breasts. She began to sob and whispered, "Please, Dr. Wesley, I am nearly fifteen years old. You are a thirty-five year old man, and you are old enough to be my father!"

His eyes locked on hers and he said, "Shut up, Yolanda, and obey me."

She felt helpless and knew that he would get her because that is all that he wanted. He took off his shirt and removed his pants. Evangeline lay motionless under his half naked body as he tore her blouse off and removed her long skirt. He ran his hands over every inch of her body and kissed her lips despite everything she said about having a fever. He placed his hand on her thigh and moved it between her legs as he removed her panties. She inhaled deeply as she prepared herself for what he was about to do to her. She was scared to try and fight back because the last time she did he threw her to the ground and who knows what else he was capable of doing to her.

He removed every piece of clothing that they wore and laid on top of her so their bare skin was touching one another. He kissed her neck and whispered, "I've longed for the touch of your skin on mine." He continued to kiss her neck and grabbed her breasts in his hands. He grabbed hold of her hand and placed it on his penis as he began to kiss her breasts. Evangeline's eyes widened in shock as she realized that this was no nightmare, this was actually happening. He parted her legs and placed his body between her opened legs as he was about to penetrate her.

Knock, knock.

"Dr. Wesley, are you in there?" It was Sister Nelly.

Evangeline sighed in relief and tried to scream but before she was able to he shoved a pillow in her face. He remained silent and continued to feel Evangeline's body. He placed his hand between her legs and began to touch her with his fingers. She tried moving her body to get free from his grasp but was unable to. He moved his hand and pushed his body on top of hers once again.

"Dr. Wesley!" Sister Nelly was still at the door and started to knock again.

Darren ignored her presence and pushed Evangeline's arms to the ground so she couldn't stop him. He began to penetrate her and heard her scream under the pillow. He moaned in pleasure and continued to rape Evangeline, "Oh Yolanda, I love you so much." She tried moving her body in hope of pushing him off of her.

"Dr. Wesley, I can hear voices and if you do not open this door immediately, I will have someone take it down!"

He continued to rape Evangeline and said, "I'm with a patient, Sister Nelly."

Sister Nelly placed her ear against the door and heard squealing sounds from a young girl. She banged on the room door and said, "I hear squealing noises so I demand you to open this door right now, Doctor!"

Dr. Wesley ignored her again so she rushed to the police station that was located two doors away from Shire Dale Academy. They returned to Dr. Wesley's door within five minutes and banged the door down. Sister Nelly gasped as she saw Dr. Wesley lying on top of Evangeline. She froze in the doorway as she stared at them in shock. The two police men grabbed Dr. Wesley by the arms and dragged him off of her and strapped his hands behind his back. Sister Nelly approached Evangeline and covered her with a blanket. Evangeline was shaking under the blanket and was horrified of what had just happened.

"Are you alright, Evangeline?" Sister Nelly gathered up Evangeline's clothes off the floor and put her arm over her shoulders.

She was shaken up and said, "He made me do it."

The police threw a blanket around Dr. Wesley as well. He looked at Evangeline and said, "I did no such thing! You are my wife, Yolanda, and that is what husband and wife do with one another."

Sister Nelly was puzzled and looked at Evangeline expecting an explanation. Evangeline turned her attention to Sister Nelly and the two police officers as she spoke, "Dr. Wesley is a mentally disturbed man and murdered his wife, Yolanda, a few years ago. He keeps calling me Yolanda as if I am his dead wife."

Sister Nelly looked up at Dr. Wesley and said, "So Benjamin did not murder my best friend. It was you that killed her. You envied the fact that Benjamin could have children and you could not." She walked up to him and slapped him in the face.

The police took him back to the police station where they placed him in a small white room and put him in a straitjacket. Evangeline told them everything that had happened along with what he had done to his wife.

Sister Nelly was best friends with Yolanda and met each other through their mothers. Sister Nelly normally would have thought of Evangeline as being dirty and a disgrace but instead she felt sorry for her.

She walked Evangeline back to her dorm and sat on her bed with her. "No one has to know about this." Evangeline looked up at her in relief. "Bury it in the back of your mind and pretend it never happened." She got up and walked out of the room but took once last glance back as she saw Evangeline begin to write in her journal.

Chapter 8

Partnership

Charles and Lawrence made their way back to Lawrence's office at his machinery company, Big Engine. He owned the company for almost fifteen years now and it was the most successful thing anyone had done in his family in a long time. The most successful machinery he created was the tractor which all farmers owned; it made farm work much easier and faster. Due to his success, he had come across many individuals who have introduced him to their creations and many of them he has accepted and taken a large percentage of the sales since he helped the machine get built. The individuals who have partnership with Lawrence needed help for their machines to be built due to the cost of the production process and that is the exact situation in which Charles has found himself in. Lawrence shut the door behind them and took a seat in his brown leather chair seated behind his large wooden desk.

Charles sat in the chair that was seated in front of the desk and removed his blueprints from his bag. He kept them in his hands and said, "Over the last four years, I have been receiving private lessons on mechanics so that I may create something amazing that will go into history. I need your help to make this happen but because it is such a large machine, it will be quite costly. Before I share this idea with you, I need your promise that you will go through with it and won't claim it as your own idea."

Lawrence was curious to know what was on his blueprints but he knew that Charles was a smart man and whatever it was it will be worth whatever the cost may be. Lawrence nodded his head at Charles and said, "Alright, Charles, I will take you up on that offer under one condition."

Charles raised his eyebrows and asked, "What is your condition?"

Lawrence smiled at Charles and began to fumble around in his desk drawer as he searched for papers. He pulled out a large brown envelope from his drawer and withdrew a white document. He read the document over once more before handing it to Charles. "This is a contract that I get all my partners to sign before we begin the construction so that way, I know that he will meet up to his end of the bargain as I have done my part."

Charles took the paper from his hand and began to read it over. "This is a joke right?" Charles pulled his eyebrows together in a frown and was not happy with the contract agreement.

"There is no humour in that contract, Charles. Every individual needs my help for something and my family needs your help in return." He skimmed over the contract again and Lawrence said, "If your invention is worth it then you will agree to that contract."

Charles sighed and said, "And if I do not survive this then all my work and effort will go to waste."

"That is not true because you will have your machine to show for it and the credit will be entirely yours. The only thing I ask of you in return is for profit shares and your participation in that contract agreement."

Charles stared at it and thought if anything this was just Lawrence's way of getting revenge on him for marrying Cecilia. "Alright, Lawrence, give me a pen." Lawrence smiled and handed Charles a pen instantly.

"Alright, now that you have signed the contract, let's take a look at your blueprints." Lawrence was eager to see the machine that Charles had created. Charles unrolled the paper and placed it on Lawrence's desk. The paper was as large as his entire desk so therefore they had to remove the items off his desk so they could see the prints. Lawrence's eyes widened as he looked at the image and he took great interest in the design before Charles even told him what it was.

Charles pointed at the drawing and said, "This is the very first steamship in the world. It can be used to transfer goods across the world or could also be turned into a battleship in time. See these circular drawings down here? Those are the propellers; They are fans that transmits the power in a circular motion to thrust the ship into movement, depending on the direction that the fan is spinning is determined on whether it is going forward or in reverse."

Lawrence looked over the design and pointed at an object that looked like a rather large pipe at the top of the ship and asked, "What is that pipe for?"

Charles was excited that he was finally able to share his idea with someone who was actually interested. "That is the smoke stack, it vents out the exhaust from the ship's boiler to the outdoors." It took nearly two hours for Charles to go over every single detail of the ship's functions.

Lawrence sat back in his chair and lit a cigar, he took a puff, and said, "I won't lie, Charles. This is a huge machine to build so it will be quite the task. It will be a very successful invention, no doubt. I'm proud of you and that you have finally made something of your life."

This was the first time that Charles was able to admit to himself that Lawrence was a nice guy after all. "Thank you, Lawrence. I really do appreciate your partnership in this project."

It was already late by the time they finally decided to call it quits for the day. Charles was dreading his long journey back to his little hut in the forest. "Charles, where are you staying at the moment?" Lawrence was locking up the doors to his company and threw the remainder of his cigar on the ground.

"Well I live quite a walk away from town so it will take me a few hours to return there. It is three hours away from here."

Lawrence raised his eyebrows in shock, "Wow, that is quite the walk! Say, how would you like to stay at my old house? You stayed there once before so you are welcome to return if you like."

Charles liked that he wouldn't have to walk back to his hut but instead he said, "That is very generous of you but I must decline your offer, after all I wouldn't want to intrude your home."

Lawrence laughed and responded, "Don't be ridiculous. I don't live there anymore. I mean it is still my property but it has been empty for many years now. I had Wilson's Architectural Design build a brand new house for me and my daughter; it is double the size of my previous house. Perhaps once the ship is finished being built, you can buy that property from me so you and your daughter have a home for yourselves, but for now, I will let you live there at no cost whatsoever." Charles wondered why Lawrence was acting so generous towards him, "I—I'm speechless but thank you." Lawrence handed Charles the keys to his old house and walked in the opposite direction from Charles.

Charles still remembered where the house was and it took him nearly twenty minutes to walk there. The house looked abandoned from the outside, the windows were boarded shut and the grass reached his knees. He made his way to the door and turned the bronze key in the key hole and pushed the door open. The house was dark and the only light that shone in was from the moons glare. He shut the door behind him and browsed the room as he noticed that all the furniture had been covered by white sheets. He walked towards what looked like a couch and removed the covering. Dust flew around him as he removed the sheets off the furniture. The lights didn't work but he managed to dig out a candle from beneath the kitchen sink where they had been fifteen years ago when Cecilia and Charles stayed there.

It was late and Charles was exhausted from his long day wondering around the city. He was overall pleased that his project was going to start being constructed the following day until it is completed but he wasn't too sure yet whether he liked that his partner was Lawrence.

Dear Journal, *May 21, 1907*

Today all my dreams came true but for a price. I spent hours in Knaresborough searching for a partner to help me build my ship but I had no luck until I was ready to call it quits for the night, Lawrence Scott took interest in my design. At first I thought to myself that I would rather the ship never be built then work with Lawrence but then I remembered that I still have a daughter who relies on me. Nobody knows why Lawrence and I hate one another so much besides us, not even our daughters ever understood the hatred towards one another.

Shortly after I married Cecilia, she conceived a child and I knew something was wrong because she was already a few months pregnant before we had even made love for the first time. I came home from work one day and found her crying so I approached her and asked her what was the matter. She responded, "Charles this is not your child that I carry." I was devastated and sat on the ground next to her and asked her what she was talking about. "A few months ago as I was cleaning Lawrence's house, I got very hot so I took off some of my clothes and I did not expect him to come home early. He put his arms around me and began to kiss me and touched me and at first I thought that it was you. I called him Charles and he still continued to kiss my neck but then when I found out that it was him I was scared. I was scared that I would lose you so I told him that I would do anything if he promised me that you would never find out what we did. I realize that it didn't make the situation much better but I just love you so much and I couldn't bear to lose you after so much we've been through. I don't expect you to forgive me but I do ask you to consider it." I didn't say a single word to her; instead I just remained seated on the ground next to her and stared at her stomach. I was furious that she had betrayed me but I could not hate her because she was the light of my life. Instead I replied, "I have vowed before God that I will be with you until death do us part and therefore I will do so. However I do ask one thing in return." She grabbed my hands and said in an eager tone, "Anything." I glanced at her stomach and then into her sad green eyes. "You will not keep that child." She released my hands and placed her hands on her stomach and looked at me in fear. "I will not murder this child, Charles." I was shocked when I heard her say those words and responded, "I don't want you to murder the child. I only ask you to give it to Lawrence when it is born so that he can have what he created. Then we may start our own family and forget about him and that bastard child that you carry." She was appalled at my tone but agreed to it considering the fact that she did betray me. She gave birth to a healthy little girl whom she let Lawrence name and care for. He enjoyed knowing that it broke my heart to know that my wife had a child with another man. He ended up naming her Frances Scott.

I have never told my daughter that she has a half-sister because I feared that it would break her heart to know that her mother betrayed us both. Perhaps one day I will tell her the truth, if it is not too late by then.

Sincerely,
Charles Welsh

The following day, Charles made his way back to Lawrence's company where they had gathered a crew of fifty men who were going to help build the steamship. Charles looked around at all the men and was happy because he knew that they were all here to help build his ship. Lawrence gathered all the men and said, "Alright, everyone, as you are aware, we are going to start the construction of a steamship which our very own neighbour, Charles Welsh, has designed."

All the men applauded for him and at the same time were also surprised because everyone knew that Charles was from the sewers. One elderly man yelled from the crowd, "Will the ship have a name?"

Lawrence responded before Charles was able to open his mouth, "She will be called Cecilia."

Charles jaw dropped as he was about to protest but he remained silent because he strangely liked it. Cecilia was his inspiration from the moment they met and as he will sail his ship she will be watching and guiding him in the right direction. He nodded his head at Lawrence and smiled, he whispered under his breath, "Cecilia."

Lawrence clapped his hands together and said, "Alright, men, let us start the construction. The sooner we begin, the sooner she is finished. Let us create history, for in time, the world will rely on ships."

The men cheered and the elderly man raised his fist and said, "Cecilia will sail the seas!" The men all cheered once again and began the construction process.

Chapter 9

Restless Night

Evangeline was so shaken up by what had just happened that it took her nearly an hour to fall asleep. It felt so good to sleep after a long and stressful day and she just wanted to escape this mad world. To Evangeline's surprise, her wish came true because that night she returned to Somnia Viveret for the first time since four months ago. She opened her eyes to find herself lying near a small river that was located deep in the forest, so she had assumed. She was puzzled because she didn't recognize the area; Sparkle didn't show her this part of the forest the last time that she was here.

As she rose off the ground, she heard a voice from behind her, "Nice legs." It was a high pitched voice coming from a female. She turned around to see who stood behind her, but to her surprise, no one was there. Instead, on a large grey rock located just alongside of the river, sat a woman who looked like a fish.

Evangeline examined here from head to toe—tail and asked, "Are you a fish or a woman?" She was amazed by this creature and wanted to know more about her.

However, she didn't seem very thrilled by her sarcastic question and responded in an irritated tone, "I am not a fish! I am a mermaid, goddess of the sea."

Evangeline began laughing and asked, "Don't you mean goddess of the river?"

The mermaid's smile turned into a frown as she raged in anger. The river beneath her turned black and large waves began to form. Evangeline got splashed by water as the waves hit the rocks and the ground near it.

"What's happening? If you are doing this, please stop."

The mermaid smiled and the water settled down, "Do not mock me, child, because I am capable of causing a tsunami or any other water related event which may cause this world the crash."

Evangeline walked closer to where she sat and looked at her purple tail and then back at her fair, toned face. She was beautiful with her long red hair reaching her waist and her ocean blue eyes. She smirked as she saw Evangeline eying her tail, "I could transform you into a 'fish' too you know."

Evangeline backed up a few inches and said, "That's perfectly alright. I enjoy my legs." The mermaid frowned at her and crossed her arms over her chest. "What is your name?"

The mermaid was puzzled by her question and asked, "My name?"

Evangeline nodded her head, "Yes, your name. I'm sure goddess of the sea is not your actual name."

She smiled and said, "Venus."

"I'm Evangeline."

Evangeline's eyes focused on the large water current that was approaching them. She stepped back a few feet thinking that Venus was going to splash her with water again. She covered her face with her arms as she expected the water to splash her but when nothing happened, she lowered her arms and saw three other mermaids before her. One of them wore a gold crown on her head and had a black tail. Her hair was black as night and her eyes were red as flames.

She spoke in an angry tone, "Marina, what are you doing upon that stone and who is this creature before me?"

Evangeline looked back at Venus and was confused why this woman called her Marina, she asked, "Who is Marina?"

The red eyed mermaid gave Evangeline a death glare and responded, "I am Venus and that is Marina. On my right is Pearl and towards my left is Melody. I am the goddess of the seas and these are my followers."

Evangeline was puzzled for a moment and turned to look at Marina, "I thought that you said you were Venus…"

Venus turned to face Marina and noticed that Marina still sat on the large stone. Venus and Marina stared into one another's eyes then Venus raised her hand in front of her and slowly formed a fist. As she did this, Marina began to make a horrid screeching noise and placed her hands around her throat as she was gasping for oxygen.

Evangeline couldn't stand it anymore so she walked into the river so she stood in front of Venus and grabbed hold of her fist, "I will not allow you to torment her so I am telling you to stop."

Venus freed Marina and turned her attention on the small girl in front of her, "You are brave to stand up to me but you are also a fool for doing so." Venus was raging in anger and turned the skies black as rain began to pour and thunder struck.

Evangeline gazed up at the angry skies and asked, "Is that all that you can do?" She smirked at Venus and acted as if the rain didn't touch her. Venus put her hand in front of her once again and clenched her hand in a fist. She was stunned when nothing was happening to Evangeline and dropped her hand.

She whispered, "But that is impossible. My powers have never failed on me before."

Evangeline asked in a puzzled tone, "Are you too afraid of me to touch me with your bare hands?"

Venus swam closer to Evangeline so their faces were only inches apart, "This is a blessed curse that I have and one of the downfalls is that I cannot touch a human but only use my powers on them. For some strange reason, I cannot torture you and it is very frustrating."

Evangeline was curious, "Why can you not touch a human?"

She looked around her to make sure no one was in sight before she answered her question, "So my powers are no threat to Sahara."

Evangeline wondered why everyone feared Sahara so much and wondered what sort of a threat Sahara was to everyone else. "What will you do if Sahara tries to attack you?"

The mermaids looked concerned by her question. Pearl, who had long curly blonde hair and green eyes, replied, "Then we will die."

Marina swam towards Evangeline and said, "She will crush us with one glance in our direction."

Melody stayed a few feet away from Evangeline and said, "You are lucky to still be a human and if you are smart then you will run, run away now!"

"Evangeline, is that you?" There was a quiet voice coming from behind her.

In that moment the mermaids disappeared into the river. Evangeline looked around but saw no trace of the mermaids; the water was calm and showed no sign of movement apart from her own.

"Evangeline, what are you doing in the river?" She turned around and saw Sparkle in midair and got out of the water.

"Sparkle, I was talking to the mermaids but they vanished when they heard your voice."

Sparkle began to laugh hysterically and said, "The mermaids do not show themselves to anyone."

"Well, they confronted me. Venus tries to make out like she is evil but in reality she is terrified because she knows that she is weak. Marina wishes she was as powerful as Venus because she puts an act on like she is the true goddess of the sea. As far as Pearl and Melody, they are just scared followers and think that Venus will protect them from Sahara but deep down they know that it isn't true."

Sparkle smiled and admired how fast Evangeline learnt about the girls. She said, "Very good but there is much more to them than just their fear."

Sparkle and Evangeline began to walk north of the river to return back to Sparkle's home. On the journey there, Evangeline asked, "Why did Melody say that I was lucky to still be a human?"

Sparkle was silent for a brief moment and began to speak, "Do you remember the first time you were here and I told you all about Somnia Viveret? Well do you remember when I said that everyone ended up suffering from Mathias' decision?"

Evangeline tried to recall the last time she was in Somnia and nodded her head. "Well the mermaids that you just met used to be the fairest ladies of Somnia Viveret. They lived in the kingdom and served as the queen's ladies and followed her everywhere she went and fulfilled her every desire. Shortly after the queen disappeared, Lance began to hypnotize King William. After everything went downhill, Sahara transformed the girls into mermaids because she didn't want competition to win over Mathias' heart. She entitled them to some powers and made them cold-hearted but she also limited what they could use their powers on. Sahara's biggest competition was Venus and that is why she is the meanest of the girls and has flaming red eyes. Mathias never mentioned anything about admiring another girl but he was friends with Venus and that was enough to make Sahara hate her."

Evangeline giggled because of how ridiculous it all sounded. "Sahara just seems like she is very jealous and doesn't like competition so she has eliminated anyone and anything that might be a threat to her just so she can get what she wants." Sparkle nodded her head and continued her journey to her city. "How did the queen disappear? Was she murdered?"

Sparkle thought about it for a moment then continued. "We aren't certain but no one ever found her so we all assume that she is dead along with King William. She was a ravishing woman and everyone adored her. Her name was Queen Teresa." Evangeline enjoyed hearing about everyone in Somnia Viveret. She felt like Sparkle was reading her a fairy tale and they were just reliving it.

Sparkle stopped midair and turned her gaze towards Evangeline. "Do you remember when I told you that you only come into our world when you are needed for something because something terrible has happened in your world and reflected to ours?"

Evangeline nodded her head and looked in front of her as she recalled the terrible incident that occurred with her and Dr. Wesley.

"Well, we need you."

Her jaw dropped as she saw a part of the forest was burnt to the ground and not just any part of the forest but Sparkle's city. All the houses that they built were destroyed and turned to ash. The trees were burnt and nearly tumbling over. There were fairies flying around everywhere as they tried to search for anything that might have survived the fire.

"What happened?"

Sparkle kept her eyes on the burnt city and began to speak, "Earlier today, a monstrous creature blew fire from his mouth and burnt down our city. He stomped on everything to make sure it was destroyed and even ended seven lives. He was a large black beast with a few orange scales on his body. He had a tail that was seven feet long and blew fire from his mouth, he was a dragon and he called himself Draco, her dark disciple."

Evangeline was confused and asked, "You talked to him?"

She turned to face me and said in a calm tone, "He was searching for me. He didn't tell me what he wanted from me but all he said was to tell you that you are no saviour to Somnia Viveret. You are its end."

Evangeline was speechless and knew that she would never be able to save a world even if it only existed in her dreams.

"Don't worry, if you were our end then I would never had opened the gate for you to come in. I never make mistakes and as far as I'm concerned you have been the best decision I have made in a long time. You will be our hero."

Evangeline was slightly irritated and said in an angry tone, "What if I fail you?"

"You will not fail."

"How can you be so certain?"

Sparkle was very serious as she spoke, "Because when the time comes, you will have a reason to fight for life."

Evangeline didn't like the idea of being the hero for Somnia Viveret because she feared that they would all be disappointed if she won't be able to save their home. She looked at the sight in front of her and was scared; scared that she would fail them. "How do I leave this place? Forever..." She kept her eyes locked on the burnt city and wanted nothing more than to return to her bed back at Shire Dale Academy.

Sparkle looked at Evangeline and said, "You cannot leave until you have finished your task. I have told you that before."

Evangeline replied in an angry tone, "I recall that but I do not wish to take part in this world. I cannot meet up to your expectations and I am no hero."

Sparkle flew in front of Evangeline and was angry now, "Our worlds are both falling apart, Evangeline! It is your destiny to save our world as you will gain the knowledge and power to save yours. You cannot just simply leave and wake up in your bed. I opened the gates for you to come through to this world and so you will either finish your task or you will live like one of us here."

Evangeline was furious and began to walk through the ashes of the burnt city to get away from Sparkle. She turned to take one last glance and said, "I will find a way to close the gates then. No one owns me." Her fast strides turned into a run and she soon found herself in a deeper and much darker end of the forest.

She slowed her pace and noticed that the sun was setting and it would soon be night. She had never been in Somnia at nightfall before and it frightened her because she knew that Somnia Viveret was a large place and she didn't know what to expect or whom she may run into. Just when she thought things were terrifying as it was, she saw him. She saw Draco. She ran and hid behind the closest tree and watched him as he flew in the dark night's sky. He was just as large as Sparkle said he was, if not bigger. He looked like he was searching for something and that's when he caught her eye. His eyes were blazing red as he stared at Evangeline and blew fire in her direction. She was terrified and began to run as fast as she could in the opposite direction. He flew behind her searching for her as she ran through the dark forest making it difficult to be seen. She screamed Sparkle's name but there was no reply or any sign of any fairy for that matter. Instead thunder rumbled in the dark sky and a sudden downpour of rain fell on the earth. She slowed her pace and looked around her but saw no sight of anyone. She continued to run however the rain did not stop Draco from flying after her. Instead it only made him more excited for the chase and thought of it as a game. She wondered whether he wanted to eat her, kill her, or give her body to Sahara.

In that instant she stopped running, stopped walking, and turned around to face the fierce dragon that everyone spoke of. He flew down to the ground and stood before her as they stared into one another's eyes. The skies continued to rumble like a thousand men banging on drums. The ground was damp with rain and puddles everywhere. Evangeline was soaking wet as her school clothes clung to her tiny body. Draco smashed his trail on the ground and made a loud bang noise.

"Look who we have here, Somnia Viveret's hero." Evangeline was shocked to hear him speak but then again, she talked to fish and a fairy. What else was new? She hated that everyone was referring to her as their hero when she wasn't entirely too sure what she was saving them from. Was it from Sahara? From Evangeline's understanding Sahara is an evil witch who has done harm to Somnia but yet is too afraid to show herself to anyone, for what reason? Is she afraid that they will defeat her or does she not even exist?

She crossed her arms over her chest and spoke back, "Look who we have here, a cowardly dog who thinks he is a dragon. Ha! You are pathetic."

Draco examined how tiny Evangeline was and thought that he could kill her in one shot but then there would be no fun. He was irritated by her sarcasm and wanted to prove to her that he was powerful so he blew fire and burnt down the trees that were surrounding them. She kept her arms folded across her chest as she looked around her at the burnt trees.

"So you can blow fire from your mouth. I can just as easily snap my fingers and make fire appear." Evangeline was bluffing to make it seem like she is bigger than she is but just to get his attention she snapped her fingers. He was appalled when he saw her fingers light with a flame. Evangeline looked down at her hand to see what he was staring at when she realized that when she snapped her fingers she truly did make fire appear. She stared at the flame and wondered how it didn't burn her hand. She formed her hand into a fist as the flame vanished. Draco was still in shock that she managed to make fire so therefore he swung his tail and knocked over the burnt trees, they turned to ash as they hit the ground.

"You might be able to make fire with your hand but you do not have strength like I do." Evangeline was curious to test that theory; if she could make fire with the snap of her fingers then what else was she capable of? She considered ripping a tree from the ground but then she remembered that he had destroyed all the surrounding trees so instead she repeatedly stomped her feet on the ground till the ground was shaking and made Draco fall on his side.

Lightening began to form in the dark sky as the thunder continued to rumble loudly. He rose off the ground and flew into the sky a few feet off the ground and said, "You may be capable of creating fire and having extreme strength but you are still no hero to Somnia Viveret. Instead you are just another demon like me who has gained black magic." In that moment Draco was struck by lightning but it was no ordinary lightning. The lightning pulled him deep into the clouds, something was controlling it. Draco's eyes flashed from blazing red into a fierce brown and back to red. Evangeline watched as he was being pulled into the clouds; Draco was terrified and even Evangeline could see the terror in his changing eyes.

Shortly after Draco vanished into the clouds, the storm passed. Evangeline stood motionless for a few minutes as she stared at the sky, uncertain of what had just happened. She looked around but there was not a sound in the world, she felt so alone. She continued to walk towards the moon in hope of finding the Empire or anything other than the dark forest. It felt like a long journey before Evangeline finally reached civilization, however it wasn't where she hoped she would find herself.

Instead Sparkle approached her and said with a big grin on her face, "You did it, Evangeline! You found your courage and stood up to the beast and because of your bravery you discovered your powers." Along with Sparkle there were many other fairies that were surrounding her and congratulating her.

"But I didn't defeat the beast, he-" she stuttered on her choice of wording for a brief second and continued, "He was showing off his powers to me when the lightning zapped him. It may sound bizarre to you but it was like the lightning grabbed him and put him into a bubble and just sucked him into the clouds."

The fairies began to whisper amongst one another and Sparkle looked puzzled for a moment. She replied, "Sahara."

Evangeline opened her eyes wide in shock, "She did that?"

"It is the only explanation. Sahara is more powerful than you might think she is. Over the years, she has given certain powers to certain people, or in your case, fictional creatures. With that in mind, those creatures have learnt how to use them and become stronger and more powerful. When Sahara feels the power is strong enough, she drains them of their power and takes possession of them. In brief, murders them when she is finished using them."

Evangeline's jaw dropped as she began to protest, "But she cannot do that!"

Sparkle nodded her head, "She does what she wants because nobody can stop her. Tonight you witnessed her steal the power of another creature." It was silent for a moment as Evangeline tried to think about whose power Sahara stole.

She gasped, "Venus!" Evangeline turned away from Sparkle and began to sprint to the south where the small river was located. Sparkle and a couple of the other fairies followed Evangeline on her search to find the river; it took nearly twenty minutes to get to the river. Sparkle and two other fairies stopped suddenly as they watched Evangeline standing motionless examining the scene. Venus, the goddess of the sea, was no longer a mermaid, instead she was a human. She was lying on her stomach beside the river. Her body was hidden by her long black hair and her crown was now only a wreath of flowers put together as a crown. Evangeline approached her body and turned her body over. Her skin was ice cold, pale as snow, and covered in black veins. Evangeline traced her finger along one of the black veins on Venus' arm and as she did so, Venus' body turned to ice from her touch. Evangeline moved back as she watched her entire body turn to ice and shatter into a million pieces.

Someone whispered, "Sahara, she, she…'"

Evangeline turned her attention to the river and saw Marina. Marina looked terrified but continued to speak, "She sucked out her soul."

Sparkle flew closer to Marina and asked, "What did Sahara look like?"

Evangeline looked confused and asked Sparkle, "Don't you know what she looks like?"

Sparkle kept her attention on Marina but said, "Sahara is a shape shifter and never takes her original form." Marina looked at the broken pieces of ice and watched it as it melted and streamed back into the river. "She was a child."

Sparkle questioned her, "A child?"

Marina nodded her head, "Yes, she was a little girl."

Evangeline was curious and asked, "What other things has she changed into in the past?"

"When she stole the fire element, she shifted into a dragon. Not one like Draco, this one was only a small one. When she stole the air element, she shifted into an eagle and consumed the power from, well like I said, an eagle. And now she has taken the water element from Venus."

Marina looked up at Sparkle and said, "She only needs one more."

They all looked concerned and Evangeline asked, "What else does she need?"

Sparkle whispered, "Me. I am the earth element. I keep balance here in Somnia Viveret and as long as I am still here, she cannot take over our world."

Evangeline was shocked and although she was mad at Sparkle earlier, she didn't want her to die. "What's going to happen if she gets to you?"

Sparkle looked up at Evangeline and said, "Our world will end, that is why I have brought you here. When you return to Somnia Viveret again you will fight for both of our worlds." She looked at the other fairies and Marina as they all looked terrified.

"What if I fail?"

"Then I will die, Somnia Viveret will be destroyed, and you will be lost in the world of unconsciousness forever."

Everyone stared at Evangeline as she grasped what Sparkle had told her. Felicia, one of the fairies, said, "You are the important one and like

God is your saviour, you are ours."

Evangeline sighed because she knew that she could not escape this situation, but then she had a brilliant idea. "What if something good happens in my world, will yours still fall or will it rise again?"

Sparkle eyed her suspiciously and said, "It is a possibility but for the time being the future remains dark."

Evangeline and Sparkle left the river and began to walk through the forest. Evangeline asked, "Am I a threat to Sahara or can she crush me with her bare hands?"

Sparkle smiled and responded, "She is unaware of your visits here but if she knew that you were here, she would try to destroy you because you hold many powers. You have yet to discover what else you are capable of but your powers are very similar to Sahara's, the only difference is that you didn't have to steal them. Whenever she gains powers, so do you."

"Why do I gain them, too?"

Sparkle thought about it for a moment then continued, "There's a bond between you two. It is your destiny to unravel the truth and destroy her with your knowledge and powers."

Evangeline wanted to ask Sparkle what she meant about having a bond but before she could open her mouth to speak, everything went black. She woke up and found herself back at Shire Dale Academy and realized that she had slept for two days straight. When she sat up in her bed, she found Sister Nelly seated on stool at her bedside, half asleep.

Evangeline asked, "Sister Nelly, what are you doing by my bed?"

Sister Nelly jumped and placed her hand over her heart and said, "Good gracious, Evangeline. You startled me!" Evangeline looked around the room and noticed that there was another lady who was in the room with them. "This is Dr. Kelly Baker, sweetie. You have been sleeping for the last two days."

Evangeline looked between the two ladies and waited as they continued to speak. Dr. Baker spoke. "How old are you, Evangeline?"

"I will be turning sixteen in a few weeks."

Dr. Baker nodded her head and wrote in a black journal as she spoke to Evangeline.

"How are you feeling right now?"

"I'm exhausted." She took a brief moment to record down everything that Evangeline told her. "May I ask what this is all about?"

Doctor Baker placed her journal and pen down in her lap and looked at Evangeline as she spoke. "I have come to the conclusion that you have a sleeping disorder called narcolepsy."

Evangeline pulled her eyebrows together in a frown and asked, "What's narcolepsy?"

Dr. Baker was very serious as she continued to speak. "Narcolepsy is a neurological disorder that affects the part of the brain which helps to regulate sleep. You show many signs of having this sleeping disorder because those who suffer from this disorder experience sleepiness and loss of muscle control which is often due to strong emotions. This is a very serious disorder because you may fall asleep instantly; you could be in the middle of class, walking to the supermarket, or even taking a bath."

Evangeline had her full attention on Dr. Baker. "A sleeping disorder? But, Doctor, you don't understand. It is not that I have trouble with my sleep. It is because I am dreaming."

Dr. Baker seemed interested to know more about the topic but before she continued she turned her attention to Sister Nelly and said, "Sister, do you mind letting me talk with Evangeline alone?" Sister Nelly nodded her head and walked out of the room, shutting the door behind her.

"Are your dreams very vivid?"

Evangeline wondered whether she had said too much already but continued to speak. "When I dream, it's not just my mind that wonders out of my soul, my body is there, too. It feels so real that when the weather is warm, I am warm, too. See look! My clothes are drenched with water from the thunder storm that just passed. Not to mention this scratch that is on my forearm. A branch scratched me as I was running through the forest to escape the dragon."

Dr. Baker took interest in Evangeline and examined her as she spoke. She looked at Evangeline's forearm and sure enough there was a large scratch, but to Dr. Baker's knowledge, she assumed that Evangeline was harming herself. "It seems to me that you have a very extreme case of narcolepsy, my dear. I understand that these dreams may seem very realistic but that is another symptom of narcolepsy: hallucinations. People often experience vivid dreams; at times it can be frightening, as well as visual or auditory sensations."

Evangeline refused to believe her and asked, "Then why are my clothes wet and I have this scratch on my forearm?"

Dr. Baker said, "You were sweating, a lot, that is why your clothes feel damp to you and while you were dreaming, you grabbed hold of your arm and scratched at it. I held your hand for a while so that you would not hurt yourself anymore."

"I don't believe you! If it was just a hallucination then why did you not wake me?"

"Believe me I tried to wake you up several times until I finally realized why I could not wake you up. It is because narcoleptics lack the stimulating neurotransmitter called hypocretin-orexin, which can make it nearly impossible to wake up."

Evangeline felt a sadness befall her as she grasped the information that Dr. Baker was telling her. She realized that it seemed like the only explanation for her bizarre dreams. A part of her felt relieved to know this so that she knew if she failed Somnia Viveret, she will still come back to reality. However, she could not stop hearing Sparkle's words repeating in her head;

"You will be lost in the world of unconsciousness forever."

Chapter 10

Crossing Over

"Frances, wake up, sweetie," said her grandmother. Frances was staying at her grandparents for the week as Dr. Wesley had mentioned earlier to Evangeline.

Frances' grandmother returned to Frances' room twenty minutes after she had tried waking her up. She sat at her side and stroked her blonde ringlets behind her ear.

She said, "Sweetie, it's nearly mid-afternoon. You must wake up." Frances was lying on her back, her hands were placed at her sides, and her legs were straight. She appeared as if she was ready to be placed into a coffin, her body was so straight. It was hard to tell whether she was breathing or not. Frances' grandmother was concerned so she shook her body but when Frances did not wake up she began to panic and called her husband. "James!"

He came running around the corner almost missing the bedroom and asked in a frantic tone, "What's the matter?" She looked at her husband and back at their granddaughter. He approached them and sat on Frances' bedside and asked, "Susan, why have you let her sleep the day away?"

"I have tried waking her! She just lies there like a porcelain doll."

James looked at his granddaughter's peaceful face then looked at her chest as he watched for signs of breathing. "She is not dead but rather in a deep sleep. Perhaps we must call Dr. Wesley over to see why she does not wake up."

Susan had fear in her eyes but nodded her head and said, "Yes, call him quickly!"

James walked over to the dining room, picked up their telephone, and began to dial the numbers. To his surprise a woman answered the phone, "Hello? May I speak to Dr. Wesley? It's urgent."

The woman responded, "Hello, sir, I'm afraid to tell you that Dr. Wesley is no longer here. He has resigned his position and returned to his home in Italy. I have replaced his position. I am Dr. Baker, and perhaps I can assist you."

James was confused and asked, "He resigned?"

"Yes, there was a family emergency back in Italy so he went back to help them in their time of need."

James wanted to question it further because he remembered Dr. Wesley told him he was from Scotland not Italy but at this moment he needed a doctor. "My granddaughter has been asleep for almost twenty-four hours and I'm very concerned about her. Do you think you could come down here and take a look at her?"

Dr. Baker remembered seeing Evangeline about the same problem just the other day and wondered whether it was the same condition as she had or not. "Of course!"

It took Dr. Baker half an hour before she made it to the Scott's mansion.

She knocked on the large door when a man in a black uniform answered, "May I help you, ma'am?"

Before she was able to answer, James walked passed his butler and invited Dr. Baker inside. He put his hand out for a handshake and said, "Hi, I am James Scott. Please follow me."

Dr. Baker followed behind James as he led her through their large home. She looked around her as they walked and admired their large, beautiful home. The walls were painted an ivory colour and on the walls were large family portraits that went back decades.

He escorted her to Frances' room and said, "She won't wake up. We have tried everything!"

Dr. Baker knelt down by Frances' beside and examined her body as it just laid there motionless. "Has she moved at all?"

Susan responded, "Not at all. She has been lying in the same position since I tried waking her early this morning."

Dr. Baker tried to lift her arm but it was like gravity was pulling it down, she was locked to her bed. "Hmm, this is strange alright. It's like her body is glued to the bed."

She used force to try and lift Frances' arm but was unable to do so. "This is a bizarre situation we have here. I was just with a different patient the other day that had a similar situation but she was not glued to her bed."

Susan tried to lift up her granddaughter's arm but did not succeed. "What is happening to her?"

Dr. Baker took a moment before she answered, "That is a good question, ma'am. However, the only explanation for this is that she has a severe case of narcolepsy and night terrors."

Susan looked up at Dr. Baker with a puzzled look, "What in the world's name is that?"

"Narcolepsy can keep the person from waking up and night terrors are worse than nightmares. You can notice on Frances that her forehead is slightly wet from her sweat; it is a sign of a night terror. Often times, people will wake up because they are so frightened but in this case, she looks like she is stuck in her nightmare and that is where narcolepsy plays its roll. Narcoleptics sleep for long periods at a time or sometimes do not. They can fall asleep at any time of day. Even if she was riding her bicycle, she could fall asleep on it and crash. Therefore narcolepsy can be very dangerous to have and she definitely shows signs of this disorder."

Susan refused to believe Dr. Baker whereas James took interest in this disorder. Dr. Baker asked, "Is Frances by any chance related to Evangeline Welsh?"

Susan looked up at Dr. Baker and said, "How dare you ask such a thing! My granddaughter is not related to that garbage."

Susan's family goes back decades and has always been a very wealthy family. Dr. Baker raised her eye brow at her and said, "I did not mean to offend you with that question, Mrs. Scott. It just happens that Evangeline Welsh also has narcolepsy and was sleeping for two days straight before she finally woke up."

Susan rose from Frances' bed and walked up to Dr. Baker until she stood an inch away from her face. "Just because the two girls both have the same disorder does not mean that they are of the same blood, Dr. Baker. I'm not even sure if I believe you for that matter. Never in my life have I ever heard of a sleeping disorder. That is just nonsense to me." As the two women were bickering at one another, Frances crossed her arms over her chest and grabbed hold of her arms as she began to move her head from side to side. She looked as if she wanted to scream but was unable to open her mouth. Her lips were glued shut just like her body was glued to her bed. The ladies turned their attention back to Frances as they watched her head twitching back and forth. In that moment, Frances dug her finger nails into her arms and scratched all the way down her forearm to her wrists. Dr. Baker ran over to her and locked her arms down at her side. Susan and James were horrified by what their granddaughter had just done.

"Please hold her arms down for me so that I may clean her wounds!" They each grabbed hold of one of her arms as Dr. Baker went to grab her medicine bag. She wet a cloth and wiped the blood from Frances' arms.

She scratched through her skin, which would leave scars. She had three scratch marks on both arms that started from her biceps and went down to her wrists.

The hairs on Susan's arms stood up in fear and she began to sweat. "Why did she do that to herself? My beautiful granddaughter has scarred herself for life; no man will ever look at her the same again!"

Dr. Baker stopped wrapping the band aid around Frances' arm and turned to look at Susan. "Excuse me? Your granddaughter is experiencing an extreme case of night terrors and you are concerned about who she will marry?"

Susan avoided Dr. Bakers question and simply said, "There is no such thing as night terrors."

An hour had passed since Frances scratched her arms and the three still remained seated in her bedroom. There was a loud knock on the door but neither of them rose from their seat to see so was there.

It didn't even take thirty seconds before Lawrence came rushing through the bedroom door. "Where is she? Where is my daughter?"

Susan got off the bed and walked towards her son. As she reached out to comfort him, he stormed passed her and froze before his daughter. He examined her wrapped up arms and noticed that she had been strapped down to the bed. "I demand an explanation as to why my daughter is strapped to her bed!"

Dr. Baker began to explain to Lawrence what had happened and what the cause of her actions was.

Lawrence knelt down on the ground beside her bed and held his daughters hand. He whispered in her ear, "Please wake up, Frances. Please." He bent his head over her shoulder and felt her body begin to twitch again. He looked up and Frances turned her head towards her father.

Her eyes remained closed but her mouth opened as she spoke, "Frances is not here, Daddy." Lawrence's jaw dropped, he listened to his daughter speak in what sounded like a foreign language.

He looked up at Dr. Baker and back at his daughter. "Frances, open your eyes, honey."

Dr. Baker whispered to herself, "Latin."

Lawrence turned to look at her and asked, "What did you say?"

She looked back at him and said, "She sounds like she has a Latin accent and if I am correct, this is just her nightmare talking."

He looked back at his daughter as her head began to twitch again and she tried to free her arms from the straps. "It almost looks like her dream is trying to cross over to our world. That's if that sort of stuff actually existed." James watched as his granddaughter suddenly stopped twitching.

Frances tilted her head backwards and opened her mouth. She screeched so loud that her family covered their ears. Frances opened her eyes as they turned from brown to black as night. She formed her hands into fists and pulled her arms out of the straps. As she did this, she pushed her family to the ground causing them to become unconscious.

Twenty minutes later...

Lawrence opened his eyes and found he was lying on the floor next to Frances' nightstand. He looked around him and found his mother, father, and Dr. Baker lying just inches away from him. He rubbed his eyes and looked to see what they were looking at. He followed their gaze towards the doorway and sure enough there she was. She was looking down at the ground as her black hair hung covering her face. Her white nightgown looked dirty and as if she was playing in the dirt. Lawrence looked over to the bed and Frances was gone.

The girl at the door kept her head down and said, "Are you looking for me, Daddy?"

He looked back at the young girl and stood up from the ground. He was puzzled and asked, "Frances?"

The young girl looked up at Lawrence and smiled. He stared into her black eyes and asked, "What have you done with my daughter?"

She began to walk closer to him and said, "I'm still myself, Dad. I just look different."

They stood inches apart as he examined this young girl who claimed to be his daughter. She grabbed hold of his hand and led him towards her bed. They sat next to one another, his hands still in hers. "I need you to do me a favour."

He turned to look and her and said, "Not until I get my daughter back."

She chuckled and continued, "Alright fine. This body will wear out soon anyways… You can have her back after you have obeyed my demands."

"And if I don't?"

Once again she laughed but became instantly serious, "Then I will consume her soul." Lawrence swallowed hard and nodded his head in agreement.

She smiled a big cheery smile and said, "Very good, Lawrence. After all she is just a bastard child. There really wouldn't be any sense in you missing out on anything. Even after you made a child with that whore, she still didn't want you." Susan remained lying on the other side of the room but kept her ears opened as she listened to their conversation.

"That is not true! She would have married me if Charles didn't pose such a threat on her. I loved Cecilia so much; I would have given the world to her just to see her smile. But in the end, fear was greater than love, because she choose Charles."

"Blah, blah, blah…So what. The woman is dead, served her right to play two men at once."

He stared at his so-called daughter and said, "She didn't know that Charles was Henry Beckem. As far as she knew, Henry Beckem always cancelled whenever he was invited to the house. He spoke to Cecilia on the telephone once and when he did she heard other women in the background. Charles Welsh does not exist."

Susan's jaw dropped as she listened in on the conversation. "Charles, or Henry, poisoned Cecilia with that filthy water when he discovered that she was going to leave him for me."

The young girl clapped her hands together in excitement and said, "Oh goody! Then that means you will have no problem going through with what I have in mind."

Lawrence looked up at her and said, "First off, you must tell me who you are and that you promise to bring Frances back to me. She is the only part of Cecilia that I have left."

She rolled her eyes at him and said, "You'll get your bastard child back but if for some reason you betray me and back down, I will end her life."

He nodded his head to inform her that he understood her terms. "Good, because I am Sahara and no man can defeat me. I am here because Henry Beckem's daughter, Evangeline, is imposing as a threat to me and I need her taken care of."

Lawrence opened his mouth to protest, "I will not kill a teenage girl!"

Sahara shook her head and said, "You humans are so difficult to get through to. I do not need help to defeat her; I want you to murder her father." He looked at her in confusion. "I changed your contract that you had Mr. Beckem sign. The only reason he signed it was because he knows that Charles Welsh is not his true identity." She held out the contract before Lawrence as he began to read:

By signing this contract I agree to share my profits with Lawrence Scott's company, Big Engine, and to both obtain equal partnership and credit. Furthermore, I also hereby agree to dedicate a year of my services to the Scott family's war corporation. I solemnly swear to fight for Knaresborough, North Yorkshire, and face the possibility of getting harmed or possibly facing death.

"As you can see I have not changed very much on your contract. I have just added that you will also receive credit for his invention and I have changed his signature to the proper name he was given therefore he cannot back out. Make sure he is murdered when he fights in your family's army."

Lawrence nodded his head and asked, "What about Evangeline?"

She smiled wickedly and said, "I have plans for her but her father poses as a threat to all of us so I need you to get rid of him."

Lawrence looked at her and watched as her eyes turned flaming red. "I will do my best."

"It's not about doing your best; it's about doing the job." Her eye's flickered from red to black and then to its original brown colour. He watched as her hair changed back to blonde and her wounds healed so that it only showed very faintly.

"Dad, why are they all laying on the ground?"

Lawrence wrapped his arms around his daughter and hugged her tightly. She didn't know what was going on but hugged him back anyways. Lawrence looked over to where the others were and watched his mother stand up with a shocked expression on her face. He tilted his head at her and asked, "Is something wrong, Mother?"

She leaned up against the wall and pointed at Frances as she began to speak, "Y—you are the devil!"

Frances was appalled by what her grandmother was saying and felt a sadness befall her. "Mother, apologize to Frances right now!"

"I saw what you became—I saw your hair turn black as night and your eyes red as flames. You are possessed!"

Lawrence got off the bed and walked towards his mother. She was still leaning against the wall, staring at Frances as her whole body was shaking from fear. "You will stop speaking to her like that. You are imagining things."

She turned to look at her son and said, "Just like I am imagining you having a child with Henry Beckem's wife?" Lawrence looked back at his daughter then grabbed his mother by the hand and dragged her into a different room.

"You will keep your mouth shut, do you understand me?"

She refused to look her son in the eyes so he grabbed her face between his palms and turned her face towards his. "You saw the witch and how she took over my daughter's body. Who knows what else she is capable of! Do you really want to find out what she would do to you if you betrayed her?"

She moved his hands off her face and said, "That is a risk I'm willing to take."

Susan retired to her room and Lawrence whispered, "Sweet dreams, Mother."

The following morning James woke up to find his wife had died in her sleep. Dr. Baker told them she had a heart attack, possibly from all the stress.

Lawrence shook his head and whispered mostly to himself, "You should've never heard anything."

Chapter 11

Maryanne

Dear Cecilia, *May 2, 1908*

There are days where I question why I did what I did, and then I remember that it was all for you. It was always you, Cecilia. I worked long days in the hot summer heat so that I could place food on the table. I sat down only for a brief moment one day at work but then I looked around me and thought about you. I thought about how you sit around all day long while I slave for you. I did it all for you. I left Scotland with you just so you didn't have to marry me. Before I met you, I was a fool and wanted nothing more than to just have fun with other women. Then when I looked into your glamorous green eyes that day, the world disappeared. I heard you speak such horrible things about me that I was forced to change my identity. I have turned myself into a brand new man for you, but for what reason, Cecilia? You betrayed me when you slept with Lawrence and you broke my heart in the process. When this ship sets sail, I will escape the nightmare you have created for our daughter and me. Our family will be reunited for I plan to take Evangeline back to Scotland, where she will meet her grandparents and see that she could have had a life all along if you wouldn't have been such a stubborn whore.

I decided to write you this one last time so that I can move on and leave you behind. However, it seems as much as I try to get rid of you the more you follow me and haunt me. Lawrence has decided to name the ship after you and if I do run away, then you will still sail the seas with me. I cannot escape you! You are corrupting my mind with hatred and negative thoughts. You were the light of my life; you were my angel. Now you are the devil who creeps behind my every step and wishes nothing more than for me to fail. You are the one who has failed because I am going to become the most successful man anyone has ever seen. I will start a brand new life with my sweet Evangeline, whereas you will remain buried in the ground to rot in hell. You were a sinner and therefore I made it easier on both of us when I ended your life.

I will always love you, Cecilia. A part of me hates you and a part of me loves you more than anything. You were my world and you crushed it. Rest in peace, beautiful.

Sincerely,
Henry Beckem

Today was the day that Charles planned on telling his daughter about his invention. It had been almost two years since he last saw his daughter and decided that he owed her a visit. He took the day off work today so that he could tidy up and get ready for his daughter's arrival.

Charles lived in Lawrence's old house for a few months before he finally decided to purchase it off of him. Even though the ship was not yet completed, Charles had already begun to make money like no other. People from all over Europe had heard about what they were building and took extreme interest in his machine. He decided to sell his idea to other contractors all over Europe but for a certain percentage of the profit, along with recognition and credit for the invention of the ship. At first he was uncertain about sharing his idea with other contractors, but when they began to negotiate with him he realized that he would soon become a millionaire, and possibly soon after, become the richest man in Europe.

Charles had tidied a room and had it fully furnished for Evangeline. He stood in the room and looked around as he made sure that everything was in perfect condition for he wanted only the best for his daughter. He had painted the room a fierce red and hung white satin drapes over the windows. Beneath the window stood a bench on which he had placed a bunch of stuffed animals. His daughter would soon turn seventeen but he still thought of her as his little girl. He never was able to provide her with everything little girls should have when they are young and he planned to make up for it now. Her room was just a start to her new life and therefore he made it perfect. There were gold, Egyptian cotton bed sheets and comforters draped over her queen size bed. Over her large bed hung canopy curtains; they were gold and shear drapes. Across from her bed was her ten foot walk-in closet that he had filled with young lady clothes that his house keeper helped pick out.

He looked around the room one last time before he shut the door behind him. He walked down the long hallway towards the sitting room.

His housekeeper, Maryanne, approached him with a glass of lemonade in her hands. “Sir, I thought I might make you a fresh glass of lemonade on account of the extremely hot weather.”

Charles glanced at her angelic face and at the drink. “Thank you, Maryanne, but I have to get my daughter now. Freshen up and enjoy that lemonade for yourself.” He smiled at her and admired her beauty as he made his way towards the front door.

She yelled after him, “Thank you, sir!”

Although Charles had become a wealthy man, he still enjoyed walking places every once in a while, besides, he wanted to surprise his daughter and approaching her school in a vehicle would ruin the surprise of his new fortunes. It took him nearly half an hour till he finally reached Shire Dale Academy. Sister Nelly was at the front of the school when he got there.

She looked at him and narrowed her eyes, "Mr. Welsh."

He nodded his head at her and said, "Hello, Sister Nelly. I am here to take my daughter home."

She turned her body towards Charles and laughed, "Ha! What makes you think that Evangeline wants to go home with you?"

His smile vanished as he stared blankly at her. "What on earth is that supposed to mean?"

She walked closer towards him till they stood inches apart. "You haven't seen your daughter in two years, Mr. Welsh. You think that she will just pretend like you never left and let you walk back into her life? I may only be a sister here at the school but I know a fool when I see one and you, sir, have broken your daughter's heart."

Charles' excitement had vanished along with his smile, he was serious as he spoke, "Excuse me, but you do not know my daughter and you certainly do not understand what my life has been like these past few years!"

"It must have been a wonderful life if you could not even spare one day to see her."

Charles was angry and had an urge to smack her cross the face for her obscure nonsense but then he remembered he was a gentleman not a monster. "She will forgive me when she discovers what I have spent my life doing, doing for her."

"Oh, I am well aware of your ship, Mr. Welsh, but is one ship worth losing two years of her life?"

His eyes widened in shock and he whispered, "Does she know about my success?"

She shook her head and laughed once again, "Unbelievable! You still only care about hiding it from her but, no, she does not know."

He sighed in relief and said, "It is not that I am hiding it from her, it is a surprise for her and I know that she will appreciate it. Now if you don't mind, I'd like to see her."

Sister Nelly made her way up the stairs towards the large brown doors of the school. Before she turned the doorknob she took one last glance at Charles and said, "I remember the day you brought your daughter into this school and remember how your clothes hung off your bodies like fabrics you picked from someone's trash. I remember seeing the sadness in your eyes as you said goodbye to her and then the excitement when you came to see her. But over the years, her faith in you coming to see her has vanished along with her love for you. Now all I see from you is your fancy clothes and excitement about your ship, not your daughter. Good luck winning her love over again, Mr. Welsh."

He was speechless but chose to ignore the hateful words that came from her. Instead he followed her in silence as she led him towards her room. She opened the room to her dorm and they stood in the doorway for a moment. Neither of them said a word, instead he stared at his daughter and watched as she sat on her bed and wrote in her journal.

He kept his eyes on her and whispered to Sister Nelly, "Is that Evangeline?"

She smirked at him and said, "Surprising how much people change, is it not? She has transformed into an amazing young lady. It's a shame you wasted two years of your life not watching her grow up." He looked at her as she continued to speak. "I watch young ladies grow up every day but don't worry, Mr. Welsh, you are not the first parent who has abandoned their child here. I will leave you two alone so you may win her love over again."

Sister Nelly left and Charles watched her as she walked down the long empty hallway. When she turned the corner he turned his attention back on his daughter. He was mesmerized by her beauty and couldn't believe how much she looked like Cecilia. He walked into the room and approached her bed. She saw a shadow appear over her journal and for a moment she simply just stared at the dark figure on her journal. She slowly closed it hoping that whoever it was didn't read what she was writing.

She heard him ask in a deep voice, "What do you write about?" She grabbed the journal and pulled it close to her chest and looked up at the man that stood before her.

"Charles?" She narrowed her eyes at him as she tried to remember what he looked like before.

He looked like her father but his clothes were far too fancy and clean. His smile disappeared as he spoke, "Yes, my sweet Evangeline, it's your father and I have come to take you home." He used to call her sweet Evangeline all the time but that was years ago when he truly cared for her, now she felt like nothing more than a stranger to him.

"I'm sorry, sir, but I am an orphan for my father abandoned me two years ago as he left me here to fend for myself."

He examined her and only found sadness and pain in her alluring green eyes. "Don't be ridiculous, Evangeline. I did not abandon you. I simply went out into the world to find a career for myself so that I might take you home one day and give you a life you deserve."

She took her journal and placed it under her pillow before she spoke again. "I am being ridiculous? I have stopped hopping for you to come back and take me home. The last time I saw you was on my fourteenth birthday and now I am nearly seventeen! That day you last saw me, you didn't even seem happy to see me therefore I felt like I was just a burden in your life. You don't know what family means."

He was shocked and said in a loud tone, "That's absurd! You are my family and I love you and care for you very much."

She smiled and said, "You cannot leave your family whenever you please and expect to walk back into my life and act like you never left." He was surprised by his daughter's attitude and felt she was being very difficult.

He sat on the end of her bed and covered his face with the palm of his hands. She moved further away and stared at him and he shook his head in frustration. "All my life, I have tried to support you and your mother and in the end I was never appreciated. Cecilia betrayed me and now my daughter refuses to even refer to me as her father."

She responded, "Have you ever stopped to consider why that might be?"

He glanced up at her and she only saw sadness in his eyes as he spoke, "I am so sorry for hurting you and for leaving you. I assure you, I never meant to hurt you, I only wanted to do more for you and I just got so caught up in my work I didn't get the opportunity to come and see you as I would have liked to."

She examined his fancy suit and asked, "Did you steal your clothing or how is it possible for you to afford such high-class clothes?"

He smiled and said, "I would much rather like to show you than to sit here in this dark, lifeless room and tell you, if you don't mind coming home with me."

She looked around the room while she considered it, "How long will I be gone for?"

He turned his body to face her and flashed his big smile at her, "Forever, I'm here to take you home for good."

She smiled at him and said, "Do you promise?"

He grabbed her hands in his and said, "Promise."

She buried her face in her flaming red hair and said, "Okay, but you are still not forgiven."

Charles helped Evangeline pack all her things which didn't take long because she didn't have very much to begin with. Sister Nelly signed her out of Shire Dale Academy and walked the two of them out of the building.

She gave Evangeline a hug and said, "I wish you the best and enjoy your life."

"Thank you, Sister."

Charles took his daughter's bag as they walked side by side through the city. After a few minutes of walking, she asked him, "Where are you staying this time?"

He kept his eyes on the road ahead and said, "You will see, princess."

She didn't bother asking anything else for she knew that he wouldn't tell her. Instead they walked in silence until they reached the large house that was located on top of a hill.

She stopped walking and stared at the house, "What are we doing at the Scott's house?"

He stood by the door and said, "This no longer belongs to Lawrence Scott. I bought it from him a few months ago." Evangeline walked slowly towards the door as she looked at the huge brick house.

"How did you afford it?"

He opened the door and said, "I have created the most successful machine anyone has seen in the longest time and have used some of my fortune towards this house." She walked through the door and looked around. Everything was spotless and beautiful; her family had never been able to afford even a small house.

Before she was able to ask him about his machine a young woman approached her and said, "Pleasure to finally meet you, Evangeline! May I offer you a glass of lemonade?"

Evangeline looked at her father and back at the woman. "Who are you?"

The woman smiled and said, "Oh how rude of me! I am Maryanne, your father's housekeeper."

She was confused and turned her attention back on her father, "What sort of job do you have that you can afford this large house and a housekeeper?"

He smiled at his daughter and said, "Once we get you settled in, I will take you to my workplace and show you. It will be easier that way."

"Miss, did you want that lemonade?"

Evangeline looked at Maryanne's innocent face and nodded her head.

Once Maryanne left the room, she approached her father and said, "Maryanne is very beautiful, I'm sure you noticed that, did you not? Is she just your housekeeper or is she your lover, too?"

He looked around the corner to make sure Maryanne could not hear their conversation, "I admit, we have had romance in our life but she is only my housekeeper."

Evangeline was shocked by her father and said, "How can you just make love to someone and then treat them like your slave after? Do you have no dignity left?!"

He grabbed her by the arm and dragged her into the sitting room for more privacy. "Maryanne is the most beautiful woman I have seen in a long time but that does not mean I love her. I only ever loved two women and that is you and your mother."

Evangeline shook her head and said loudly, "Mom is dead. She is never coming back! You need to move on and find someone else who can make you happy."

He smiled, "That's why I brought you home again..."

"You are impossible!"

Maryanne walked into the room with two glasses of lemonade in her hands and said, "I don't mean to interrupt, but I have brought your beverages."

"Thank you, Maryanne. You may go home early today. I would like to get better acquainted with my daughter."

She looked between the two and smiled, "Of course. Thank you, sir. Evangeline, it was a pleasure meeting you."

After Maryanne left, Charles led his daughter upstairs to show her the rest of the house, along with her bedroom.

As they walked down the long hallway, she said, "I must ask you one thing. Why did you choose to buy a huge house for just two people? A small house was not good enough for you?" She remembered the very first time she dreamt about Somnia Viveret and how she had judged Sparkle for choosing the smallest house while she could have had the largest of them all.

Charles looked at her in confusion and thought about it. "Because I can afford it now and I am making up for all the times when I couldn't even afford a shack for us to spend the night in. A small house would do, but why settle for less when you can have more."

She shook her head in disapproval and said, "Fortune has corrupted your mind to think like a wealthy individual…"

He said nothing to her smart remark but rather directed her towards her new room and opened the door. She walked in the room and looked around her.

She was speechless as she examined the large bed and the huge closet. "Wow, this is amazing. I admit this is a beautiful room."

He showed her where he placed everything and said, "Maryanne helped pick out the outfits and helped arrange the room so it is her that you should thank."

She smiled and said, "I will remember to do that next time I see her. Maryanne really seems like a wonderful woman. Are you sure you don't love her in return?"

He narrowed his eyes at her and said, "In return?"

"Oh come on, Father, you cannot tell me that you don't notice the way she admires you when she looks at you. She is head over heels for you and would do anything for you. Her eyes lit up when she looked at you or when you gave her the slightest bit of attention."

Charles blushed and turned away from his daughter. "A woman will do anything for a man just so she can get to his money."

"That is nonsense! You cannot tell me that you honestly believe in that! Maryanne is a kind hearted woman and she clearly adores you.

You are either too blind to see it or your heart is lost at sea along with our mothers."

He smirked as she spoke these words and whispered to himself, "If it is lost at sea, then I must set out to find it."

"Pardon me?"

Charles looked back at his daughter and said, "Nothing, sweetheart. Come on, let's go. I want to show you where I work and my most recent project."

Evangeline narrowed her eyes at him and asked, "Your most recent project? I thought that there was only one…"

He raised his eyes brows as he found the proper words, "Well technically yes, but it is such a success that I have made different models of it and sold it to other parts of Europe. Some are smaller and some are the same size as the one that we are still working on."

"Alright then, let's go so I can see this amazing invention of yours and see why it has made you so wealthy." Charles flashed his daughter a big smile and grabbed hold of her hand as he directed her out of the house.

It took them nearly twenty minutes to reach the harbour. There were men everywhere as they ran back and forth hulling wood and metals. Evangeline glanced around her as she watched the men carry large pieces of metal over their shoulders and hull it towards a large, unfinished ship.

Her jaw dropped as she stared at the huge ship that was tied to the docks. "You—you built that?"

She kept her eyes on the ship and Charles laughed at her reaction, "No, I designed it. I have put my fair share of work into the ship but these men here are the contractors who have put my design together and created this beautiful ship before us."

She kept her eyes locked on the large ship and slowly began to walk towards it. She looked around her as the men walked back and forth, hammering and placing pieces of metal and wood together. Some men stood off to the side and ate their lunch that their wives had prepared for them. They glanced back at her and smiled for women never came to the construction site because it was dangerous and anyone could get hurt. She continued to walk towards the ship until she stood only inches away from it. She stretched out her arm and gently slid her index finger along the side of the ship.

A young man approached her and gently grabbed hold of her hand. "You must be careful, miss. You could fall in the river or hurt yourself. This is no place for a lady to be."

Evangeline looked down at their hands and followed her glance up his arm to his face. Her cheeks turned rosy as she blushed at the sight of this charming young man. She stared at his charming hazel eyes and wavy bronze hair that lit up his handsome face. She kept holding his hand because she feared if she let go he would disappear and only remain a mirage.

"My—I'm Evangeline." He smiled at her and led her away from the dock and to her disappointment he released her hand.

"Pleasure to meet you, Evangeline. May I ask what you are doing by the docks?"

"My father created this ship." The young man was surprised and slightly impressed as well.

"Mathias! Leave the young lady alone and get back to work."

Evangeline's jaw dropped as she discovered his name was Mathias and was left speechless. "Yes, sir, but you must be careful of this one so she doesn't fall overboard." Mathias winked at her and returned to his work.

She watched as he walked away and asked, "Who was that?"

Lawrence looked over at Mathias and back at Evangeline and responded, "That is Mathias, and he's a very nice young man and very hard working, too. It's a pity his family left him when he was just a child.

He has provided for himself since he was nearly a boy so I hired him and only seen him transform into a wonderful man. If he was well off then I would allow him to have my daughter's hand in marriage but I do not want my Frances to live in the sewers or be the one who brings in the income. It truly is a shame; she had her eyes set on that boy."

Evangeline looked up at Lawrence and was beyond irritated by his hurtful words. "Excuse me, Mr. Scott, but as you and I both recall it was not long ago that my father and I were living in the sewers and now you are making money off of him."

Lawrence looked down at Evangeline and said, "Oh yes, that is correct, but the difference between your father and Mathias is that when you grow up with money, you will do anything in your power to regain the wealth, but when you are born into poverty, it is about surviving not about becoming a millionaire."

Evangeline narrowed her eyes at him and said, "And the difference between me and your daughter is that she grew up with a big mouthy father and became a stuck up bitch. Whereas I have become courageous and not afraid to stand up to jerks such as yourself."

Lawrence raised his eyebrows at her and was about to protest until he realized that she was nearly seventeen and still a lady. "You and Frances are more alike than you will ever know."

"Ha! She has blonde ringlets and brown eyes; I have green eyes and red hair. She is spoiled and I am fortunate. She is a disgrace and I am, well I am me."

Lawrence's jaw dropped as he listened to Evangeline's hateful words. "Do not speak about my daughter in such a rude manner. There is another difference and that is that she is a lady and you are a savage."

Charles approached them and said, "Sorry, I was held up by Jimmy, he wanted to know where to put..." He stopped talking as he glanced between the two as they stared at one another. Evangeline had fire in her eyes and looked like she wanted to sprint at Lawrence and attack him.

"Did I miss something here?"

Lawrence turned his attention on Charles and said, "Yes, perhaps your daughter needs to attend Shire Dale Academy for another few years to perfect her manners a little more rather than to say such cruel things about my daughter."

Evangeline looked at her father and smiled innocently. "I just told Mr. Scott here that his daughter is a stuck up bitch and that she is everything that I am not."

Lawrence and Charles stared at one another for a brief moment for they knew the truth and that was that the girls were sisters whether they liked it or not.

"Alright, Evangeline, that is enough. Apologize to Mr. Scott."

Evangeline stared at her father in disbelief and said, "Are you serious? I have only ever heard you say cruel things about Lawrence Scott and now you are defending him over your own daughter?"

Charles sighed for he knew that his daughter was right. "Apologize to Mr. Scott, Evangeline."

Evangeline rolled her eyes at her father and said, "Sorry that I am so outspoken."

Lawrence nodded his head at her and said, "You're forgiven." He turned his back to them and began to make his way towards his office. It was located in a large bricked building that was located near the docks. After they had begun the construction of the ship, he wanted to be closer to the project so he had his crew build a new building by the docks.

After Lawrence had disappeared in the large brown building, Evangeline turned to face her father and asked, "Why do you defend the man you once hated over your own daughter? Have you gone mad?"

Charles began to walk along the docks and said, "Lawrence is my partner in building this ship. I didn't have very much money and therefore I needed to find someone who did and he happened to walk into my life at the perfect time."

Evangeline walked beside her father and said in a snobby tone, "Next, he will walk down the aisle with you and pronounce you as man and wife."

Charles laughed at her sarcasm and said, "You are silly and so much different than I remember."

"Yeah that tends to happen over the years, especially if you're left to discover the world on your own. You learn to fight your own battles and know the importance of your own life."

He nodded his head, "I found it rather amusing how you spoke to Lawrence. If he wasn't my partner in this ship, then I would have stood there and watched the show a little more."

Evangeline tried to hide her smile and continued to walk alongside her father.

They made their way back to the office shortly after and Charles said, "I have to help Lawrence with some more designs on the ship. You are welcome to go back home if you'd like."

She looked around and said, "Um…I'm not entirely too sure which way home is from here." Charles crossed his arms over his chest and stared into the distance. He smiled as an idea had crossed his mind and he began to walk towards the workers.

"Mathias, I need you to take a break from the propellers and take on a different task."

Mathias stopped what he was doing and wiped his greasy hands on a dirty blue rag. "What is it, sir?"

Charles smiled at the young man and pointed at his daughter as he spoke. Evangeline turned her eyes away as her cheeks felt warm and turned rosy. It wasn't long before her father returned to his daughter, "Alright, I have made arrangements for Mathias to walk you home. He said he will just clean the grease off himself. Those propellers sure can get messy!"

Evangeline couldn't help but smile and had an urge to hug her father but decided not to act like a little schoolgirl.

He leaned in closer to his daughter and whispered, "I saw you light up when you met him at the docks earlier today and figured you would enjoy the company." He winked at his daughter and made his way into the building.

She watched the door shut behind him and suddenly felt a tap on her shoulder. She turned around, startled, and was facing Mathias.

He smiled at her and said, "Alright, Miss Welsh. Shall we go before the sun sets?"

She nodded her head and they began to walk alongside one another. During the first few minutes of the walk neither said a word and Evangeline wondered what he was thinking, he was so difficult to read.

She knew that within the next fifteen minutes, they would arrive at her house and not a word had been said between them. She glimpsed at him and saw sadness in his eyes but also bravery. He felt eyes on him and turned to look at her but in that moment she returned her attention on the road before her.

He smiled and finally said, "How does it feel to go from poverty to wealth?"

She looked at him but his eyes were still set on the road ahead. "I'm not sure yet. I've only felt it today and I feel like those before me misuse money and act like ignorant fools. I'm not sure if I like my father anymore and sometimes I fear that I will turn stuck up, too."

He giggled and said, "You are very insightful, so it appears. It's nice to see another individual who see's life from more perspectives, rather than just trying to decide on what pair of shoes you will buy today."

Evangeline laughed and said, "Clearly you spend too much time around Frances Scott."

They laughed together and he turned to look at her. "I know that we have just met but could I ask you to promise me something?" They slowed their pace so that they could have more time together. Evangeline nodded her head as he said, “Do not let wealth and power corrupt your mind. I saw the way you stood up to Mr. Scott and I couldn’t help but admire your courage and bravery. No one has ever dared to say anything to him.” They reached her house by then and they stood by the drive way, he grabbed her hand and looked into her green eyes. She felt her heart skip a beat as she stared at their hands and then back at his hazel eyes. “I won’t leave here until you promise me to never change.”

Evangeline blushed and buried her face in her red hair. “What if I didn’t want you to leave?”

Mathias smiled at her and pulled her closer to him and said, “You have a beautiful heart and a face that’s hard to miss.”

Evangeline had butterflies in the pit of her stomach; she had never felt like this before. “I promise, but you must promise me to not disappear.”

Mathias resisted the temptation of kissing her red lips and said, “Promise.” He released her hands and let them fall at her sides. “Have a good night, Miss Welsh.” He turned away from her and made his way back to the city.

She stood in her driveway for a few moments and stared after him. When he turned to take one last look at her, she quickly made her way towards the front door of her new house.

Before she was able to touch the doorknob, someone from the inside had opened the door.

Maryanne had a big grin on her face and said, “Good evening, Evangeline!”

Evangeline smiled and wondered how her father didn’t love this woman. She was beautiful beyond belief and so kind hearted. “Hello, Maryanne.”

Maryanne led Evangeline to the kitchen where she had prepared supper for her and her father. The aroma of the spaghetti and meatballs made Evangeline’s stomach growl as she had forgotten how hungry she was. She sat down at the table as Maryanne began to clean the stove.

Evangeline took a bite of the spaghetti and said to Maryanne, "Have you eaten already?"

"Oh heavens, no. I don't eat here."

Evangeline's smile turned serious and her eyes wondered on the huge plate of food what was in the centre of the table. "Did you eat before you came?"

Maryanne stopped cleaning the oven and turned to face Evangeline. "No, but this is not my home, sweetheart. I only do as I'm paid to do."

"Did my father pay you to sleep with him?"

Maryanne's eyes widened in shock and she stuttered to answer, "I—I don't know what you are talking about."

Evangeline placed some spaghetti into the empty plate on the table and gestured Maryanne to take a seat next to her. "I live here now, too, and I insist you eat rather than starving yourself. There is plenty of food." Maryanne did as she was told and smiled shyly at her. "I'm sorry, I shouldn't have asked that but I was curious."

Maryanne and Evangeline ate their dinner in silence but the question still lingered the room.

While Maryanne cleaned the kitchen, Evangeline remained seated at the table and watched her. "I may only be sixteen, but I know love when I see it and you light up like a star in the midnight sky when you look at my father."

Maryanne smiled and turned to face her. "He is locked in the past and forbids moving on, whereas my heart is set on him." She sat down across from Evangeline and looked up at her. "You must hate me…"

Evangeline was shocked and asked, "Why on earth would you say that?"

"Because I'm in love with your father, but his heart is set on your deceased mother."

Evangeline rolled her eyes at her and smiled. "My mother died when

I was ten years old. It's alright if you are in love with my father. Charles, on the other hand, is finding it much harder to let her rest in peace than me. Just don't give up, okay? He will come around when he realizes that he's in love with you, too."

Maryanne stood up and walked over towards the sink and looked out the window. She stared up at the dark night's sky and looked for the brightest star and remembered what Evangeline had said. She whispered, "I may shine brightly in the midnight sky but I am still invisible to him."

Evangeline got out of her chair and made her way to the sitting room. She was still amazed at how large the house was and how beautiful it looked. She walked towards the large chestnut bookshelf that was located on the west side of the room. She dragged her finger across each book and found herself staring at a large blueprint of her father's ship; it was hung over the fire place. Evangeline stared at it and tried to figure out how it worked and wondered what made her father come up with a ship.

"I saw you with that young boy before. Mathias."

Evangeline jumped in fright and placed her hand on her chest. She turned around and looked at Maryanne's chocolate brown eyes and said, "You startled me!" Evangeline grabbed a random book off the shelf and walked towards the red chair; she opened the book and pretended to read.

"Did you hear about what happened to his family?" Evangeline peeked over her book in curiosity but never said a word. Maryanne smiled a weary smile and took a seat across from Evangeline. "Mathias' father, Franklin, and his wife, Caroline, moved here twenty years ago to escape their family feud in Ireland. Franklin was arranged to marry a woman named Cynthia Rose and just days before their wedding, he met a woman named Caroline. His family hired her to help around the house. With the wedding approaching, they needed an extra hand around the house. Caroline was their housekeeper and walked into Franklin's room one day to tidy it. She wasn't aware he was in the bath just a room away. As she had almost finished cleaning his room, he walked in with just a towel wrapped around his body. Caroline dropped the clothes she had in her arms and stared at his muscular chest and arms. She quickly turned her back to him and said, 'I'm terribly sorry, sir. I am the new housekeeper here and wasn't aware you were bathing.' Franklin laughed at her and said, 'That's fine. I wasn't aware we had a new housekeeper. You look awfully young. How old are you?' She kept her back towards him and answered, 'I'm eighteen, sir.' He giggled and said, 'You don't have to call me sir all the time. My name is Franklin.' She smiled and said, 'Caroline.' She walked out of the room and let him get dressed shortly after.

"The next day, he spent the majority of his time around the house and kept his eye out for Caroline for he hoped to run into her again. 'Caroline!' His mother yelled from in the kitchen. He got up and went to see what all the commotion was about. "Caroline, you forgot to clean the silverware. Now look at it; it looks filthy! I cannot let our guest come to a dirty house especially with the silverware. They could get sick.' Caroline looked over her shoulder and saw Franklin in the doorway. 'I'm terribly sorry, ma'am. It slipped my mind. I won't let it happen again.' She nodded her head and said, 'Indeed you won't. You no longer have a job here.' Caroline raised her eyebrows in shocked and said, 'Just because I forgot to clean the silverware? I'm sorry, ma'am.' Franklin's mother shrugged her shoulder at Caroline and said, 'Do not make me get someone to show you where the door is.' Caroline began to whimper and ran out the front door. Franklin shook his head at his mother and said, 'You are impossible to please. It amazes me that people are still employed here at all.' He ran after Caroline and caught her by the arm. 'Hey, Caroline.' She wrapped her arms around him and sobbed in his arms. 'I have no source of income; I don't know how I will survive…' He wrapped his arms around her waist and stroked her hair. 'Then let me be your saviour.' She looked up at him and asked, 'I thought you were marrying Miss Cynthia Rose tomorrow.' He looked around to see if anyone could see them. 'Not unless that is your name.' Caroline dropped her arms but his remained tight around her waist. 'Why are you doing this, Mr. Strong? You realize why your mother found a reason to fire me so suddenly, do you not? My mother worked here years ago and stole a bracelet from her and she found out and had her locked away. She thinks I will do the same and when she found out that she was my mother, she made it her goal to fire me.' Franklin took her by her hand and guided her back into the house towards his bedroom. Caroline sat upon his king size bed as he began packing bags and said, 'If that is how she feels, then I have no other choice then to run away with you.' 'Have you gone insane? You could lose everything you have!' He grabbed a scroll that lay on his dresser and said, 'Not entirely, besides if I have you what else does a man need.'

"They ended up moving here and shortly after, Franklin Strong got a job working for Lawrence Scott. Two years later they had a beautiful baby boy named Mathias Strong. When Mathias was four years old, Franklin took the scroll he had taken from his home before they left Ireland and gave it to Lawrence. It was blueprints for a grain cart that he and his father had worked on for years. Lawrence agreed to start the construction of the machine but for a price. He had to sign a contract to take part in his family's war for a minimum of a year. He agreed to it but was killed in an explosion. Caroline was devastated when she heard the terrible news that her husband had been murdered.

"Lawrence delivered the news to her personally and said, 'If you expect to receive any profit from his machine, then you will pay a price.' She asked him what he wanted and he responded, 'You must leave your son and let him fend for himself. When he is old enough, I will offer him a job at my company so he can make a living for himself.' She began to protest and held her son tightly in her arms. 'If you do not obey my instructions, he will serve the remaining seven months in the war that your husband did not. He could get murdered just like Franklin did.' She looked down at her two year old son and said, 'Why must I leave him? Can he not work for your firm anyways?' Lawrence shook his head and said, 'I always need more men and women pose too much of a distraction whether it be someone's mother or wife.' 'And what do you suggest I do? Pretend that I do not have a son? Let him rot in the sewers while I live in the riches with the income I will be receiving from my dead husband's invention?' He smiled and said, 'I did not say you would become rich but I like that you dream. You will drop your son off by the bridge near the river this evening and I will have another who lives in poverty watch over your boy. Never in your lifetime will you tell him that you are his mother. You may live in this town but if I know that you spoke a word, I will personally murder you.' Lawrence touched Mathias' cheek and made his way to the door. Just before he shut the door he said, 'Do what you are best at and go clean houses; it's what women are best at.'

"That evening, Caroline hugged her son tightly in her arms and cried her eyes out. The poor child cried along with his mother and put his hands on her cheeks and said, 'Please don't cry, Mommy.' She packed his things in a large duffle bag and brought him to the riverside. She knelt down beside him and said, 'Someone will come get you and take care of you. Mommy has to go back to finish some work. Don't be scared, my sweet Mathias. You are a strong little boy and you can take on the world. I love you, Mathias.' She gave her son one final hug and began to walk away. Mathias stood alone by the river and watched his mother walk away. 'Please don't leave me, Mommy.' It broke her heart but she knew that his life meant to much to her to see his life end the way her husband's did. He never found out who his mother was but there was word around town a few years ago that he was searching for her."

Evangeline was silent for a brief moment as she found herself filled with anger and wanted to yell in Lawrence's face and hurt him like he had hurt Mathias and his family. She asked, "Does anyone know where Caroline is now?"

Maryanne shrugged her shoulders and looked towards the window. "Locked in a house somewhere."

Evangeline followed her gaze and then looked back at her. "How come you know so much about his family's past if Caroline wasn't able to tell anyone?"

Maryanne remained silent and rose from her chair. "I must go finish polishing the silverware."

Evangeline rose and walked after her, grabbing her by the arm. "You are Caroline, aren't you?" Evangeline was shocked beyond belief as the information sank in.

Maryanne turned to look at her and whispered, "Caroline disappeared years ago. Don't be ridiculous, Evangeline."

Evangeline smiled. "Then why did you become so defensive? Caroline might have disappeared but that is only because you replaced her with Maryanne."

Maryanne looked around and whispered, "You must never tell anyone, not even Mathias. I will never risk losing him."

Evangeline's jaw dropped as she was amazed that beautiful Maryanne was Mathias' mother. It was by far the last thing she would have suspected. "You have done a wonderful job at hiding yourself, if I do say so myself, for I would have never suspected you to be his mother let alone Irish. You have no accent whatsoever."

Maryanne giggled the slightest bit and said, "I have done my fair share of practicing to hide it."

"He is a wonderful young man, Mrs. Strong."

She smiled for no one had called her Mrs. Strong in years. "As he is the star that lights up your world and adds life to your gloomy world." She smiled and made her way towards the kitchen.

Evangeline followed her and said, "I don't know how Lawrence can be such a greedy and hateful man! It is preposterous. It makes me wonder what sort of terrible event had occurred in his previous life that makes him the way that he is."

Maryanne questioned her curiosity, "What makes you think something terrible occurred in his previous lifetime?"

"There is a reason for everything mankind does and I want to find out what his reason is."

Maryanne began to clean the silverware and said, "Perhaps it has something to do with Frances' mother."

Evangeline giggled, "Yeah, maybe he shipped her off to war, too."

Despite her sarcasm, the question lingered in the room.

Chapter 12

Blind-folded

Evangeline woke up the following morning and found herself on the couch in the sitting room. She squinted her eyes as the sun's rays were beaming on her face. She sat up and noticed that Maryanne had covered her with a blanket and placed a tray on the table before her. On it was a slice of toast, scrambled eggs, and a glass of orange juice. Evangeline reached over and grabbed the toast and glanced around the room. She stood up and walked towards the window and smiled. "For once, reality is better than my dreams." She stared into the horizon as she watched the sun rise and wondered if her father had stayed out all night.

Evangeline felt a tap on her shoulder and jumped, "Good morning, Evangeline." Maryanne began to gather up her dishes and brought them over to the kitchen.

Evangeline followed after her and sat down at the table as she watched Maryanne clean up. She examined her and asked, "Do you ever think about telling Mathias you are his mother?"

Maryanne turned around and had fear written all over her face, "That is preposterous. I will never risk such a thing for my son." Maryanne walked towards Evangeline and bent down in front of her. She grabbed her hands in her and looked up at Evangeline. "I give you my blessing to become friends with him, but I ask you to never mention me."

She looked into Maryanne's pleading eyes and nodded her head. "If Franklin only needed to serve for another few months in the war, then how come Lawrence can keep Mathias for however long he pleases? Not to mention have you hidden here in our home and miss out on his life..."

She rose from the ground and sat on a chair next to her and covered her face with her hands. "Because Mathias is not joining his family's war."

Evangeline shook her head as she tried to understand it all. "He cannot take someone's child from them!"

"He did."

Maryanne returned to her chores as Evangeline sat at the table for another few minutes pondering everything they had been discussing. After a short while, she rose off the chair and made her way towards the stairs. She went to her bedroom and browsed through her large closet. She stared blankly at the variety of clothes that hung in her closet and wondered how she would decide what to wear. When she attended Shire Dale Academy, she only ever wore the same uniform and before that, she wore rags that hung off her body and were soaked in dirt.

Evangeline closed her eyes and ran her fingers across the clothes and choose an outfit, blindly. She opened her eyes and removed the dress off the hanger and made her way to the bathtub. Next to her closet was her very own bathroom that had been cleaned spotless and the towels organized from smallest to largest alongside the wall. She began to undress and let her clothes hit the floor. She filled the bathtub with hot water and slowly stepped over the edge as the water touched her bare skin.

After she finished bathing, she slipped on the white summer dress she had chosen from the closet. The dress flowed just below her knees and hung off her shoulders. It was covered in green and yellow daisies. She looked at her reflection in the mirror and wondered who the girl before her was. She had never worn a dress such as this one in her entire life. She felt beautiful and continued to look at her reflection. Her thick, wavy, flaming red hair reached her mid back and complimented her skin's complexion. Her eyes were a fierce green and her plump lips were as red as her hair.

"Evangeline, are you in there?" Maryanne knocked on the bathroom door and grabbed hold of her attention. Evangeline opened the door and saw Maryanne standing before her with her mouth open. A huge grin crossed Maryanne's face as she said, "You look absolutely beautiful Evangeline! I am speechless." She smiled shyly and walked passed her towards her closet. Beneath her clothes was a column of shoes that had been arranged according to colour. Evangeline grabbed a pair of one inch, white heels. Maryanne looked at the heels and said, "Why don't you choose ones that have a bigger heel?"

Evangeline blushed as she felt embarrassed that she had never worn heels before. "I'm afraid I will fall if I wear those." Maryanne laughed and nodded her head. Evangeline grabbed a purse that hung on a hook in the closet and placed it over her shoulder. In it she had her journal, some money her father had left her, and a pen.

She walked passed Maryanne and headed for the front door of the house. Maryanne followed after her and asked, "Where are you headed?" Before Evangeline shut the door behind herself, she said, "I'm going to go to the docks and see what my father is up to."

Maryanne smiled and said, "Don't you mean Mathias?" She winked at her as she closed the door behind Evangeline.

When Evangeline finally reached the docks, she browsed the crowd for a young man named Mathias. He was nowhere in sight so she walked around the working men as she searched the crowd for him. From all directions men whistled at her shouted, "Are you lost? This is no place for a beautiful lady. Someone might kidnap you." She ignored their rude comments and walked towards the ship. She looked at it as it looked the same as it had the day before.

Mathias approached her from behind and spoke in his Irish accent,

"Are you looking for me?"

She turned around as he had startled her. "No, I am looking for my father…"

He smiled his sweet smile and wrapped his arms around her and directed her towards a large brown building. "He is in there."

She turned around to face him and said, "Alright so you caught me. Perhaps I was looking for you."

He giggled and examined her from head to toe, "You clean up very nicely, Miss. Welsh."

She blushed and looked down at her new dress, "My housekeeper bought clothes for me and there were just so many to choose from so I closed my eyes and selected this."

He rolled his eyes and said, "The dress is lovely, but I was referring to your face. I saw you walking up the dock but remained hidden behind the propellers as I watched you find your way back to where we first met. You leave me breathless every time I look at you." He whispered, "I'm trying very hard not to kiss you right now."

Evangeline blushed and wanted him to kiss her. "You should stop resisting the temptation, Mr. Strong."

He smiled at her and said, "Everything about you is alluring, you put me in a trance—how do you know my last name?"

Evangeline widened her eyes and looked over at the ship. "Umm, my father told me. You are his worker, after all."

He nodded his head and teasingly said, "For a moment there, I thought you pulled out my documents and did a criminal record check on me. I must warn you, do not believe them when they tell you that I murdered that man…"

He winked at her as he spoke and began to laugh. "Oh ha, ha Mr. Strong…"

"Mathias!" Lawrence made his way towards the young couple and did not seem very pleased. "Miss Welsh I see you have come to distract my crew once again."

Evangeline smiled and said, "Well if they are distracted then maybe you can step out of your office and actually do some work yourself. Tell me, Mr. Scott, have you ever actually welded anything in your lifetime?"

Lawrence frowned at her as Mathias fought back his smile. "You are trouble, Miss Welsh. I hereby order you to stay off this property. It is not safe and we wouldn't want to get your pretty little dress all dirty."

"That's ironic that you say that."

He eyed her curiously and asked, "Why do you say that?"

"Because your suit is so clean, there isn't even a single hair on it."

Lawrence smoothed out his suit and smiled a cocky smile. "I am not going to argue with you but could you please leave my men alone. They are not getting paid to stand around." Evangeline nodded her head and watched as Lawrence walked away.

Mathias placed a kiss upon her hand and began to walk away. She followed after him and shouted, "Will I see you again?"

He glanced back at her and said, "That is a ridiculous question. You already know the answer to that." He continued to walk towards the propellers and began working.

She watched him for a brief moment then walked towards the brown building.

"Evangeline, how was your sleep?" Her father sat in a large office and worked on more blueprints.

She looked around the room and said, "Fine."

He looked up at her and said, "Wow. You look stunning."

She smiled and suddenly began to dislike all the attention she was receiving. "What made you decide to create a ship?"

He crossed his arms over his chest and leaned back in his chair. "When your mother died from cholera, I went to the river and wanted to drink from the stream as well. I couldn't get the nerve to do it because I still had you to care for, so instead I watched the water flow. Up on the water floated leaves and it made me wonder where they were going and how they stayed afloat. I bent down and touched the water and wondered where the water would take me." He stopped speaking for a brief moment as he stared out the window. "A ship, I thought. I wanted to build it for three reasons: one, to make an income that we can survive from; two, to make history; and three, to take you home."

"But I am home."

He looked up at his daughter and said, "Not exactly." She was puzzled and walked closer to her father as she waited for him to give her answers. "I feel like the life I have lived has been a lie to both you and me."

She took a seat in the chair across from him and asked, "What part of your life has been a lie?"

"All of it and the worst part is that my own daughter doesn't even know who I am." He sighed and peered up at her, "You will never forgive me if I tell you."

Evangeline got up and shut the door and said, "I will never forgive you if you do not tell me."

They sat across from one another as Charles began to speak, "Many years ago, I was arranged to marry your mother but at the time, I was not ready to settle down and was seeing other women. Her father hired me to work part-time on their farm so Cecilia would fall madly in love with me without realizing that I was the man she had to marry. I went by the name of Charles Welsh, and as time went on, I fell in love with her, too. I was mesmerized by her beauty and charm. One day, I saw her and her father arguing about her upcoming wedding and she stormed off into the wilderness. I was ordered to follow her and so I did. She asked me to run away with her and at first I did not want to leave because I was so wealthy. My family was one of the richest families in Scotland. But I was in love with this woman and the idea of running away with her excited me. She became my main priority and soon, money was the last thing I thought about. Shortly after we moved here, Lawrence was kind enough to invite us into his home. Turns out that he was madly in love with Cecilia and while I was at work one day, he became very intimate with her. They made love in his bed and I went on living my life while I was kept in the dark. The more she saw him, the more she fell in love with him and I could sense she was becoming too fond of him so therefore I suggested we get married. It was not long after that I discovered she carried a child. She betrayed me but I still loved her more than anything in the world. Therefore I agreed to forgive her as long as she gave the child to Lawrence to take care of. Show him what responsibility feels like. It was not long after that we had you…"

Evangeline interrupted her father and said in a loud tone, "Frances Scott is my mother's daughter?"

He nodded his head but refused to look at her.

"So I am her sister?"

He nodded once again.

"Frances Scott is everything that I am not. I despise her; she is a disgrace to society. I refuse to consider her my sister. She was my whore of a mother's mistake, not mine."

Charles looked at his daughter in disbelief and said, "Do not call your mother a whore!"

She was shocked as she spoke, "How can you still defend her after she broke your heart and slept with another man?"

He smirked and said, "I have not been completely honest myself so therefore we were on the same boat. I am not Charles Welsh; I am Henry Beckem and your ancestors are beyond wealthy. I needed to create this ship to get us back home where you can have the life that you should have always had."

Evangeline's jaw dropped as she listened to her father's words. "Henry Beckem? I have heard about the Beckem's in my history class and they are beyond rich. Why in the world would you lie about something so huge, especially to your own daughter?"

He buried his face in the palm of his hand. "I did it all for her and for you. I was so in love with her I would have given her the world if she asked for it."

Evangeline stood up and walked over towards the window. She looked at the large ship that sat above the water and wondered where home really was. She kept her attention on the ship but continued to speak, "I cannot believe that you would lie to me, even about your name. I'm not sure what to call you anymore."

Charles glanced up at his daughter and said pleadingly, "Call me father."

Evangeline giggled and turned to look at him. As much as she wanted to pity him she could not for he didn't deserve her pity. "I'm not sure you know what a father is, Mr. Beckem."

Charles licked his lips and nodded his head before he began to speak. "I admit that I have lived a life full of lies but the only regret I have is not telling you the truth about who I am. I do ask you, my daughter, to please respect me and my decisions and continue to refer me as your father or Charles." He walked towards his daughter and continued to speak, "At least until we depart from here."

They stood only inches apart and Evangeline's eyes were filled with anger as she listened to everything her father had just told her. "Then what will happen?"

He sighed and bowed his head. "Then you may do as you like, whether that is hating me for my mistakes or staying with me because I am your family."

Evangeline smirked at him in disbelief and said in a loud tone, "I have no family! I fight my own battles and walk these empty streets of Knaresborough alone." Evangeline stumbled towards the door and took one last glance back at her father and said, "I may be your daughter by blood, but as far as I'm concerned, I'm an orphan. You are a coward and stuck in the past. You won't even give Caro—Maryanne a chance to win your heart over!" She slammed the door shut behind her as Charles stood motionless in his dark room.

He stared blankly at the door and for the first time in his life he felt completely alone.

Chapter 13

Gone

Despite what Lawrence had told her, Evangeline returned to the docks the following day and searched for Mathias. She wandered around the docks but Mathias was nowhere in sight. She was upset with her father so she decided to avoid going anywhere near or even inside of the big brown building.

Evangeline had been home for a week already and not one of those nights did Charles come home. He practically lived in his office; having a house seemed like a waste of space. Evangeline walked towards a pile of two by fours and sat down. She pulled out her journal from her purse and began to write. The last time she had written was when she was still at Shire Dale Academy. After Frances had found her journal that one time, she decided to carry it on her everywhere she went.

It was already mid-afternoon and Mathias still had not shown up for his shift so Evangeline decided to call it a day. She realized that she looked strange sitting on a pile of wood and watching the men work. She didn't know how else to reach Mathias other than seeing him at work and she really wanted to spend more time with him. She got up and gathered her things and made her way home. To no one's surprise, Charles never came home that night.

Maryanne and Evangeline knew more about each other than Charles knew about his daughter. They became very good friends and spent hours on end talking about the joys and downfalls of life. Tonight, Maryanne had promised to teach Evangeline how to make stuffed shells. All Evangeline learnt when she attended school was intellectual things but she had never cooked a meal in her life so Maryanne decided to teach her how to cook.

"What exactly are stuffed shells?" Evangeline was used to eating small portions of food and ate everything that was served on her plate. Growing up with no money made her become grateful and appreciate everything that was given to her. She wasn't a picky eater at all but if she had to choose her favourite; she loved pasta.

"I know that it doesn't sound very appetizing, but it tastes very good. First we need to fry up some ground beef and boil these large noodles that we stuff the meat into afterwards." Evangeline placed the meat in a frying pan on the stove as Maryanne cut up onions and peppers to add into the meat. "This just adds extra flavour to the meat." Evangeline loved the time they spent together; it made her realize that this is what having a mother would have felt like.

Evangeline watched Maryanne as she chopped the onions and wondered how her father did not love this woman in return; she was so lovable. "Evangeline!" Maryanne pointed at the pot behind Evangeline in a panic.

She turned around and noticed her noodles had caught on fire. She hurriedly removed the pot off the flame and ran it under cold water. Maryanne opened some windows to let the smoke out of the room then made her way over to Evangeline. Once the smoke had vanished, Maryanne looked over at the pot of burnt noodles and began to laugh hysterically.

"Evangeline," she began to speak but found it hard to fight her laughter. "You were supposed to put water in the pot and wait for it to boil then you add the noodles. You didn't add any water, sweetheart."

Evangeline looked down at the black noodles and began to laugh in embarrassment. "I am a woman; I should know how to cook."

Maryanne wrapped her arm around Evangeline's shoulder and said, "You just need some more practice and then you can open up your own restaurant." They looked at one another and began to laugh, "Alright, maybe you shouldn't. The place might only stand for one day if you ran the kitchen."

Evangeline's jaw dropped but she laughed because she knew that there was sarcasm in her voice.

Maryanne filled the pot with water and placed it on the stove, "I can finish supper if you'd like to go read or write in your journal some more."

Evangeline walked over to the dinner table and stared at her journal. She opened it up and reread what she had written in it earlier today.

Dear Journal,

I have discovered that my life is a lie. My father claims to be a man named Henry Beckem whereas I have referred to him as Charles Welsh my entire life. I feel as if I have no family anymore; from this point on I am an orphan. I have not dreamt of Somnia Viveret in almost a year and I sometimes wonder if that was a lie, too. Perhaps I am no one's hero and really am Frances' sister. I am outspoken as is she. I am in love with Mathias, as is she. We are both in the middle of our fathers' war. I hate to admit that she is my sister but a part of me knows that I cannot hate my family. Then I think about how I was left to fend for myself for four years while my father lived his life to the fullest. What do I really know about those around me? Nothing.

I sometimes think that my dreams of Somnia Viveret were not real. I was shocked when I found out Mathias had the same name as the prince of Somnia Viveret. I can't help but wish to dream of it again so that I can meet the Prince and see if Mathias is Prince Charming in both reality and my fantasy world. I must be insane. That or in love. Whatever love is.

Where were you today Mathias…?

Sincerely,
Evangeline "Beckem"

"Dinner is ready." Maryanne placed the supper in the center of the table.

Evangeline glance up and said, "Wow, it looks and smells amazing." The room smelled of tomatoes, melted cheese, ground beef, and oregano.

They ate supper in silence that evening, both thinking about something. Maryanne finally broke the silence and said, "Does your father ever ask or speak of me?"

Evangeline glanced up at her chocolate brown eyes and said, "Rarely…" Maryanne looked down at her supper and tried to shrug it off. "I think he feels for you but is afraid to admit it."

She smiled and asked, "How is my boy?"

Evangeline loved when Maryanne talked about her son or asked questions. She loved how every time she told her about Mathias it lit up her whole world. "I have not seen Mathias around the docks in the past two days. Perhaps Lawrence has him doing a different task inside the ship so that I cannot distract him from his work." Maryanne giggled but showed a sign of concern. "Don't worry, Caroline. I'm sure your son is fine and has not been shipped off. If that was the case, then I would personally murder Lawrence."

Maryanne touched Evangeline's hand and said, "You should not say such cruel things."

Evangeline pulled her hand away and looked at her in disbelief. "Unbelievable." She stood up from her seat and grabbed her journal.

Maryanne looked up at her in confusion and asked, "What's the matter?"

Evangeline shook her head and began to speak loudly. "Why is everyone defending Lawrence Scott?! All he does is cause pain in people's lives and yet everyone is beyond polite to him. I don't understand why you don't just slap him or scream in his face. He is one man; he can be stopped!"

Maryanne whispered, "I'm afraid of what he would do to my son." Evangeline rolled her eyes and made her way to her room.

Evangeline was disappointed when she woke up the following morning and was still in Knaresborough. She wondered what sort of horrible thing had to occur for her to wake up in Somnia Viveret. She wanted nothing more than to be in a world where she felt important and could change lives. Here she felt like her life was on pause and the only thing that kept moving was the feud around her.

Every day for the next few weeks, Evangeline went to the docks to see if she could spot Mathias. Every day she was disappointed to find out he was not there. After a while, she began to go only once a week and she still did not see him. She celebrated her seventeenth birthday a week ago and received many gifts from her father. She decided not to open any of them. Instead she put them in her closet where they remained unopened.

Charles asked, "How come you don't want to open your gifts?"

Evangeline replied, "What more do I need?" The conversation ended at that and it was now two months after her birthday and the gifts still sat in her closet.

Evangeline spent the majority of her time in her room writing in her journal. She had given up cooking after Maryanne defended Lawrence over her own son. Evangeline's pen had just touched her journal when Maryanne came storming in her room. She was panting and raging in anger and fright.

Evangeline got off her bed and rushed over towards Maryanne.

"What's the matter?" She led Maryanne towards her bed and sat next to her.

Maryanne whispered, "I did it..."

Evangeline was puzzled and asked, "Did what?" There was a brief moment of silence before Evangeline asked again, "What did you do, Maryanne?"

Maryanne began to laugh which was followed by tears. Evangeline wrapped her arms around her shoulders and wondered what could have happened. "I—I slapped Lawrence Scott. I slapped him real hard across the face."

Evangeline was silent but could not fight back her laughter. Within seconds, they were laughing and hugging one another. Evangeline stopped laughing suddenly as she realized that Maryanne was still crying. She pulled away from her so their faces were inches apart. "What happened, Maryanne?"

Maryanne whimpered as she began to speak. "After the day you lectured me about standing up to Lawrence over my own son, I began to think. For weeks I ignored the subject, until recently that is. I noticed that you stopped going out to the docks and didn't seem full of life anymore and it concerned me. I knew that it had something to do with my son. Therefore I decided to go down to the docks myself and see if Mathias was there. I was unsure of where to start looking so I just began to browse around the yard. I asked an elderly man if he knew where I could find Mathias, he responded, 'Are you talking about that handsome young fella?' I nodded my head and he continued to speak, 'Heck, I haven't seen him in a couple months! The last time I seen that boy was when Lawrence pulled him into the office for a little chit-chat, or so I guessed. Come to think of it, I never did see him leave the building.' I thanked him for his time and made my way over to the office.

"I entered the building and made my way to Lawrence's office in a hurry so that I would not run into Charles. I quickly shut the door behind me and walked towards Lawrence's desk. He placed his newspaper down on the table and removed his reading glasses as he looked up at me. He blinked and smiled as he was surprised to see me, 'Ah Caroline, or should I call you Maryanne? How are things?' Lawrence Scott is a handsome devil and always made me shy but in that moment I was as brave as a soldier. I spoke in a loud tone. 'You know damn well why I am here today. What have you done with my boy? Where is Mathias?' Lawrence shook his head at me in disappointment and gave me his full concentration as he began to speak. 'Dear Caroline, you have broken your promise that we made years ago. I am not a fool, nor am I blind. You have shared the truth about your past with another individual and therefore you and your son are both suffering the consequences.' I was raging in anger and walked so that I stood in front of him and said, 'Where is my son, Mr. Scott?' Lawrence sat back in his reclining chair and smirked at me. 'He is finishing the job that your husband was unable to go through with.' My eyes filled with tears and anger and in that moment I remembered your words. With full force I struck Lawrence across the face with the palm of my hand. He placed his own hand against his cheek and looked up at me in disbelief. He rose off his chair and pushed me against the wall. 'Caroline Strong has finally found her courage after all these years.' He held me locked to the wall; I looked over his arm and spat in his face. 'Lawrence Scott has finally discovered that he doesn't own me.' He laughed and said, 'Oh but I do. I really, really do. Or have you forgotten about your son already?' I glanced up at him in anger as he continued to speak, 'This is my town, and you cannot hide anything from me. I am aware of your newly developed relationship with Miss Welsh and I can notice the bond and honesty that is shared between the two of you. It does not take a genius to figure out that after spending so much time with a person that you will eventually fall in love with them and treat them like your own.' I defended you and myself. 'Evangeline is wonderful young lady who has done nothing wrong. Now for heaven's sake, Lawrence, where is my boy?' He released his grip on me and said, 'I have already told you that he is finishing your deceased husband's unfinished job. But do not worry, Mrs. Strong, it has been almost three months that he has been there and he is not dead, yet. He is a strong young man and I'll be damned if he does get murdered.' I had the urge to attack him again but instead I let my arms fall to my side as I realized that my baby boy was off in a war zone somewhere. A grin crossed Lawrence's face as he realized that my heart was broken. He opened the door to let me out but before I left he said, 'In a way, you should thank me, Caroline, because now you can tell your beloved son the truth…if he makes it back alive. But I must warn you, be prepared for the worst because he may hate you for lying to him.' I left the docks and made my way back here. The entire walk here, I thought about how my son would react to the truth or if he would believe me or not." She paused for a brief moment as she continued to sob, "I have not cried this much since the day I was forced to leave my son and now it seems to have been a waste because in the end, he was sent off to the war anyways. I did an awful job at protecting my son. I will never forgive myself."

Evangeline wrapped her arms around Caroline and let her cry the pain away. "Perhaps before you tell him the truth I could get the chance to spend more time with Mathias and talk to him more about his family. I understand that this very hard for you and that it breaks your heart but only time can heal your wounds."

Caroline pulled away from Evangeline and glanced up at her green eyes and smiled. "You are amazing. You are the daughter I never had and the best friend anyone could ever wish for. I cannot help but to feel pity for you from time to time because of the terrible things that you went through and how your father spends more time at work than here."

Evangeline looked at the ground and realized that everything Caroline said was true. "My father saw me three times in the four years that I was at Shire Dale Academy. I have been home for a few months already and he has not spent a single night at home. I don't understand why he bought a house if he is never even home, especially one that is so large. I sometimes wonder about that man. His heart is set on that ship and he is not giving anyone else a chance to enter his life, including me. I think the only reason he brought me home was because I remind him of Cecilia."

Caroline shook her head and said, "That is not okay. His reason to bring you home should have been because he missed his daughter and wanted to catch up on all the years that he missed. What does your father truly know about you?"

Evangeline got off her bed and walked towards the window. She glanced passed the land and saw the small city in the distance. "He knows that I am his daughter and that I resemble his deceased wife."

"Is that all?" Caroline was astonished by what she was hearing. "Never in my life has he ever asked me what I wanted, he only assumes. He told me once the ship is finished being built that he plans on taking me home to Scotland." Evangeline turned around to face Caroline and said in a desperate tone, "I don't want to leave Knaresborough. I know that I have lived a difficult life here and am not liked by many, but this is my true home. Not to mention my father lied to me my entire life!" Caroline took interest in her and patted her hand on the bed next to her. Evangeline walked towards her and took a seat, "Has he ever told you about his past or the feud between him and Lawrence?"

Caroline was puzzled and asked, "I thought that Lawrence and Charles were great friends?"

Evangeline exploded into laughter and said, "My father hates Lawrence Scott with a passion! I do not understand why because they are so much alike. They are both traitors who deserve to sink on that ship together!"

Caroline's eyes widened in shock and said, "Evangeline, that is preposterous. I understand that he has hurt you a lot but you should never speak about someone in such a manner."

"You are far too defensive, Caroline. Charles and Lawrence are both terrible people and all you see in good in them. You need to stick up for yourself and see the truth in people but instead, you only choose to ignore the hateful and hurtful things they do."

She smiled and nodded her head, "I choose to give everyone a chance because everyone is beautiful in their own bizarre way. You, on the other hand, are beautiful inside and out and I admire your motivation and courage to speak your mind but I am not like you, sweetheart. I know I stood up for myself today but I'm not sure that I will be able to be that brave again."

"You frustrate me..." Evangeline began to giggle and shook her head. "I must be insane to still love you after you defend morons."

Caroline hugged Evangeline tightly and said, "I love you like you are my own. I'm sorry that Charles fails to show you what love is and therefore I will give you all the love in the world."

Time crawled by and both Evangeline and Caroline worried about Mathias. Evangeline took on her cooking lessons again and managed to cook a meal without burning the house to the ground. On days that she was not learning how to cook she wondered around the countryside and thought how her father could want to leave this beautiful place. Sometimes she wished that something would go wrong and the ship would never get finished.

Evangeline took the knowledge she developed at Shire Dale, put it to use, and began painting. She planted her own garden that spring and accidently stepped on one of the tomatoes. She bent down and picked it up and looked at the vibrant colours of the red tomato and remembered she had taken a couple art classes with Sister Nelly. That evening, she asked Caroline to go to the city with her so she could purchase paint and a canvas to start up a hobby. Caroline was excited when she heard her ask and agreed to take her immediately. They walked side by side through the city and made their way to a small shop that was filled with art supplies and home fashions. The store was small and cramped; the lighting was dull and smelled of wet paint. She ended up purchasing a few things as well as a type writer. She loved the creativity that art allowed an individual to do and wanted to pursue her career in that direction. Not only would it allow her to keep busy but also keep her mind occupied rather than worrying about Mathias.

It had been nearly a year since Mathias was shipped off to the war. Evangeline packed her art supplies in her knapsack but before she left she said to Caroline, "I'm sorry to bring this up again, but I thought Mathias was only required to serve for a few months in the war."

Caroline stopped doing the dishes and dried her hands off on her apron. "Yes, but because it has been so long since my husband died, Lawrence told me he increased it so Mathias must serve for a minimum of two years."

Evangeline felt a sadness befall her; she missed him so much. "Two years? That is not fair."

Ever since Mathias was shipped, off Caroline's smiles were always sad. "Yes, sweetheart, it is definitely not fair. Please don't think about it too much; it only makes you sad and I love seeing that beautiful smile upon your gorgeous face."

Evangeline gave her a hug and smiled as she grabbed her knapsack and made her way out the door. She walked a few miles down the gravel road until she came to a fork in the road. She turned down the narrow path that was surrounded by large trees. It was nearly noon and the trees made it look like nightfall due to the dark shadow they casted around her. She continued to walk down the path until she began to see light at the other end. Evangeline enjoyed going on adventures and seeing where the road would take her and this was her first time taking this path so the scenery was all new to her.

She reached the end of the road and stopped walking as she stared at the sight ahead. She was in a trance as she admired the beautiful landscape ahead. It was all open land and the fields went miles and miles back. On the land stood a large abandoned house that must have been built a century ago. It was much larger than the one she was currently living in but this house looked like it was in terrible condition. The wood had turned into a grey and was falling off the house. The windows were smashed and boarded up with wood. On the deck stood a lonely rocking chair and alongside was a crib that clearly must have been for a child. Evangeline walked closer until she stood a few feet away from the house. *This was a true piece of history*, she thought, *not a ship*. She opened her knapsack and pulled out a large canvas and her paintbrushes. She sat cross-legged on the grass and began to paint the scenery before her.

Evangeline had spent nearly the entire day painting but when the sun began to set, it made it difficult to see what she was painting. She didn't dare to enter the house because she feared someone would possibly be inside. Instead she remained seated on the grass the entire day and painted the house and the fields around it. When the sun had almost finished setting she packed her belongings and made her way back home. The entire walk home, she wondered what was inside the house and whether she should have gone in or not. Tomorrow she would go back and finish her painting since it was almost finished. Not only did she enjoy painting the beautiful, antique house, but she loved to be around it because it gave off a sad but interesting vibe and she wanted to study it and figure out what happened to the house.

By the time she finally got home it was pitch black outside. Before she was able to open the door, Caroline opened it from the inside. Tears were streaming down her cheeks; her eyes were all red and puffy.

Evangeline's smile vanished as she approached Caroline, "What's the matter?"

Before Caroline spoke she wrapped her arms around Evangeline and gave her the tightest hug ever. “He’s gone, Evangeline. My baby is gone.”

Evangeline was horrified as she thought the obvious and asked, “What do you mean he’s gone?”

Caroline fell to the ground and began to sob. She leaned against the wall and brought her knees to her chest. She wrapped her arms around her knees and buried her face. “I’m a terrible mother. I let my son get murdered in a war zone.”

Evangeline’s eyes widened as she grasped what Caroline was telling her. She bent down before her and touched her arms softly as she tried to remain calm. “Caroline, you need to tell me what happened.”

Caroline peered through her hair and whispered, “Lawrence stopped by today and he told me that Mathias and a few other soldiers were killed in an explosion.”

Evangeline’s jaw dropped as she froze in shock, “There must have been some sort of misunderstanding, and how do they know it was him?”

“They saw him going there. I will never live with myself knowing that I am the cause of his death.” The only sound was the leaking of the tap in the kitchen. Caroline rose off the ground and said, “He just turned twenty years old yesterday and his life was over before he even got a chance to live it. I am going to call it an early night, Evangeline. I hope you do not mind. I need to be alone and cry my pain away.” She gave Evangeline a hug and walked out the door.

Evangeline stood motionless in the doorway as she watched Caroline walking away. The person she loved the most had just lost their entire world. Evangeline was head over heels for Mathias and it broke her heart to know that he was gone. She began to sob as she realized that she had never felt so alone before. She retired early that night as she wanted to clear her head. She wished that she would wake up the next day and realize that it was all just a dream. Evangeline cried herself to sleep that night.

Evangeline's eyes were puffy from crying as she woke up the following morning. She showered and washed her eyes as she decided that from this point on she would no longer shed tears. This world was full of sick and twisted things and it just so happened that lately everything was happening to her. She decided that today would be a good day and she would finish her painting. She put on her baby blue embroidered British muslin gown and brushed her wavy red hair and made her way to the sitting room with her knapsack. To her surprise, Charles was in the sitting room. He had his face buried in the palm of his hands and looked up when he heard Evangeline approach him.

"What are you doing home?"

He patted the seat beside him and she sat down. "There is something I need to talk to you about, sweetheart."

Evangeline eyed him curiously and asked, "Is it another lie that you want to confess to me about? Because if it is, I don't think I want to hear it."

He smiled but the smile vanished as fast it appeared. "Last night, Maryanne committed suicide."

Evangeline's jaw dropped and her eyes widened in shock. She wondered what else would go wrong. It was official; she was completely alone in this world. It was surprising that last night she didn't dream of Somnia Viveret.

"They found her early this morning by the docks. She hung herself off the ship with a note attached to her body. The note read: *You killed me without even touching me*. I'm not sure what she meant by that or who it was directed to, but it broke my heart to see she was suffering. I never knew that Maryanne was hurting so much and it makes me sad. She practically lived in this house since the day I bought it and I never stopped to ask her what she was feeling."

Evangeline rolled her eyes and said, "You didn't just do that to her, you know that right? Am I invisible to you, too? Do I have to commit suicide as well just so you will notice me?"

Charles looked at her with sad eyes and said, "That won't be necessary, Evangeline. Your death would be my end." He was mesmerized by his daughter as he examined her fully, "You look beautiful."

Evangeline stood up without saying a word and walked out the front door. She broke her promise as tears streamed down her cheeks.

Chapter 14

Bloody Wound

Evangeline began to walk down the gravel road once again and couldn't help but feel sad about Caroline's death. Her note broke Evangeline's heart: *You killed me without even touching me.* Only Evangeline and Lawrence would ever know the truth behind her words. The saddest part of all was that Caroline lived a lie and she never got a chance to hold her baby boy in her arms again. Why such terrible things happened to such great people was a question that lingered in Evangeline's head day and night.

When she reached the house, she pulled out her canvas once again and continued her painting. Two hours passed before she did the final touch ups on the painting. She held the painting up in front of her and compared it to the scenery in front of her. She glanced back and forth between the canvas and the house to make sure they were identical. In that moment something passed by the window and startled Evangeline. She put her hand against her chest and dropped the painting on the ground. She leaned forward and squinted her eyes as she tried to look through the one window that was not boarded up. There was no sign of anything or anyone and she began to wonder if her eyes were playing tricks on her. She stood up and left her painting lying on the ground alongside her knapsack. She slowly began to walk closer to the old house and looked around her to see if there was anyone around. With every step getting closer, her heart began to beat faster.

Evangeline reached the old, rotten stairs and slowly walked up them as she feared that they would collapse on her at any moment. The house was so old she wondered how it still remained standing. As she stood on the porch, she looked over at the old rocking chair and crib and wondered if a mother sat there as she cradled her baby to sleep. She walked towards the broken window and peered in to look. To her relief there was no on in sight but a bunch of covered furniture. She backed away from the window and walked towards the old door. She slowly turned the doorknob as she hoped it wouldn't fall off as she grabbed hold of it. She slowly pushed the door open and stuck her head in as she looked around. When she knew there was no one around, she walked in and shut the door behind her. Evangeline covered her face as dust flew off the door when she shut it.

She walked forward as she looked around the house. She walked towards the sitting room and stood before the old fire pit. Above the fire pit hung a large family portrait. In the portrait were a beautiful mother, a father, and a little boy. She looked up at the picture and wondered if they were killed in the fire. It was clear that the house had been through a fire but it was strong and still stood. She turned around and began to walk towards the kitchen. Before she reached the doorway, she saw a trail of blood on the hardwood floors. She stopped walking as her eyes followed the trail and led around the corner. She pondered for a moment whether she should see what was around the corner. She feared she would see a dead animal or even worse, a person.

She whispered to herself, "I will never know if I continue to stand here and question it." She slowly walked alongside the blood and asked, "Hello? Is someone there?" No one responded but instead she heard a moan. It startled her as she realized it was a man. She peeked around the corner as she saw a solider covered in blood, lying on the floor. She rushed around the corner and knelt down beside him and said, "Are you alright, sir?" The man held his leg tightly and moaned in pain. Evangeline looked down and pulled his pant leg up. His leg had pieces of iron stabbed into it. It looked like something exploded and all the little pieces flew in his leg. Evangeline was bewildered at the sight of his leg and rushed over to the sink. She began to open all the cabinets as she searched for a pail. She filled the pail with warm water and grabbed a rag from a drawer. She knelt back down beside the solider and said, "I really need to get the iron pieces out of your leg. This will hurt a lot so I need you to be very still, sir."

Before Evangeline did any more she searched for a knife and a pair a tongs in the kitchen. She was relieved that the fire did not burn everything completely. She returned to the soldier and cut his pant leg off and tied it around his thigh to stop the blood circulation. She grabbed hold of the tongs and carefully started to remove the pieces of iron. Some pieces were deeper in his skin than others so she was forced to cut his skin so she could remove the iron. She heard him moan in pain but didn't bother to look up. She knew that this man would bleed to death if she didn't help fix his wound. If she went to get Dr. Baker, he would be dead by the time they got back.

It took Evangeline nearly half an hour to remove all the iron pieces that were in his leg. When she had finished, she washed the wound and stitched it up. She took a different towel and wrapped it around his leg. She looked down at her dress as it was drenched in blood and looked up at the man as she realized she never even saw his face under all the black ashes. She wet a rag and began to wash the dirt off his face. He was as pale as a ghost but alive was all that mattered.

When his face was cleaned she dropped the rag on the ground and he whispered, "Thank you, Evangeline. You are my saviour; I am so fortunate to have you in my life."

Evangeline's eyes widened in shock as she stared into Mathias' hazel eyes. She wanted to ask him where he had been and what happened to him but instead she leaned in and kissed him. The blood was rushing through her veins as she suddenly felt ashamed of her childish actions. "I'm sorry I should not have kissed you, Mathias. I just thought you were dead and I just can't bear to lose you again!"

Mathias stared at Evangeline in shock but considering the situation he simply smiled and placed his hand against her cheek, "Never apologize for loving someone." She smiled shyly at him and was blessed that he was not dead and realized that she truly was his saviour. He began to shut his eyes and whispered, "I just need to rest. Please stay with me."

She lay down beside him and looked at him and whispered, "How did you get here?" His eyes remained shut as he spoke, "I followed my feet and this is where they took me." Evangeline had so many questions that she wanted to ask him but when she glanced back at Mathias he had already fallen asleep.

Evangeline and Mathias had slept through the night in the big rotten house. She woke up to the sounds of chirping birds and the sun shining on her face. She sat up and rubbed her eyes. She looked around and realized that last night was not a dream. She turned to face Mathias and to her surprise, he was awake and looking back at her.

He smiled innocently and said, "I cannot thank you enough for your bravery last night." He put his hand on Evangeline's cheek and leaned closer as his soft lips met hers. He glanced up at her and whispered, "No one can know that I am alive." Evangeline pulled her eye brows together as she was puzzled by his request.

"But you have completed your service at the war; they would have no right to send you back."

He nodded his head in agreement and said, "That may be so but who is to say that will stop Lawrence from sending me back. I do not understand why I was put there in the first place. I always thought that

Lawrence favoured me and thought I was a hard worker. He was the closest person I had to family but he betrayed me and left me to die."

Evangeline sighed and walked towards the window. Mathias struggled as he lifted himself off the ground and limped over towards Evangeline.

He wrapped his arm around her waist and looked up at her as she stared at the horizon before her. "Have I said something that upsets you?"

Evangeline smirked but could not get herself to look at him. "Mathias, do you ever wonder what happened to your parents?"

He turned his attention on the scenery before them as he spoke, "I do not waste my time on them for they did not bother to waste theirs on me."

Evangeline's eyes fell to the floor and then looked up at his hazel eyes. "I knew your mother."

Mathias stared at her blankly and eager to know why she knew his mother and he did not. "That is ridiculous. My mother left Knaresborough when I was a child. She could not take care of a child and therefore left me to fend for myself." Mathias became serious and defensive towards Evangeline. Thus, she turned her attention before her once again but Mathias placed his hands on either sides of her face and turned her attention back on him.

"Why would you try to hurt me like this, Evangeline?" Evangeline reached into her apron pocket and pulled out a dirty, white piece of paper. He released her face and looked down at what she held in the palm of her hands.

He took the paper from her hands and read in a whispered, "You killed me without even touching me." He was puzzled and looked up at her for answers.

"Your mother was my housekeeper and when Lawrence told her that you were murdered in an explosion, she killed herself."

He stared at her blankly as he waited for her to say more.

"Don't you see? Lawrence Scott ruined your family as he has ruined mine. He was the death of my mother and the death of yours. Your father died three months after he was put into the war and therefore your mother let you go. Lawrence made her depart from you otherwise you would serve the remaining year at war that your father was unable to do. She changed her name from Caroline to Maryanne and served as a housekeeper for my father. From time to time, she passed by the docks to see her lovely boy and make sure he was alright. She was devastated when she found out that living her life a lie was a waste because in the end you were sent off anyways. So do not hate your deceased family, Mathias. It is Lawrence Scott that you should hate." Mathias was in shock and plopped himself on the ground. Evangeline knelt down beside him and said, "I envy you because love is rare to find. Caroline had a beautiful heart and talked about you constantly. I would like to murder Lawrence Scott."

Mathias glanced up at Evangeline and said, "You should not say such hateful words, my dear. Although, I understand where you are coming from; I never got a chance to meet my mother and therefore I envy you." Neither one of them spoke a word; instead they glanced in opposite directions and wondered why they were stuck in this cruel forsaken world.

Evangeline walked out of the house and found her painting lying on the ground. She picked up the canvas and to her surprise, it was not damaged, not even a scratch.

From a distance, she heard Mathias saying, "What have you got there?"

She glanced up and noticed him leaning against the doorway. His leg still in pain, he tried not to put too much pressure on it. "It's my painting." She stared at it for a moment before she walked towards Mathias. When she stood only inches away from him, she turned the painting over for him to see.

He nodded his head and widened his eyes as he spoke, "Wow, Evangeline that looks really good!"

She smiled at him and said, "After you left, I began to spend the majority of my time painting and gardening. Caroline helped me learn how to cook and sew." She eyed his leg and continued, "That's why I knew how to sew up your wounds." He glanced down and saw his bandaged up leg. His pant leg had been cut above the knee, whereas the other one remained untouched.

He returned his attention to Evangeline and said, "I cannot continue to wear these rags, but I also cannot leave this house otherwise my return will be announced."

Evangeline pouted her lips and said, "I suppose I should go grab you some fresh clothing then."

He smirked at her and replied, "I cannot force you to do anything you don't want to do, but I would very much appreciate that."

She nodded her head at him and said, "Alright, I will leave now so that way I am back before the sun sets."

She turned away from him as she began to walk away, but before she could take another step, he softly grabbed her hand and pulled her near him. She glanced up at him as he slipped his arm around her waist and drew her closer. He closed his eyes and kissed her lips passionately.

Mathias whispered, "I will be here when you return."

Evangeline kissed his cheek and freed her hand as she began to walk away. He stared after her and suddenly felt sadness befall him, for he realized that his whole world was leaving his side.

When Evangeline finally reached her house, she realized that her father was waiting for her in the sitting room. He got off the couch when he saw his daughter walk in the room. He glanced at her from head to toe and was horrified. Her baby blue dress was drenched in blood and dirty from mud. She noticed his gaze and looked down at her dress as she had completely forgotten that she was covered in blood.

He slowly approached his daughter and said, "Please do not tell me that you attempted to commit suicide?"

Evangeline began to giggle and said, "Don't be ridiculous, Henry! You have already killed me, what more do I need to do?"

Charles was appalled by his daughter's words and replied, "I am your father, and you do not call me by my name. That is both disrespectful and hurtful." Evangeline turned away and began to walk up the stairs. "Evangeline, I am not finished speaking to you!"

She froze as she got to the top of the stairs and said, "What else could you possibly have left to say?"

He began to climb the stairs and asked, "Why is your dress drenched in blood?"

She tried to think of a way to hide the truth from him without lying so she said, "I met a man the other night who was badly hurt. At first I was afraid because I didn't know who he was or what to expect. Turned out he was a very nice man who was struck by a four wheeled steam buggy. The driver didn't stop to see what he hit and left the man to die. I was lucky to have been walking in that direction to notice him otherwise he would have been dead by sunrise. After I helped him with his bloody wounds, he asked me to stay with him for the night so that I could watch over him while he slept. He feared someone else would try to harm him some more so I agreed to stay."

Charles stared at her blankly as he searched her eyes for the truth. He sighed and said, "There is a lie in your words but I will believe your story because it is better than thinking you tried to kill yourself."

Evangeline made her way down the long empty hallway and towards her bedroom. She looked through her closet as she grabbed a fresh pair of clothes for herself. She quickly bathed herself and washed her thick red hair. She brushed her hair behind her ears and slipped on her ruffled, red satin dress. It reached just beneath her knees and slipped on a pair of ruby red slippers. She glanced at her reflection in the mirror and thought she looked like she was ready for a blood bath, that or looked like Little Red Riding Hood. She turned away from the mirror and sneaked into her father's room. She looked around his large bedroom and realized that he really was obsessed with his ship. All along the walls of his room were blueprints of his ship; someone had painted them to the walls. Evangeline shook her head in disappointment. If her father would have shown Caroline the slightest bit of interest then perhaps she would have reconsidered killing herself. Evangeline wondered if she had meant nothing to Caroline after all. Caroline always told her that she was like a daughter to her and would do anything for her.

"Anything but live..." Evangeline whispered to herself and she made her way to her father's closet. His closet was the same size as hers but with a different selection. She grabbed a knapsack off the rack and stuffed a bunch of clean garments into the bag. Evangeline threw the bag over her shoulder and made her way towards the kitchen. She opened the cupboard and grabbed a stash of money that her dad left in a cookie glass for Caroline to buy groceries with.

She walked into the sitting room and realized that he had already left for work. Therefore Evangeline grabbed a piece of paper and a fountain pen from the desk drawer. She began to write:

I will be away for a few weeks but I cannot tell you where I have gone to, and do not try to find me, Henry. I will return but only when I am ready to. I know your secrets and if you try to set out on a quest for me then you may kiss your ship goodbye.

Evangeline knew how much his ship meant to him so she knew that using his secrets and lies against him would prevent him from searching for her. It was both harsh and clever. She placed the note on the kitchen table and walked towards the front door. She looked back into the house and thought it looked so sad and empty without Caroline's glow. She smiled as she knew that Caroline would be reunited with her long lost husband.

She whispered, “I will take care of your son and tell him only good things about you.” She shut the door and hurried back to Mathias. She didn’t look back at the house at all and knew that it would be a while before she returned.

Chapter 15

Bonding

A week had passed since Evangeline found Mathias in the big old house. His leg began to heal nicely and he was not limping as much as he had a week ago. They had uncovered all the furniture in the old house and treated it as if it was their own. Evangeline had snuck back into her old house a few times to gather more of her belongings to bring into this house.

Evangeline sat on the deck as she began to paint the pathway that lead to the old house. "You know, I was thinking that perhaps we could fix up this house and live here."

Evangeline stopped painting as she looked up at Mathias and considered his idea. She remained silent as she rose off the rocking chair and walked away from the house. Mathias remained on the deck as he watched Evangeline walk further away from the house. When she stood a few feet away, she turned around and faced the house. She tilted her head to the side as she examined it from all angles. Mathias crossed his arms over his chest as he looked at her in confusion and couldn't help but wonder what she was thinking.

She smiled as she looked up at Mathias and began to approach him. "This will require a lot of hard work and dedication if we plan to turn this house into our home."

He wrapped his arms around her waist and said, "Think of it as one of your paintings. You can create a beautiful masterpiece from nothing."

She glanced up at him and remembered all the reasons why she adored him so much. Her smile vanished in that moment and she dropped her arms to her side. She walked toward the garden she had begun to plant a few days ago. Mathias was puzzled by her sudden sadness and followed her like a shadow. She bent down by her garden and began to pull out the weeds.

He placed his hand on her shoulder and asked, "Have I said something that has offended you?"

She continued to pull the weeds as she said, "Not at all."

He glanced around at the empty fields and said, "Then what is bothering you?"

She stopped pulling at the weeds but kept her eyes locked on the growing plants in front of her. "Do you not find it weird that we plan to live together but are not married?"

Mathias bent down beside her and said, "I suppose it is but we love each other and cannot afford to risk the news of my return to Lawrence."

She glanced at him and said in frustration, "I do not understand why no one can stand up to that man!" Mathias sighed and placed the palm of his hands on either sides of her face.

They stared into one another's eyes as he said, "I love you, Evangeline, and you fill the empty gap in my heart."

She smiled but continued, "I love you too, Mathias, but I hate not being able to live like man and wife."

Mathias thought about what she said and realized what she was referring too, "Believe me when I say that I really want you, but I am a traditional man and want to wait until we are married before we make love."

Evangeline began to laugh and stood up, "You make me sound ridiculous!"

He rose off the grass and asked, "How so?"

Evangeline began to walk towards the pathway and said, "You are such a gentleman, Mathias."

Mathias didn't follow her, instead he yelled from the distance, "Where are you going?!"

She didn't turn to look back but said, "I will return with help for the construction of our new home."

Mathias didn't say a word but was concerned to find out what she had in mind.

It took Evangeline nearly half an hour until she finally reached the city. She walked towards the docks as she glanced around for men who looked like they would be suitable for the job. However, before she approached anyone she walked into the office to see her father. When she opened the door, he was already standing there. He was beyond surprised and excited to see his daughter and without thinking he wrapped his arms around her and gave her a big hug.

She awkwardly patted his back with one hand and said, "Hi."

He pulled away from her to look at his daughter and asked, "Where have you been?"

She shook her head and said, "That is none of your concern."

His smiled disappeared as he directed her into his office for more privacy. When they were in the office, Charles began to pace back and forth in frustration and said in an angry tone, "I do not understand why you are hurting me this way. Does it make you happy to see your father in pain or to be sad? I—I just do not understand who you are."

Evangeline sat down in his big reclining chair and said, "I am a stranger to you because all my life, you have failed to take interest in me, so do not blame me for my cruel words and uncalled for behaviour. As far as I'm concerned, the only reason we are related is because we share the same blood. Apart from that, you are just another person who walks along the streets of this mad world."

Charles buried his face in the palm of his hands and plopped himself on the ground. "How can I show you that I truly do love you?"

Evangeline hesitated to answer. "You can take a break from your ship to help me build a life for myself."

He glanced up at her in confusion and asked, "What do you mean?"

She glanced around his office and said, "I need help to reconstruct a house that I have found. However, we cannot do it on our own and do not have the proper materials for it."

Charles looked at his daughter and asked, "Who is we?"

She smiled and said, "I will give you a chance to regain my love and trust if you help us and remain silent about it."

Charles asked again, "Who else is there, Evangeline?"

Evangeline sighed in frustration and said, "My soldier."

He raised his eyebrows as he recalled what she told him a while back. "Is this the man you found on the side of the road?"

Evangeline said, "Something like that. So do you agree to help? We will need a few other men to help as well."

Charles stood up and walked closer to his daughter. He put his hand out in front of her for a hand shake. She looked down and at it and shook his hand. "Alright, Evangeline. If this means regaining your love, then I will do anything for you."

Evangeline knew that her father loved her, but she often wondered whether it was only because she looked like Cecilia or if he felt like he had to. She knew for a fact that it wasn't for her personality because he hated how outspoken she was and felt that she wasn't very lady-like at times. Evangeline and Charles began to gather a group of men together that would be interested in a job constructing the house. They gathered all the materials that would be needed for it and filled three large wagons full of wood, paint, windows, and other necessary supplies. It took them the majority of the day to gather everything they would need for the following day. Evangeline had spent that night at home with her father. To her surprise, he came home with her and cooked a meal. He roasted a chicken and made a potato salad.

Evangeline was surprised to see him in the kitchen and asked, "Since when do you cook?" Charles glanced up at his daughter and smiled.

"Maryanne used to teach me how to cook. She would tell me that every woman likes a man that can cook a meal every now and then." He placed food in their plates and smiled mainly to himself.

Evangeline stared at him and said, "What happened between you two?"

Charles sat down and stared at the food on his plate before he began to talk. "Shortly after I purchased the house, I realized that it was much too large for me to take care of, not to mention I was hardly ever home. I saw an ad in the newspaper to hire a housekeeper and so I called and I interviewed a few women because I wasn't just letting anyone into my home. I was just about to give up when Maryanne showed up at the door. I opened the door and was mesmerized by her beauty. She must have thought I was a fool because I didn't even say hello to her, instead I simply stared at her and smiled for she took my breath away. She smiled back at me and said, 'Good day, sir. I am Maryanne and I've come for an interview for your housekeeping position.' I blinked my eyes a few times and shook my head. 'Oh that's right! I apologize I completely forgot that was today.' In truth I didn't forget, I just didn't want her thinking that I was a fool for staring at her so blankly. I gestured her into the house and directed her into the sitting room. I nearly fell over my feet as I walked. I made such a fool of myself that day and I could tell she was really trying hard not to laugh at me.

"She sat down on the couch as I sat across from her. I crossed my arms and stared at her angelic face and began my questions with, 'Are you married?' I realized it wasn't an appropriate question and it threw her off. She glanced over at the fire place as she spoke, 'I was married many years ago but he was murdered on the battlefield.' I felt pity for her but as arrogant as it may sound, I was also glad to discover that she had no lover. I replied, 'I was married many years ago as well, but she has also passed away.' She glanced back at me and said, 'I'm sorry for your loss mister…' I realized I had not introduced myself and stuck out my hand and said, 'I'm terribly sorry! You can call me Charles. Charles Welsh.' She smiled and said, 'Well, Mr. Welsh, would you like to ask me some actual housekeeping questions or do you ask everyone about their personal lives?' She smirked at me and I giggled at her sarcasm. 'I apologize for that too but I cannot help but wonder how someone as beautiful as you cleans homes for a living.' She avoided the compliment and said, 'Beauty does not bring food to the table, Mr. Welsh. It is just a bonus.' I liked her the moment I opened that door and fell madly in love with her the more we spoke. She had such a beautiful heart and I knew that I would give her the position but before I did I was curious to learn more about this magnificent woman before me. 'Did you and your husband ever have children?' She was silent for a moment and looked sad, 'We had one child, a boy. He passed away when he was just two years old.' I knew that I should not have asked more but she interested me and I wanted to learn more about the mysterious Maryanne. 'May I ask how he died?' She hesitated to answer but said, 'I took my eyes off of him for a few seconds and he had wondered off. I searched everywhere for him but could not find him anywhere. I felt like such a terrible mother! A few hours later the sheriff came to my house and when he tipped his hat I instantly knew that he had bad news. He told me that my son drowned in the river and that they found his body floating near the docks.' I felt so sorry for Maryanne, I wanted to reach out to her and comfort her. Instead I asked, 'What was your son's name?' She stuttered to answer, 'M—Damian.' She smiled and looked at me as she asked, 'Did you and your wife have any children?' I smiled and said, 'We have a beautiful daughter named Evangeline. I haven't seen her in the longest time because she is staying at Shire Dale Academy boarding school. Sometimes I feel like I am such a terrible father because I do not see her often but I feel like I must accomplish more for her before I can bring her home. You see, the thing is that my wife and I never had any money and we were constantly on the move. I cannot bring her back into that world because she deserves so much more than that.' She nodded her head and said, 'I understand what you mean but have you ever told her that?' I shook my head and said, 'I want to surprise her. Everything I have done, I did it all for her.' She smiled at me and said, 'You are a gentleman, Mr. Welsh but I must warn you that it isn't just as simple as that. She is older, I presume, and living the life of an orphan. She may feel like you left her there to rot especially because you didn't let her know about your project.' I knew that she was right but I choose to ignore the truth. 'It is hard to please everyone.' She smirked and said, 'You should not be trying to please everyone. You should only be giving your love to her.' We talked for hours about you and about how terrible of a father I was. I felt like I could tell her anything and everything and she would still appreciate me in the end.

"Two weeks later was her thirty-fifth birthday and I had asked her to come in to work two hours later than usual. She didn't bother to ask why but just simply agreed. When she came in to work that following day, I had the entire house decorated in blue and white streamers and balloons tied on everywhere. The entire house was lit by candle lights and dinner was prepared on the kitchen table. In the centre of the table, I placed a vase of white lilies. On the rails of the stairs, I wrapped small white Christmas lights that shone brightly and beautifully. When she walked through the door, she froze. She dropped her purse near the coat rack and shut the door behind her. Her jaw dropped as she saw how beautifully the house had been decorated. I handed her a glass of red wine and said, 'Happy birthday, Maryanne.' I kissed her softly on the cheek and said, 'You are an amazing person so I decided to celebrate this special day with you, if you would like my company.' She glanced around the room and back at me with a big grin across her face, 'Thank you, Charles. This is by far the sweetest thing a man has done for me. See, you really do have a gentle and beautiful heart. The house looks amazing.' She looped her arm through mine as we walked towards the kitchen together. I pulled the chair from beneath the table as she sat down. We ate dinner and talked and laughed. She made me feel so happy.

"After dinner, we walked up the staircase, hand in hand. She glanced around at all the lights and I said to her, 'There are not enough lights in the world to show you how much you light up my world.' She smiled at me as I leaned in and kissed her lips softly. She glanced up at me and kissed me once again. We made our way down the long hallway towards my bedroom. We made passionate love that night, a night that I will never forget."

Evangeline smiled and thought that they had such a romantic love life. She asked, "If you claimed to be so madly in love with her, why did you treat her as if she was nothing when I arrived?"

Charles sighed and said, "A few months passed after we had begun to secretly see one another. Lawrence came over to discuss business one day and I saw him look at Maryanne in a strange way. We went into the sitting room and he asked me, 'Is that your housekeeper?' I nodded my head and said, 'Yes, that is Maryanne, she's a wonderful woman.' He kept glancing at her and whispered, 'Maryanne, huh?' I nodded my head but I guess he didn't see. 'Don't tell me you are sleeping with that woman, Charles.' I looked at him with a puzzled expression and said, 'Why is that of your concern?' He said, 'You will stop seeing her, Charles. Otherwise I will prolong your contract agreement to two years minimum.' I felt angry and confused so I asked, 'What do you have against her, Lawrence?' He smirked and said, 'She is a whore and puts on a nice act. In truth, all she wants is your money. Don't let her beauty fool you, dear friend. Take this as a warning.' After that day, I began to think differently of her and felt as if she truly did put on a show because no one could ever be that nice. She questioned why I was acting so strangely and I simply told her that she was my employee and that it was not right to be seeing each other. She wanted to quit so she would no longer be my employee and we could continue to see one another. However, I said, 'That will be impossible, Maryanne. Please, you still have your job here but we cannot continue this relationship. It must end here.' She never questioned it after that. I was torn that she would play me like that and then just rip my heart out with her beautiful hands."

Evangeline shook her head and said, "First of all, Maryanne truly was a beautiful woman inside and out and loved you very much. She would never use you for your money because she was well off already. Secondly, prolong what contract?"

Charles pulled his eyebrows together and asked, "She was well off?"

Evangeline's eye's widened as she realized, "You have agreed to participate in his family's war, haven't you?"

Charles stared at his daughter and asked, "How do you know about that?"

She shook her head in disappointment and said, "Because that is how Maryanne's husband died. After his death, she inherited money from his invention and worked as a housekeeper to keep herself occupied."

"How do you know so much about her?" Charles envied the amount of information that Maryanne had shared with Evangeline and was also shocked to hear the truth.

"Because she let me into her life, unlike you. You only blocked her out because of what one man told you. Do you even know why she killed herself?"

Charles shook his head and said, "I honestly thought that it might have been because I mistreated her because of what the note said, but then if that was the case, she would have done it a long time ago so I have no idea why she ended her life."

"Maryanne was not her true name. It was Caroline Strong and her husband was not finished serving his time in the war so Lawrence had her son serve the remaining time…"

"Charles interrupted her and said, "How could he if her son died as a child?"

Evangeline felt as if she could reveal the truth now because Caroline was dead anyways. "Her son is not dead. He was taken away from her when he was a child by Lawrence Scott. Her son is Mathias."

Charles widened his eyes and whispered, "Mathias?"

Evangeline continued, "Lawrence told her that he was killed in an explosion in the battlefield and therefore she committed suicide. She felt as if her entire world ended in that moment she discovered he was dead."

Charles was silent as he rethought everything his daughter told him and realized that it all made perfect sense. "I feel responsible."

Evangeline had never had such a serious conversation with her father before and although they spoke about Caroline's history, she enjoyed it because they both missed her.

"I should have followed my heart and married her." Evangeline stared at her father as she waited for him to continue. "I was planning on proposing to Mary—Caroline the next day but then Lawrence told me such horrible things. A part of me knew that she was not the person he claimed she was but I was such a fool to believe him. She would smile but it was always forced upon her face…You brought life back into her and then Lawrence took it away again. I understand her note now; you killed me without even touching me."

Evangeline reached over the table and placed her hand on top of her father's. He glanced at her hand and then into her green eyes as he smiled. "I am sorry I have been such a terrible father to you. Caroline will be reunited with her husband and child."

"Well she will be reunited with her husband but Mathias never died in that explosion."

Charles looked up at his daughter in shock and said, "Is Mathias the solider you saved the other day?"

Evangeline nodded her head and said, "You must promise me that you will not tell anyone! If Lawrence finds out, he will send him back."

Charles nodded his head as he agreed, "You have my word." There was a moment of silence before either one spoke again. "Do you love him?"

Evangeline began to blush and buried her face in her hair. "His heart is as beautiful as his mother's was."

Charles smiled and said, "Then you have my blessing to marry that boy."

Evangeline thought to herself that she would have married him either way but knowing that her father supported her meant a great deal to her. She walked around the table and gave her father a proper hug.

Chapter 16

Reconstruction

The following day Charles, Evangeline, and the group of men made their way to the old house along with the three wagon's full of building supplies. It was a bumpy ride there and a tight squeeze through the path towards the house. Mathias heard a noise from outside and peered through the living room window. He didn't recognize the men and began to wonder if these were the true owners of the house.

He suddenly became concerned and whispered, "Where are you, Evangeline?" He watched as they started to climb off the wagons and counted a total of eleven men and one girl. He tried to look closer at their faces but found it hard to make them out. The girl began to walk closer towards the house so Mathias went and hid behind the staircase.

The door opened slowly as the young girl stepped in. He saw the green chiffon material of her gown and noticed she began to approach him. She peeked around the staircase and began to giggle, "Hi, Mathias."

Mathias glanced up as he realized that it was Evangeline. He crawled out from under the stairs and examined her from head to toe. Her dress hung off her shoulders and had a beaded design under her bosoms. "You are stunning."

She smiled and handed him the knapsack that she had filled with clothes. "Go change your clothes then come meet the men that we have gathered to help us rebuild our home." Evangeline went back outside and contributed ideas with the other men as to what needed to be done or added onto the house.

A few minutes later, Mathias made his way outside. Evangeline glanced up and back at the men. As fast as she could blink she looked back up at Mathias and smiled.

He walked towards her as she whispered in his ear, "You look handsome."

He smiled and said, "How did you gather all these men?"

Evangeline turned around as she looked for her father.

Mathias felt a tap on his shoulder and turned to face Charles. "Good afternoon, Mr. Welsh."

Charles tipped his hat and said, "Mathias, it is so good to see you are in one piece! Evangeline has shared your story with me and do not worry, your secret is safe with me. These men here do not know who you are so you have nothing to fear."

Mathias nodded his head and shook Charles' hand, "I appreciate that, sir."

The crew had spent the entire day stripping the rotten wood off the old house and replacing it with fresh wood. In the first day, they had finished building the frame of the house and began to put up the walls. They set up a campsite on the big open field for the workers and themselves so that they did not have to travel the long distance each morning. Evangeline helped design the house and choose the interior such as flooring, wallpaper, paint colours, cabinets, etc. The men worked nonstop and it only took them three months to finish the entire house. Charles came out to the property whenever he was able to get time off work, which sometimes was only once a week but he didn't want to make it obvious to Lawrence that he was up to something.

The day after the house had been finished, Evangeline invited the men and their wives over for a barbeque in appreciation of their hard work.

That evening Charles tapped Mathias on his shoulder and said, "Mathias, let's go for a walk."

Mathias looked at Evangeline suspiciously but walked alongside Charles anyways. The two men walked far out into the field and for the longest time neither one of them said a word.

Charles glanced back at the house and said, "Everyone did such an amazing job on the house."

Mathias nodded and agreed, "Evangeline looks to design and paint so she did a great job designing it."

The house was huge, the bottom half of the house had black bricks while the top half was painted a dark grey. They enlarged the porch and added a deck to the back of the house where guests could come to spend time. They planned to add a barn but wanted to wait a few years before they added more to the house.

"Do you plan to marry my daughter now that the house is finished?"

Mathias kept his eyes locked on the sunset before him. "I have considered it."

Charles nodded his head and said, "Because you have my blessing, a man and a woman cannot live in the same house for very long without wanting to crawl into bed with each other."

Mathias wanted to tell Charles that all they had done was kissed one another but felt shy to tell her father about their personal life together.

"Is money what concerns you?" Mathias was unsure how to answer so instead, he remained silent. The two men stopped walking and turned to face each other.

Charles dug in his pocket for something and said, "When your mother died, I wanted to keep a memory of her so I took her engagement ring and wedding band off her finger. She told me that your father died but she told me that wearing the rings made her feel closer to him."

Charles dropped the rings into Mathias' hands and said, "Perhaps you and Evangeline can both keep her dear to your hearts as well and use her wedding bands as your own."

Mathias glanced up at Charles and gave him a one armed hug as he said, "Thank you, Charles. I really appreciate this."

Charles smiled and said, "As much as it hurts to see my baby grow up, I know that I cannot prevent it from happening. Over the last couple months, I have gotten to know her so well and I know why you love her so much. She is nothing like me or anything like her mother. She is unique and madly in love with you."

The two men made their way back to the house.

All the guests left shortly after, everyone was exhausted from the long, hot day in the sun.

Charles was the last to leave and gave his daughter a hug as he said, "Don't be a stranger, you know where I live. Goodnight, sweetheart. Goodnight, Mathias."

They shut the door behind him and retired for the night. They both had their separate bedrooms because Mathias wished to wait till marriage before sharing a bed with his bride.

Evangeline woke up at noon the following day and took a bath. She slid on her ivory, knee-length dress and wore her gold slippers. She opened her door and made her way to the kitchen for a bite to eat. To her surprise, Mathias had made her an omelet and placed it on the kitchen table for her. She ate the omelet and began to search for Mathias. She found him nowhere in the house and decided to see if he was chopping more firewood. She saw a small figure far out in the field and walked towards it. Mathias was sitting on a blanket he had laid out on the grass and next to him laid a steel-string guitar.

Evangeline sat next to him and asked, "I didn't know that you knew how to play an instrument."

Mathias smiled and began to explain, "When I was living at the orphanage, they had a room filled with instruments and every day after class, I would go there and play the guitar. One day after class, the professor caught me playing with it but he didn't get mad at me. I was young at the time so I feared he would hit me but he never did. Instead, he sat next to me and grabbed another guitar and started to play. From that moment on he would give me private music lessons. He gave me this guitar before he moved back to his home in Ireland."

Evangeline loved it when he told her stories of his past. "May I hear you play something?"

Mathias' face lit up as he said, "I wrote a song for you." Mathias picked up the guitar and stared into Evangeline's eyes are he began to strum his guitar. He kept his eyes locked on hers the entire time he played the song. She smiled at him as a tear rolled down the side of her cheek. He placed the guitar on the grass and said, "I have struggled all my life to survive and to please those around me. Then I met you and suddenly no one else mattered to me. I was mesmerized by your beauty and adored your courage and bravery. You introduced me to a world that is worth living in and I am deeply and madly in love with you. Would you do me the honour of being my wife?"

Evangeline nodded her head and began to sob as she threw her arms around Mathias. "Yes, I will marry you. I love you, Mathias."

Mathias dug in the pocket of his dress pants and pulled out a small gold ring. It was a sixty-karat gold band with a square ruby diamond in the centre and a diamond halo. Evangeline glanced at the ring as it looked familiar.

"This belonged to my mother and I would like you do have it."

Evangeline smiled as she let Mathias slide it onto her finger. "I would be honoured to wear her ring." Evangeline threw her arms around Mathias and kissed him passionately. The couple spent the remainder of the day planting the garden and tending the fields.

A month later...

"Evangeline, we need to get your hair done. The bride cannot be late for her own wedding."

Evangeline walked towards the stool and sat down. Charles had helped pay for the entire wedding and decided to have it at Evangeline and Mathias' new house. He hired a hair stylist, Veronica, a cook, a priest, and also a few guards to make sure no uninvited guests got into the party, especially Lawrence or Frances.

It took Veronica forty minutes to do Evangeline's hair, considering the fact that her hair reached to the end of her spine. Evangeline picked up her Victorian vanity mirror and looked at her reflection. She smiled and wondered who the beautiful woman in the mirror was. Veronica had curled her hair and pinned half of it up with a beautiful old butterfly hair clip that belonged to her mother. The butterfly was a faded gold colour with green gemstones on it. Evangeline walked over to her closet where her dress waited for her. The dress was still in the closet and hung on a hanger to prevent it from getting wrinkled or ruined. Veronica took the dress off the hanger and brought the dress over to Evangeline. Evangeline untied her house coat and let it fall to the floor. She then put on a gored skirt and over it she wore a crinoline cage. Veronica helped Evangeline put on her wedding gown. The gown had lace trimmings and pleated bertha; a collar-like trimming. Her gown was white silk satin, with needle lace, cotton, and whalebone strips.

Evangeline glanced at her reflection in the mirror and still could not believe that it was her reflection that she stared at. She glanced down at her ruby red engagement ring and knew that today was the day that she was marrying the love of her life.

Evangeline jumped when someone knocked loudly on the door, "Sweetheart, are you ready? The wedding is about to begin."

Veronica opened the door to let Charles in the room. Charles glanced up at his daughter and froze in the doorway. His jaw dropped and his eyes became moist as he saw his stunning daughter before him.

Evangeline smiled and walked towards him, "Let's not stand here all day, Father. I have a man waiting for me at the end of the aisle."

Charles smiled at his daughter as she lopped her arm in his. Veronica grabbed hold of her veil's train so it would not drag on the ground.

They made their way towards the field in the back of the house and Charles whispered to Evangeline, "You are breathtaking, beautiful."

She glanced at him and said, "I love you, Dad." It was the first time Evangeline had told her father she loved him since she was just a child.

His face lit up as he said, "I love you too, sweetheart." Over the past couple of months, Evangeline and Charles had bonded and created the father daughter relationship that she had always wanted.

Evangeline stood at the end of the aisle as the harp began to play a beautiful melody for her to walk to. There were only one hundred guests that attended the wedding due to the fact that they wanted to keep a low profile. Evangeline held a bouquet of white calla lilies as she walked alongside of her father down the long aisle. They walked on a long, gold-coloured carpet that reached the priest's stand. She kept her eyes locked on Mathias the entire walk down and couldn't help but smile the entire time. Her stomach turned with butterflies as her heart began to race.

Mathias stared at Evangeline as she walked down the aisle and couldn't take his eyes off his beautiful bride to be. She was absolutely breathtaking and he wondered how he was lucky enough to win her heart over. Mathias felt as if his smile was frozen upon his face and longed for the touch of her lips on his.

Charles lifted the veil then kissed his daughter softly on the cheek as he gave her away. Evangeline was eighteen years and he was twenty one. The ceremony took slightly longer than half an hour. It was then followed by the after party that was also hosted at their house. The entire backyard was lit up with small white Christmas lights, just like Charles' story. Evangeline shared a few dances with her father as well as her guests and of course with her new husband. It was nearly one in the morning by the time the last guest left their house. Mathias and Evangeline were exhausted from the long day.

Together they walked up the long staircase and down the long dark hallway. Evangeline took off her crinoline cage and removed her butterfly clip from her hair. As she began to brush through her long luscious hair, Mathias wrapped his arms around her waist and whispered into her ear, “My beautiful wife.”

He began to kiss her neck softly and slowly unzipped her dress. Evangeline shut her eyes as she longed for his touch. Mathias slid the straps of her dress off her shoulder and began to kiss her shoulders. Evangeline turned around to face Mathias and kissed his soft, red lips passionately. Mathias pushed her dress down her arms and off her waist till it slid down to her ankles. Evangeline stood before him wearing nothing but her corset and panties.

She unbuttoned his white dress shirt and slid it off his arms and threw it on the ground. Mathias directed her towards the bed and pushed her on it gently. Evangeline lay on their king-size bed and looked up at him as he pushed himself on top of her. They kissed one another passionately and fiercely. Evangeline slid her hands around the rim of his pants and down to his zipper as she unzipped his black dress pants. Mathias kissed her neck as he untied her corset and removed it from her skin so the only fabric she wore was her panties. The couple continue to strip one another of their clothes until their bare skins were touching one another.

Mathias kissed her ear lobe and whispered, “I love you, Evangeline.”

They began to kiss one another again and pressed their warm bodies together. Evangeline bit her lip as Mathias began to penetrate her. She ran her hands over his bare back for she had longed for the touch of his skin on hers. The couple made passionate love that night.

Chapter 17

Amelia's Cameo

It has been nearly seven months since the couple got married and Mathias began to feel lifeless as he was never able to leave the house. In a week was Evangeline's nineteenth birthday and he wanted to buy her something special, but he felt as if the money he used to purchase things was money from her father. He worked hard all his life and decided that today he would go into the city and seek a birthday present for his beautiful wife. There has been no word that Lawrence has suspected anything about Mathias being alive and therefore he would risk his life today to browse around the streets of Knaresborough.

It was humid outside and slightly foggy so Mathias decided that it would make it difficult for people to realize that it was him walking on the sidewalk next to them. Evangeline had an art class today so it was the perfect time for him to leave without her knowing he left. Mathias walked around the town and looked into a couple stores but did not find what he was looking for. He walked into an antique shop and glanced around at the large, darkened room. The walls were painted a rich gold with hardwood floors beneath his feet.

An elderly man approached Mathias and asked, "Is there something that I can help you find, young man?"

Mathias glanced at his unfamiliar face and smiled in relief, "I am looking for a birthday present for my wife." Mathias turned around to look behind him as he heard a book hit the floor.

Frances Scott hid behind the bookshelf in shock to discover Mathias was alive and most of all, had a wife. She used to go down to the docks on a daily basis and watch him work from a distance as she would admire his charm. She was secretly in love with him and hearing him saying "wife" broke her heart.

Mathias didn't see anyone and returned his attention on the elderly man before him. The man was beaming with a smile as he said, "I have a perfect gift that she would love!" The man turned around and began to walk towards his desk. "Come follow me." Mathias followed after him and stood patiently waiting as the man searched for something. The man stood up from behind his desk with a large blue velvet box in his hands. "This cameo necklace used to belong to a Serbian Princess named Amelia. She was shipped overseas when she became very ill and the people believed that there was healing water that could save her. It turned out that the water helped her regain her strength and her health improved. They decided to take her back home considering the good news that she was cured. Unfortunately, shortly after Amelia returned home, she began to have periods of ill health. Her father bought her this rare and expensive cameo to celebrate her wellbeing but when she started getting sick again she stopped wearing it. Amelia died at the age of twenty-seven from tuberculosis."

Mathias looked down as the elderly man snapped the velvet box open. Inside the box laid a cameo necklace featuring a beautiful ivory lady silhouette cameo that was resin. Around the lady was a rose gold Victorian pendant frame. It was an eighteen inch rose gold chain. Mathias touched the cameo and glanced up at the man, "How much are you asking for this?"

The man glanced down that the necklace and said, "Three thousand euros."

Mathias widened his eyes in shock and repeated, "Three thousand euros?!"

The man glanced at Mathias and said, "Young man, do you not recall the story I just told you about how this belonged to a princess?"

"But how do I know that is true?"

The man removed the necklace from the velvet box and placed it in the palm of Mathias' hand, "Look on the reverse side of the necklace." Mathias flipped the necklace over and pressed his finger on the engraved writing that read, *For my daughter, Princess Amelia*. Beneath it was a signature from her father. Mathias knew that three thousand euros was a large sum of money but Evangeline was worth every penny of it.

"I am interested in the necklace. Can I make payments on it or does it half to be a flat out payment?"

The man thought about it for a moment and asked, "What is your name, son?"

"Mathias Strong."

Frances gasped as she heard the words come from his mouth.

"Well, Mathias, I will make a deal with you." Mathias nodded his head as he waited for the man to continue. "You see I am an old man and cannot do as much as I used to be able to do. Tomorrow I plan to have a sale at my shop and clear out my store. If you help me run the store and deliver parcels, then you may have the cameo for free. All you have to do is help me out for a couple of days maximum."

Mathias glanced down at the cameo and said, "That is more than generous of you and you have yourself a deal." Mathias stuck out his hand and shuck hands with the man.

Frances tried to sneak out of the shop but as clumsy as she was, she bumped into a mannequin that wore an old ivory wedding dress. Both Frances and the mannequin hit the floor and make a loud bang noise. Mathias and the old man both turned and looked over at the mess on the floor.

Mathias placed the cameo on his desk and rushed towards the young woman on the floor. "Are you alright, miss?"

The girl's blonde ringlets were covering her face as she grabbed hold of Mathias' hand. He helped her get back on her feet and she smoothened out her dress and parted her hair from her face. She glanced up at him and said, "Hello, Mathias."

Mathias froze as he stared into her brown eyes. "Frances Scott."

The elderly man began to pick up the mannequin as they stared at one another. The man said, "I take it she won't be surprised anymore about her gift."

Mathias glanced at him and said, "Pardon me?"

The man pointed at Frances and said, "Your wife. She is gorgeous; you two make a splendid couple."

Frances blushed as she stared at Mathias' hazel eyes. Mathias began to laugh and said, "That is not my wife, just an old friend."

The old man glanced between the two and said, "Are you sure that was all?"

Mathias nodded his head and glanced over at Frances with narrowed eyes.

The man returned to his desk and grabbed the velvet box and walked back towards Mathias. "Take the cameo and return tomorrow before the sun rises. My name is Earl."

Earl walked away and left the two standing awkwardly before one another.

"She must be very special if you are giving her Princess Amelia's cameo. I used to come in Earl's shop all the time and he would tell me stories behind almost everything in the shop but Princess Amelia's was my favourite."

Mathias and Frances had never spoken to each other this much before; the most they ever said to one another was when Lawrence introduced them. They walked out of the shop together and walked alongside one another down the streets of Knaresborough.

"I thought you died in an explosion."

Mathias stared into the distance as he spoke, "I was hurt very badly but I did not die, as you can see. I managed to make my way back to Knaresborough when I found an old house outside of the city. I stayed in the house for a day before she found me and saved my life. We fell in love all over again and married one another a few months ago. She truly is my hero, my world, and the love of my life."

Frances couldn't help but to feel jealous of his mistress and asked, "May I ask who she is?"

Mathias hesitated to answer but figured that she already knew he was alive so what more was there to hide. "Evangeline Welsh, well now she is Evangeline Strong."

Frances' jaw dropped as she stopped walking and stared at him. "You cannot be serious."

Mathias raised his eyebrows at her and asked, "Why do you say that?"

Frances shook her head and said, "This is unbelievable. I don't understand how someone can go from living in the sewers to living in high class. She is beyond beautiful, wealthy, happy, and is married to you. I only have my father's money."

Mathias grabbed hold of her hands and looked her in the eyes as he spoke, "Now, now, don't put yourself down. She has worked so hard to be where she is; perhaps you need time away from your father so you can discover who you truly are as well."

Evangeline was finished with her art lesson and made her way out of the building. She froze on the staircase as she stared at the couple across the street. Mathias was holding Frances' hands and was just inches away from her face.

Frances glanced over Mathias' shoulder and saw Evangeline staring at them in disbelief. Frances leaned in closer to Mathias and pressed her lips against his for half a second before he pulled away.

"What are you doing, Frances? I am a married man."

Evangeline hurried across the street and pushed Frances up against the brown building behind her. Evangeline locked her to the wall by her throat and said, "After all these years, you are still an immature child whose goal is to hurt people and ruin people's lives. You are a pathetic bitch and I cannot believe that I am your sister!" Evangeline backed away as her eyes widened and she covered her mouth with her hand.

Frances and Mathias both stared at her and said, "Your sister?"

Evangeline glanced between the two but remained silent. Frances walked towards her and said, "You only wish I was your sister, Evangeline. You are the pathetic one."

Evangeline stepped closer to her so they only stood inches apart. "Perhaps I am, but never in my life would I wish to be related to you in any way. At least my father loves me enough to tell me the truth."

Frances was furious and demanded, "Well, you tell me the truth then!"

Evangeline shook her head and said, "This is the reason why I did not believe the truth. Because you are obnoxious!"

Frances crossed her arms over her chest and sighed. "Fine, please tell me the truth… better?"

Mathias stood there as he stared at Evangeline in disbelief and wondered why his wife never told him about this.

Evangeline told Frances the truth about the relationship that their mother had with both of their fathers. Frances stared at the ground as she was shocked to discover the truth and realized that it made sense that she had never seen her mother before.

"I cannot believe that I have been lied to all my life!"

Evangeline replied, "That is a topic that you are to discuss with your father, Frances. However, I do ask one thing from you in return…" Frances glanced up at her as she waited for her to continue. "You must promise not to tell your father about Mathias and me."

Frances glanced between the couple and said, "Our lives are already both ruined, Evangeline. What more could hurt?"

Evangeline and Mathias stared after her and Frances began to run down the foggy streets of Knaresborough. She wanted to escape before the couple tried to hold her captive or give her another bloody nose.

Evangeline and Mathias walked alongside of one another as they began their journey back home. For the longest time, neither one said a word to the other.

As they reached the end of the city streets, Evangeline turned to Mathias and said loudly, "If something is to happen to you, this will be your fault for risking your life and going into the city!"

Mathias stared at her in disbelief and said, "Me?! I apologize for wanting to do something special for my wife. You don't understand how boring it is to stay in that one area for months on end! And do not judge me, Evangeline, for you have lied to me as well."

Evangeline shook her head and said, "I did not lie to you Mathias. You never asked me if I had any siblings nor did this topic ever come up."

The couple walked the remainder of the way in silence. When they reached the house, Evangeline made her way to the kitchen to prepare dinner. As she rinsed the vegetables off, she felt Mathias wrap his arms around her waist.

"I'm sorry."

Evangeline turned around and stared into his hazel eyes as she said, "As am I." Mathias leaned in closer and kissed her softly.

Days passed and Mathias had gone through with his agreement with Earl and helped him clear the store out. It was an overall success but a couple days after the huge clearance, Earl passed away from tuberculosis. The man must have known his end was near and that was why he wanted to close the store as fast as he could. All the profit he made from his antiques went to his children and one fourth of it went to Mathias for his generosity and help.

The day finally came when Evangeline turned nineteen. Charles invited the couple over for a home-cooked meal and invited a few other guests as well. It was a formal event so Mathias dressed in his best black suit and wore a red bowtie. Evangeline slipped on her ivory silk taffeta and chiffon evening gown. The gown had ecru lace insertions with chiffon flowers embroidered on it. Her hair was wavy and put into a bun with loose curls framing her face. She applied soft tones of makeup that made her look more elegant and soft. The couple stayed at Charles' house until shortly after midnight. It was a small celebration but Evangeline always liked small gatherings better than huge parties. Later that night when the couple returned home, they sat in the sitting room as Mathias dug in his pocket for her gift. He pulled out a blue velvet box and handed it to her.

Evangeline snapped the box open as Mathias said, "Happy birthday, Evangeline."

Evangeline's jaw dropped as she stared at the beautiful cameo in the velvet box. She traced the lady silhouette with the tip of her index finger and glanced up at her husband.

"This is beautiful! Thank you, Mathias." Evangeline leaned in to kiss him and said, "Could you put it on me?"

She removed it from the box and wrapped it around her neck. Mathias grabbed hold of the ends and closed it behind her neck. He kissed her softly on her neck and wrapped his arm around her waist. Evangeline stood up and took hold of his arm as she led him to their bedroom.

Chapter 18

Anchors Away

"Evangeline, wake up!" Evangeline squinted her eyes as she heard her father yelling at her to wake up. "Evangeline, we have to leave now!"

She sat up in her bed as she watched her father filling a knapsack full of her clothes. "What are you doing?"

Charles continued to stuff her clothes in the bags when she asked again, "Dad, why are you packing my things?"

Charles threw the bag over his shoulder and walked towards his daughter. "We are in danger and we must leave now before Lawrence and his men get to us first!"

Evangeline stood up and realized she was still wearing her ivory silk taffeta and chiffon evening gown from the night before. "Where is Mathias?"

Charles hesitated to answer, "He—he is waiting at the ship."

Evangeline eyed him curiously and asked, "The ship?"

Charles nodded his head as he grabbed his daughter by the hand, "Please let's go now before the sun rises."

Evangeline grabbed her white housecoat off her bed rail and followed her father out the house. "How come Mathias left without me?"

Charles continued to power walk towards the docks as he said, "I needed his help to start the engine and told him that I would come for you shortly." The men had finished the ship a couple of days ago and it had never been sailed before.

It took Evangeline and Charles nearly half an hour to make it to the docks. Evangeline glanced around as she realized she had never seen the place so empty and peaceful before.

There were a few men who began to untie the ship and yelled out, "Miss! We must board the ship now. She is going to set sail."

Evangeline took one last look at Knaresborough and wondered if she would ever return. Evangeline walked towards the steamship and walked over the board to load onto it. The men untied it and quickly followed after her. The last man was forced to take a big leap onto the ship as it had already begun to sail the water. It occurred to Evangeline that it had been so long since she last saw the ship and seeing it completed was strange. It was bigger than she remembered and looked beautiful. She was amazed at the craftsmanship on the ship and wanted to explore and discover it. She began to walk around the upper deck of the ship and watched as Knaresborough began to disappear in the distance. On the deck were ten smaller boats in case the ship began to sink, then they would have an emergency boat. Evangeline walked towards the doors that led into the ship. She opened the door and peeked in at the fancy interior. The carpets were ivory and the walls were painted a warm brown. She walked down the long hallway and dragged her fingers across the wall. She came to a curve and followed it as it led her to a case of stairs. She walked down the metal stairs and it started to become hot and steamy from the boilers. Evangeline continued to follow the stairs and thought maybe she would find Mathias helping with the engine as her father had said.

Evangeline reached the basement and began to wander around. It was hot and men were working hard to keep the engine going but to her disappointment, Mathias was nowhere in sight.

She approached a middle aged man and said, "Excuse me, have you seen Mathias?"

The man was puzzled and said, "I don't think this is a place for a lady to be."

She rolled her eyes at him and asked again, "Have you seen Mathias?"

The man shrugged his shoulders and said, "Sorry to disappoint you, sweetheart, but Mathias died in the war."

Evangeline was getting frustrated with him and said, "No, my father said that he was in the basement helping with the engine."

The man shook his head and said, "Then I'm afraid your father has lied to you." Evangeline backed away from the man and glanced around the room for her husband. When she finally realized that he was nowhere in the basement, she made her way back to the upper deck to search for her father.

Evangeline froze as she stared at her father at the front of the ship. He looked so peaceful and happy. His dreams were finally coming true as he had worked so hard for his ship to set sail one day.

Charles turned around as he heard his daughter approaching, "Evangeline! How do you like my ship?"

Evangeline glanced around and said, "I think it looks amazing, I am very proud of you."

Charles glanced at the water ahead and said, "It's like floating on a sea of dreams."

Evangeline nodded and remember the real reason she had searched for him. "Where is Mathias?" Charles kept his eyes at the water ahead and she continued, "I searched the boiler rooms and the man in the basement told me he wasn't here." Charles remained silent and kept his attention on the waves that the ship made. Evangeline started to become frustrated with him and said loudly, "Dammit, Dad! Where is my husband?"

Charles didn't look at his daughter as he spoke, "He is with Lawrence."

Evangeline's body began to shake as she grasped at what her father had just told her. "Pardon me?!"

Charles turned his body towards her and stared into her green eyes as he said, "Lawrence found out about Mathias' return. Frances had told him. She said she ran into him the other day. When Lawrence found out, he came barging into my house shortly after you left and demanded answers. He had a crew of men with him and threatened to kill me if I did not tell him where you guys were. He promised me he wouldn't hurt you for it was Mathias he wanted."

Evangeline was terrified and scared; she plopped herself on the deck and asked, "Why does he want him so desperately?"

Charles sat next to his daughter and wrapped his arm around her shoulder. "He told me that after his men have finished surviving their time in the war, he ships them out to a deserted place. He told me that he does this so that the men can start a new life somewhere they have never been before and if they find their way back to Knaresborough, then he will leave them alone for good. With them, he gives the men a large sum of money from their creation to help them survive."

Evangeline stared at her father in disbelief and replied, "That is the stupidest thing I have ever heard! What does it matter what one does with themselves after they have fought for the war? He only wishes to cause pain in a man's life." Tears began to roll down her cheeks as she said, "So my husband is lost in the world somewhere?"

Charles nodded his head and said, "Unfortunately yes."

"How do you know he is not lying?"

Charles sighed and said, "Because I have known many individuals who have been shipped away and never have I seen one return to Knaresborough."

Evangeline stood up and said loudly, "We must turn back!"

Charles remained seated on the ground and said, "I'm afraid that won't be possible."

"Why is that not possible?" Evangeline stared into the distance as she tried to spot the city. The sun was rising and the city was disappearing.

"If we turn back, I am a dead man and Mathias won't even be in Knaresborough anymore. There is nothing left for us there."

Evangeline kept her eyes locked on the sight ahead as she began to spot a small black figured miles away. "You are already dead to me. What makes your life so special anyways?"

Charles felt a sadness befall him as her words struck him like a million needles piercing at his heart. "The only special thing about my life is you and that is the reason I refuse to go into the war. I cannot risk dying and never seeing my beautiful daughter again."

Evangeline rolled her eyes and wondered where her husband was. Her eyes were moist as the tears continued to fall. She bent over the rails and stared into the moving water. Charles rose off the ground and stared at the small approaching figure.

He asked, "What do you suppose that is?"

Evangeline glanced up and said, "If Lawrence Scott is capable of placing someone on the other side of the world, or putting someone into the war, or even building this great ship, then I am sure he was capable of building his own ship for situations like these."

Charles stared at the approaching figure as it started to become larger and clearer. Evangeline was right and he knew it; Lawrence would stop at nothing, especially if Charles signed a contract.

Charles smiled as he remembered something, "The contract I signed cannot fall through because I signed as my false name, not as Henry Beckem."

Evangeline tilted her head at him and said, "One signature cannot save your life any more than a ship can."

Charles rushed off the deck and made his way to the boiler room.

"Listen up, men! We need to get her going at full speed! We have an approaching enemy and he is getting closer by the second."

The men nodded their heads and began to work even harder than they already were. Charles rushed back to the upper deck to see the captain that drove the ship. "There has been a slight change of plans and I'm going to need you to head south rather than going west and please hurry as our enemy is approaching!"

The captain turned the steering wheel all the way left. The ship's speed had increased due to the men's extra hard work in the basement and therefore made the ship turn sharply.

Charles stared at the sight ahead and widened his eyes in horror as he screamed, "Evangeline!"

The captain informed the crew to stop the engine as Charles ran to the front of the ship. Due to the extreme speed and sharp turn, Evangeline had flipped over the rail of the ship and fell overboard. Charles reached the front of the ship as fast as he could but Evangeline had already hit rock bottom. Without hesitation, Charles jumped into the water after her.

When he lived in Scotland, his father placed him into a boarding school where he had learnt to swim and therefore he was lucky to put his knowledge to use. Charles opened his eyes under the water as he swam further down searching for his daughter. Evangeline never learnt how to swim like he had and knew that she would drown if he didn't find her. After a few seconds, Charles returned to the surface to get more air before he dove in again. He swam back a few feet and dove beneath the ship when he spotted a dark figure floating near the rear of the ship. He swam towards it and noticed that his daughter was caught on the bottom of the ship. Her gown got caught in the propellers. He was relieved that the captain had shut the engine off when he did otherwise Evangeline would have been chopped into tiny pieces. He began to untangle her but found it impossible to get her dress out. He reached into his pocket and pulled out a small black pocket knife. He began to cut the dress off her body. When he finally freed her, he wrapped his arm around her and swam with her to the surface. He glanced at her with horror as he realized that she was not moving.

When Charles finally reached the surface, his crew threw down a raft at him. Charles got on the raft as the men pulled it back onto the ship. When they were finally back on the ship, they placed Evangeline on the deck. Charles moved his body above hers and began to breathe in her mouth. He then placed his hands on top of one another and began to push on her chest.

He repeated this multiple times until one man said, "Sir, I think she's gone…"

Charles ignored the man and continued to give her CPR when suddenly she began to cough up water. Evangeline's eyes remained shut as she spat water out of her mouth. Then suddenly she stopped and remained lying on the ground. Charles was puzzled at what just happened and placed his head on her chest as he listened for her beating heart.

He sat up and turned to face his crew, "She is alive."

The middle aged man she saw earlier that day said, "Then why does she not open her eyes?"

Charles glanced back at his daughter as he said, "Because she is sleeping, Craig." Charles got up in a hurry and glanced out on the water as he realized that the ship was approaching faster by the second. "We must get the ship going again before they catch up to us! Hurry, men. Get back to work!" Then men rushed back to their posts and started up the engine again. Within minutes the ship was moving at a fast speed.

Charles lifted his daughter off the ground and carried her into one of the rooms down the long hallway. He placed her on the large bed and requested one of the female cooks to change her into warm clothing. The woman began to strip Evangeline of her wet clothes and threw them into a laundry hamper. She walked towards the brown oak dresser and took out a white night gown. She lifted Evangeline's arms and placed the dress over her head and let it fall over her body. The woman was nearly the same size as Evangeline, so when she was finished, she called for Charles to help her get under the covers. Charles came into the room and lifted Evangeline as the woman rolled the blanket down. He then placed her on the bed as the woman covered her with the covers. Charles placed his finger on her throat to make sure he could still feel her pulse.

He sighed in relief and kissed his daughter on the cheek, "Sweet dreams, Evangeline." Charles shut the light off and closed the door.

Chapter 19

In a Daze

Evangeline's head was pounding and her ears were plugged from falling into the water. She rubbed her eyes for a brief second and glanced around the room. The room was much smaller than the one she had back in Knaresborough and definitely a lot emptier. In the room were a queen-size bed, one oak dresser, and a nightstand. The room was simple and nice but it was not her home. Evangeline sat up and buried her face in the palm of her hands as her head ached in pain. She glanced down at her clothes and wondered who had changed her last night. She crossed her fingers as she hoped that it wasn't her father who undressed her. Evangeline got off the bed and walked towards the oak dresser that stood in the corner of the room. She opened the drawers as she began to look through them for clothing to wear. She pulled out an outfit that she didn't even know she owned and put it on. She glanced down at the floor length evening gown with a short train. It had white net studded with glass beads over the grayish-pink silk taffeta. Evangeline searched the room for a pair of slippers to put on. She found a selection of sandals hidden underneath her queen bed. She put on a pair of gold sparkly slippers. She stood in the middle of the room and glanced down at herself and wondered who she was.

Evangeline walked towards her room door and opened it. She froze in the doorway as she stared the horrible sight in front of her. Her eyes widened in shock as her questions were finally being answered.

She whispered, "Somnia Viveret."

The last time she dreamt of Somnia Viveret was almost four years ago. She expected this day to come sooner but because of the prolonged time, she began to think it wasn't real to begin with. One thing was certain: Sparkle warned her that the next time she came back, she would have to save their world. Evangeline thought about it for a moment and it made perfect sense why she had returned now rather than before. Evangeline's world was crashing down on her and from the look of things; Somnia Viveret had been taken over. The skies were dark and gloomy and the trees were burnt of all their leaves. The ground was black as coal and cracked. There was no grass, no flowers, and no sign of life anywhere. Evangeline took a few steps forward as she continues to stare at the horrible sight before her. There was nobody around and for the first time ever she felt as if she was the only person in the world. Throughout her life, she has felt alone and abandoned by her father and betrayed by those around her. When she met Mathias, he made her feel like she was the world. As she was standing in the destroyed and deserted land, she felt the same as she did years ago, alone.

Evangeline began to walk around the empty land as she glanced in every direction in hope of finding someone, anyone. She brushed her finger tips along the dead branches of the withered trees. She glanced up as she heard a scream coming from the distance. There was no sight of anyone so Evangeline began to walk in the direction in which the scream came from. She walked miles on end before she finally reached a long bridge. The bridge was broken in the centre and looked like someone blew it up with a bomb. Evangeline began to walk across the bridge and stopped where the bridge ended. She glanced over the edge of the bridge as it was forty feet from the ground. The water smelled like rotten sewers as dead fish were floating above the water. There was a thick layer of green algae on top of the dying river. Evangeline crinkled her nose at the horrible smell and began to back away from the edge.

Evangeline turned around quickly as she bumped into someone. She covered her mouth with her hands as she looked down at the miserable, green creature. She narrowed her eyes at him as she examined his appearance.

"What are you looking at?" said the green creature. His ears were massive and pointy as they stuck out on either side of his head. He stared at her with his hazel eyes as he waited for her to answer his question, "What?"

Evangeline remained silent as she couldn't get over his strange green skin tone and his long and pointy nose. He crossed his large arms over his chest as he slouched before her. She glanced down at his massive and bare feet. The only fabric that was covering him was a piece of cloth that covered his pelvis. The creature flashed his razor sharp teeth at her and growled in a deep snarl.

"You do not frighten me." Evangeline smirked at him and crossed her arms over her chest to mock him.

He narrowed his eyes at her and said, "How can I frighten you if you are the hideous one?"

Evangeline dropped her arms at her sides and stared at him in disbelief. "You are the one who looks like vomit."

He peered up at her and snapped, "I am a goblin!"

They stared at one another as they were both getting irritated with each other.

"Then I have discovered that I do not like goblins." Evangeline pushed her way past the goblin and began to walk away. He stared after her for a brief moment before he sped after her. In the blink of an eye he was at her side. Evangeline stopped walking as she glanced down at him and back to the broken bridge. "You are extremely fast for someone who has such short legs."

He rolled his eyes and said, "Do you have an insult for everything?"

Evangeline giggled and replied, "Do you know how to smile?" He narrowed his eyes at her and shook his head in frustration. She stuck her hand out before him and said, "My name's…"

"…Evangeline. Yeah, yeah, everyone knows that."

She looked at him with puzzled eyes as she asked, "Everyone? I have not seen a single person since I arrived here over an hour ago."

He glanced around the flat land and said, "They are too afraid to come out of hiding." He leaned in towards her and whispered, "They are afraid of the queen."

Evangeline was confused and said, "Sparkle never mentioned anything about the queen. As far as she was concerned, the queen died."

The goblin grabbed hold of Evangeline's arm and directed her towards the bridge. "We must go somewhere where no one can hear us."

They went down the steep slope and sat on a large rock just beneath the bridge. "Before you tell me anything else, what is your name? I cannot continue to call you the goblin or little green creature."

He glared at her and said, "Damian."

She nodded her head and repeated, "Damian."

He rolled his eyes at her and began to speak, "I take it Sparkle told you how your world and our world are connected?" Evangeline nodded her head as he continued, "Yes our worlds are connected but the years here do not pass nearly as quickly as they do in your world. It has only been three weeks since you were last in Somnia Viveret."

Evangeline narrowed her eyes as she began to protest, "How is that possible? Four years have passed since I last dreamt of this world."

Damian shook his head and said, "In your world, perhaps, but here it has only been three weeks."

Evangeline wondered how that was possible but instead of questioning him further she nodded her head as she waited for him to continue.

"Shortly after you left Somnia Viveret, Sahara's evil disciples began to attack different towns and cities. They took them down one at a time until there was nothing left of them but ashes on the ground and dead trees." Evangeline glanced around at the dead land. "Sahara took possession of Draco..."

Evangeline interrupted him and asked, "The dragon that was pulled into the sky?"

"I suppose so, anyways... Draco became her pet and tool. He destroyed the majority of our land with his fire and extreme strength. Perhaps when he was pulled into the sky, like you said, it was the work of Sahara because shortly after you left, he began to destroy everything."

She widened her eyes as it all became clear to her, "That makes perfect sense because as Draco was being pulled into the clouds, he looked terrified and confused. I knew it was not him that did that because his eyes began to change in colour and he looked like he lost control of his body. At the time, I didn't care why that happened because he was trying to kill me."

Damian was getting frustrated that she kept interrupting him while he was trying to tell her about what had happened. "Do you want to know what has happened or would you like to tell me the story?"

"Sorry, you may continue."

"The land was dead, the trees withered, the people are scared, and the prince was gone. According to the rumour that has spread around, Prince Mathias walks these very grounds but does not recall who he is. Sahara's men killed his guards and broke into his castle in the middle of the night. She leaned over him as he was sleeping and held a knife to his throat, and that was when he woke up. He wasn't scared because he knew that this day would come. She said to him, 'Killing you would be much too easy. I intend to make you suffer and your people will pay for your mistakes, Prince.' Mathias glared up at her red eyes and said, 'You will never get away with this.' She smiled at him and said, 'I already have.'

He glanced at her soldiers and back at her piercing eyes. She glanced down at the knife she held to his throat and transformed it into a black wand. She stood up and pointed it at him and said, 'I will transform you into a creature and give you brand new memories. You will have no memory of your life as a prince or anything that happened in your previous lifetime. Instead, you will walk the land of Somnia Viveret as a completely different character. As of right now, I am Somnia Viveret's new queen and people will bow down before me. You are nothing but dust in the air and to find you will be like looking for a needle in a haystack.' Sahara's eyes were glowing with flames as she pointed her wand at him and changed his character. When Prince Mathias woke up the following day, he was not in the palace. He is somewhere in Somnia Viveret and no one knows where or what creature she has turned him into.'

Evangeline tilted her head and asked, "How do you know all of this?"

"Everyone knows everything here in Somnia Viveret, hence why everyone knows who you are."

Evangeline nodded her head as she understood what he was referring to. "If Sahara is murdered, will everything change back, including Prince Mathias?"

Damian shook his head and said, "Somnia Viveret would change back to its natural environment and the creatures would return to their normal human form. However, Prince Mathias would remain a creature for the rest of his life and would never recall his previous life."

"Why would Mathias not turn back into a prince?"

Damian stood up from the rock and walked onto the broken bridge. Evangeline followed behind him as he continued to speak. "Because that is his curse and only he can break it."

"How can he break it?"

He glanced up at her green eyes and said, "He must discover who he is before she kills you."

Evangeline blinked her eyes and said, "What does my existence have to do with his?"

He pointed into the horizon and passed the mountains and said, "On the other side of this bridge and up in the mountains is where Queen Sahara is forming her army. If she murders you before he discovers who he is, then you will be dead and he will be cursed forever. Somnia Viveret has turned into hell and your existence will save us. Therefore we must go on a quest and find Prince Mathias before Sahara gets to us first."

Evangeline glanced at the mountains and asked, "How will we know if we have found him or not?"

Damian turned around and began to walk away from the palace as he said, "We will just know."

She followed after him as she glanced back at the broken bridge. "Does she know that I am here?"

He nodded his head and said, "That is why we are going in the opposite direction from her, so we may prolong your life."

Chapter 20

Sleeping Beauty

Evangeline had only been in Somnia Viveret for twenty-four hours but as Damian had mentioned, the years pass quicker in her world than in Somnia Viveret. Charles and his crew had finally reached their destination: Scotland. Lawrence continued to follow them but had fallen back a few miles because Charles' ship was much faster than Lawrence's was.

As the ship docked, the men rushed to gather their belongings and get away before Lawrence would reach the docks. They placed Evangeline onto a stretcher and brought her onto the land with them. Charles and his men rode together to Cecilia's parent's house. They owned a massive house out in the country and he knew that Lawrence would not think to look there. It took them nearly an hour before they reached the farm. The car dropped them off at the end of the street and the men walked up the long driveway with their belongings and Evangeline.

There was a total of twenty-five crew members that walked up the driveway and in that moment an elderly man walked out onto the porch and held a shot gun in his hand. The men stopped walking, all expect Charles.

"Who are you and what do you want from here?"

Charles continued to approach him slowly and calmly as he said, "Good afternoon, Steven."

Steven lowered the gun and blocked the sun with his hand as he tried to take a closer look at the man who stood before him. He widened his eyes and gasped, "Henry Beckem." Steven flared his nostrils in anger and pointed the gun at Henry's head.

Henry raised his hands in the air and said, "You can shoot me if you like but first, we must help my daughter and your granddaughter."

He lowered the gun once again and said, "My granddaughter?"

Henry glanced back at his men and waved them over.

Steven watched as the men carried a stretcher towards him and on it laid a beautiful young lady. He stared at the girl with big eyes and touched her arm and said, "This is my granddaughter? She is beautiful."

Henry walked on the other side of her and said, "Her name is Evangeline and during our voyage here, she slipped off the ship and has been in a coma ever since. She is not dead because she is breathing and her heart is still beating. It has been almost a month since the incident and she still does not wake up. We would have arrived here sooner, but Lawrence was on our ass the entire time."

Steven examined his granddaughter and placed his finger on her neck as he felt for her pulse. "Come bring her in the house and I will call for a doctor immediately."

Henry glanced back at his men and said, "My crew needs a place to stay until Lawrence leaves Scotland. I know that it is a lot to ask, but for now, can they stay here, even in your barn would be great. They are good men and will work for you until it is safe to leave."

Steven sighed and nodded his head, "In the barn, but let's get Evangeline into the house."

Steven called for the doctor and in the meantime, had the men bring her into Cecilia's old bedroom. They placed her on the bed and left the two men alone.

Steven sat on a chair next to her and lifted her arm, "We need to get food into her body, her arms are so thin and she will die if she does not get the necessary nutrients."

Henry sat on the bed next to his daughter and buried his face in the palm of his hands. "I've been such a terrible father. My wife is dead and now my daughter is in a coma."

Steven glanced up at him in anger and asked, "Cecilia is dead?"

Henry looked down at his daughter and said, "She died from cholera nine years ago and I have been doing everything in my power to bring Evangeline back home. I did not intend on this happening and if she dies, then I give you permission to shoot me."

Steven felt a sadness befall him and could see how much Henry had suffered and was still suffering. "If you wouldn't have run off with my daughter, then she would still be alive and Evangeline would be awake and living her life right now. Instead you killed my daughter and put my granddaughter into a deep sleep. You have only hurt the people around you, did you even actually love them or do you just think that you did?"

Henry pulled his eyebrows together in a frown and said, "How dare you say that! I loved Cecilia with all my heart and would have given the world to her. Evangeline is the only reason I am still here. If I lose her too, then I have no purpose on Earth."

Steven was about to ask a question but was interrupted when he heard a knock on the door. He got off his chair and opened the door only to see Dr. Walter standing in the doorway.

Steven stuck out his hand and shook Dr. Walter's hand, "Please come in, Doctor." He directed him over to where Evangeline laid and told him everything that had happened to her.

Dr. Walter asked the men to leave the room while he examined his patient fully and thoroughly. He was in the room for over an hour before he opened the door to let the two men back into the room.

"Please have a seat, gentleman."

Henry and Steven exchanged a look with one another before they sat down. Steven had just met his granddaughter and he was already in love with her and they didn't even have a conversation yet. They were both worried and feared what the doctor was going to tell them.

Dr. Walter remained standing and looked over at Evangeline. "It is obvious to say that Evangeline is in a coma but her case is very strange. I have never seen anything like this in all my years of being a doctor. Not only is your daughter in a coma but she also has a severe case of narcolepsy. It appears that she is in such a deep sleep that she thinks she is awake but really she is just dreaming. If you look closely at her face, you can see her eyes moving back and forth as if she is looking around and her mouth moves from time to time as if she is speaking to someone."

Henry was puzzled and said, "So what are you trying to say, that we can't wake her up?"

Dr. Walter shook his head and said, "Oh no, Evangeline is awake." Steven and Henry looked at her and back at one another in confusion. "She is dreaming, but to her, she is awake. She won't wake up until she finishes whatever she is meant to do in her dream and until then, she will remain asleep."

Steven got off the chair and walked towards his granddaughter and touched her arm, "She is starving! She will be dead before she wakes up if we do not get food into her body!"

Dr. Walter stood next to Steven and said, "I will come back later tonight and hook her up to a tube that will go down her throat and we will get nutrients into her system so she stays strong and we do not lose her."

Henry scratched his head and laughed. "This is a joke right? She can't be living in a dream. That's just a sick joke, Doctor."

Dr. Walter grabbed his first aid bag and pulled it over his shoulder as he walked towards Henry. "There is no humour in this, Mr. Beckem. Watch your daughter carefully as she is as wide awake as you are. I will return in a few hours with my assistant and we will hook her up to the tubes. Hopefully she is almost done her task because one can only live for so long off injected sugar water."

Dr. Walter left the house and returned in a few hours like he said he would. With him was a middle aged woman, Heather. She would assist him and care for Evangeline, making sure she got the nutrients that she needed and that her heart was still beating.

Later that evening, there was a loud knock on the door. Henry glanced at Steven in fear and knew that it was Lawrence. He had put together a search crew for him and his men.

"Please, Steven. I need you to cover for us!"

Steven sighed and said, "Alright, alright. Heather, please bring me to the door in that wheelchair." Heather didn't ask any question. Instead, she got the wheelchair. Steven sat in the wheelchair and she pushed him to the front door. They banged on the door loudly just as she slowly opened the door.

Steven made himself look incredibly tired and asked, "Can I help you?"

Lawrence glanced at him and back at Heather and said, "Yes I am looking for a man who goes by the name of Henry Beckem. That or perhaps Charles Welsh. He is with a large crew of men and arrived earlier today. Have you seen this man?"

Steven stared at the man with confused eyes and said, "Henry Beckem?"

Lawrence nodded his head and said, "Yes! Have you seen him?"

Steven glanced down at the floor and back at Lawrence, "I was good friends with his father but I have not seen Henry since he was a teenager. Last I heard he ran away with Cecilia and no one has seen them since. It's actually quiet tragic, if you ask me. Why are you looking for him, if I may ask?"

Lawrence eyed him curiously and said, "He has not gone through with his agreement to a contract and therefore he will be hanged when we find him. If you see him, you tell Mr. Beckem that we will find him if it's the last thing we do."

Steven nodded his head and said, "I'll be sure to do that but I cannot guarantee you that he will come this way." Lawrence peeked over Steven's head as he tried to glance around the house but to his disappointment, he saw no signs of Henry. He turned his back to Steven and walked away with his crew of men.

Heather closed the door and Steven sighed in relief that they left. They returned to Evangeline's room shortly after he left.

Steven approached Henry and said, "I demand answers! I want to know who Lawrence is, who is Charles Welsh, why Cecilia died, and what kind of contract did you sign?"

Henry sighed and sat down for he knew that it would be a long conversation.

Chapter 21

Quest

Damian and Evangeline had been walking for nearly twelve hours and there was still no one in sight.

Damian looked around carefully and said, "The people of Somnia Viveret are very good at hiding and I'm sure we have walked passed many already."

Evangeline looked around and wondered where they could possibly hide. Sahara and her disciples had burnt everything to the ground expect the old palace and the broken bridge. She bumped into Damian as he had stopped walking and said, "What is it?"

He stared at the sight before him and said, "It looks like Sahara missed a spot."

She looked up and in the distance were green trees, grass, and mountains. Evangeline began to walk towards it as a smile crossed her face. She looked back at Damian and asked, "Do you think that Mathias could be up in the mountains?"

He began to follow after her and said, "That is a possibility but one is never too sure." They began to walk towards the mountains which seemed like an eternity.

Dear Mathias, *1911*

I have discovered why I returned to Somnia Viveret and that is to find you. You have disappeared in both of my worlds and I will find you if it is the last thing that I do.

I have made a new friend, his name is Damian and he is a goblin. I have met many different types of creatures in this world but Damian is different than all the others. He is so miserable all the time and I have never seen him smile since I have been here. I have made it my goal to place a smile upon his gloomy face. I enjoy his company because I feel that we are very alike but very different. I cannot help but to feel sorry for him and wonder what has happened in his previous lifetime that has made him so dull. I hope that I can save his life as well as save yours.

I love you, Mathias, and I will never give up. I will search for you until the day that I die so please hurry home. My arms are spread wide open for you and my love for you will never die.

Sincerely,
Evangeline Strong

"What are you thinking about?" Damian noticed that Evangeline had been very quiet since they began their journey.

She looked over her shoulder at him and said, "I like to write journal entries and because I do not have my journal with me, I imprinted one into my head."

Damian rolled his eyes and shook his head as he said, "You are such a strange girl."

Evangeline smiled because she knew that her life was bizarre and another person or creature telling her she was strange didn't make a difference anymore. She whispered, "Yeah, you're one to talk."

"What was that?"

She looked straight as they had just reached the green scenery before them. "I just said look, we're here."

He eyed her suspiciously and began to walk through the huge oak trees. It was already nightfall and not even the moon was out tonight. "We better find shelter and get some rest." Evangeline and Damian walked towards a raspberry bush and hid behind it. "This should be fine for the night. Quick, Evangeline, grab some leaves and cover yourself with them so you blend in with the bushes." Evangeline gathered a bunch of leaves and branches and curled into a ball while Damian placed the leaves on top of her.

She watched him as he buried her under the leaves and said, "I suppose you don't need to be covered up since you blend in just fine on account of your green skin tone."

Damian lied down next to her and whispered, "Without me, you would have been dead already."

Neither of them said another word, instead they fell asleep instantly.

"Hello!" A sweet, pitchy voice screamed. "Is anybody out there?"

Evangeline woke up to the sounds of someone screaming. A little girl, she guessed. She sat up and all the leaves and branches fell off her body. She peered through the bush and saw a little girl, a human, wandering around the forest. She looked like she was no older than six years old. Evangeline opened her mouth to talk but before words escaped her mouth, she felt a large hand cover her mouth. A large green hand. It was Damian. She turned around to face him and saw him hold his index finger to his lips to silence her. Within a few minutes, the little girl wandered off and Damian freed Evangeline.

"Why didn't you let me go help her? She looked lost and she was a human!"

Damian plumped himself on the ground and spoke with caution, "Don't be fooled by one's innocence because that was no ordinary little girl. That, my dear, was Queen Sahara."

Evangeline looked through the bush again but there was no sign of the girl. She was confused and said, "That was a little girl!"

Damian sighed as he started to become irritated with her, "Do you not listen to anything that I tell you? Sahara is a powerful witch and if she has the power to transform others into creatures, then she sure as hell can change herself, too. You have to be careful who you run into and who you talk to. One way of knowing that it is her is because she can only shift herself into the form of a human. She can become a man or a woman and differ in age ranges, too."

They stood up and walked on the other side of the bush as they began their journey again.

"So you're pretty much telling me to avoid anyone that is a human?"

He nodded his head and said, "Including Prince Mathias. She tends to change into him every now and then and lures in more of our people. Once she has them in her grasp, she puts them into her prison for slavery."

Evangeline and Damian made their way through the long, thick grass and the huge forest. The trees were twice the size of the ones back home and some were shaped strangely. Evangeline ran her fingers across a tree that looked like it had been shaped into a chair.

Damian saw her and answered her question before she could ask it. "Somnia Viveret is a huge world and it is easy to get lost here. One of the most popular ways to mark one's territory is to shape and engrave trees with unique symbols or shapes. That one that you are touching right now has been shaped into a chair; it most likely was a trade mark for a leprechaun. If you take a look around, a lot of the trees in this area of the forest have been shaped into different objects. Leprechauns are very crafty creatures and build their furniture from these trees. From the looks of things, it looks like there was a population of a hundred leprechauns here."

Evangeline looked around at all the different shaped trees and asked,

"Is that a leprechaun?" She narrowed her eyes as she tried to look at a small creature that was hiding behind a pear-shaped tree.

"You see one?"

Evangeline slowly walked towards the pear-shaped tree. As she reached the tree, the small creature ran in the opposite direction at the speed of a lightening bullet. "Wait!" He stopped running and stood frozen in place as Evangeline ran up to him. "Please don't run away. I'm not going to hurt you. My name is Evangeline and that over there is Damian."

The small creature turned around and looked up at her with his innocent blue eyes. "I'm Bonzi."

Evangeline stuck out her hand and said, "It's a pleasure to meet you, Bonzi!"

He smiled at her and he said, "No, no, it's a pleasure to finally meet the great Evangeline. We have been waiting for you to return and save our world!"

Damian approached them and stood there with his arms crossed over his chest. Evangeline went up to Damian and whispered in his ear as Bonzi watched them with curiosity. Damian nodded his head in approval as Evangeline returned to Bonzi's side.

She said, "We are on a quest to find Prince Mathias and we would love it if you'd accompany us on our journey. It would make it a whole lot easier if we had more people—creatures that could help us find him."

Bonzi looked between the two and jumped up with joy. Evangeline began to laugh as she watched the little guy dancing in circles with a huge grin across his face. She glanced over at Damian as he rolled his eyes at the two.

"It would be my honour to serve with you." Evangeline smiled at him and wished that Damian would ease up and enjoy life even on its dullest days. "Where are we going first?"

She looked passed Bonzi's head and pointed, "Up the mountains."

Bonzi turned around and looked at the mountains and said, “It will take us a few days to make it there but we can do it. Might I ask what makes you think that Prince Mathias is in the mountains?”

Evangeline was speechless for a brief moment and realized she didn’t have an answer for him.

Instead, Damian began to walk towards them and said, “It would make perfect sense to leave him stranded somewhere far and where someone would never think to look.”

Bonzi giggled and said, “That’s ironic that you say that because you thought to look there.”

Damian snarled under his breath, “This is going to be an awfully long journey.”

Damian walked a few feet ahead of the other two; he couldn’t stand the sounds of their laughter. He glanced down at the pendant that hung around his neck and traced his large index finger along the rims of it. The pendant was a circle with the centre cut out with fancy designs. The outside of it was a smooth circular cut.

“Ouch!”

Damian stopped walking as he felt a small creature bump into his chest.

“Would you mind watching where you walk, you miserable goblin?” The fairy crossed her arms over her chest and eyed him angrily.

“Perhaps you should be the one who watches where you are flying. I’d gladly pluck your wings for you so you can learn how to walk on the ground like everyone else.”

Her jaw dropped as she stared at him in disbelief, “I will have Sparkle ban you from the forest and let the evil queen eat you for dinner!”

Evangeline and Bonzi caught up to Damian and heard the two fighting. “Did you say Sparkle? Do you know where she is?”

The fairy looked over Damian’s shoulder and said, “No, but when I find her, I will have her ban him. She disappeared when Sahara killed the land."

Evangeline eyed the fairy and said, "Felicia is that you?" Evangeline met Felicia the last time she visited Somnia Viveret and she was surprised that she even remembered her name.

Felicia flew around Damian so she could see Evangeline better and said in a cheery voice, "Evangeline! It is so good to see you again." Felicia flew up to Evangeline's shoulder and wrapped her tiny arms around her neck to give her a hug. "Our world is falling apart and our prince is gone! Only you and Mathias can save our world from being completely destroyed."

Evangeline invited Felicia to join their pack to find the prince. When nightfall came around, the pact was forced to climb into an old oak tree and spend the night there. It was the safest place for them to hide so the evil queen could not find them.

Evangeline woke up that morning feeling very stiff from the uncomfortable sleep in the tree. *Trees were meant to be constructed into a bed first*, she thought. The rest of her crew was still sleeping expect for Damian; he was nowhere in sight. Evangeline was concerned and climbed down the tree in a heartbeat. She could not afford to lose her crew, especially Damian. She had begun to grow fond of him. Despite the fact that he is constantly miserable, she sensed innocence from him. She looked at the ground and saw large footprints in the mud and began to follow them. When she reached the river, the footprints stopped. She looked in every direction but there was no one in sight. The water was calm and blue as ever. She knelt down to the water and scoped up a handful of water and drank it. She looked at her reflection in the water and saw a dark shadow fall over her. The figure was very large and held a large pointy spear in their hand. Evangeline felt the spear poke her in the back and a deep voice commanding her to get up. She rose off the ground and held her hands up to surrender. She turned around to face the man and noticed he was no ordinary man. He wore a suit of armor except his face was not covered. He only had one eye in the centre of his face, his teeth were rotten, and snot hung from his nostrils.

Evangeline crinkled her nose at his stench and said, "What do you want with me?"

He flashed his rotten teeth at her and said, "Lunch." He pointed the spear at her chest and tilted his head as he smirked at her.

She glanced down at the spear and back at him, "Sorry, creature, but not today." Evangeline grabbed hold of the spear and slid it out of his grasp. She pointed the spear at his face for it was the only part of his body that wasn't hidden behind a sheet of armor.

He smiled at her and said, "You cannot kill me! I am protected by the queen's shield and no creature or human can get past it."

Evangeline tilted her head and said, "Watch me." In that moment, she struck him through the eye with the large spear. He fell to his knees and then on his face. Evangeline stared at the large beast that lay dead on the ground before her and wondered what she had just done.

"Evangeline, are you alright?" Damian came out of the bush in a run and stared at the large beast that lay on the ground in front of her.

She looked up at him with wide eyes and said, "I killed him."

He nodded his head and lifted the beasts arm and let it fall to the ground. "Yes, I see that."

She stared at the creature with puzzled eyes and said, "He told me that I wouldn't be able to kill him because the queen had placed a shield around him and said I wouldn't be able to get past it."

Damian took the spear from Evangeline's hand and tried to spear the beast. As the spear touched the creature's body, Damian flew back a few feet because he could not pass the queen's shield.

Evangeline ran after him and said, "Are you alright?"

Damian sat up and stared at the creature and at the broken spear. "Only you can get past the queen's protection spell."

She eyed him suspiciously and asked, "Why only me?"

He glanced up at her glamorous green eyes and said, “That is why you are here. This all makes perfect sense now. I wondered how a girl could save our world but it is clear that you are the only one who is immune to her powers.”

Evangeline looked back at the creature and said, “What makes me so special as opposed to everyone else?”

He kept his eyes locked on hers and said, “Because you are her sister.” Evangeline’s jaw dropped as she consumed the information. “You are a witch, too, and you just haven’t discovered how to use your powers yet.”

Evangeline stood up and looked down at him. “That is impossible! There is no way in hell that Sahara is Frances.”

He took up and said, “The great Frances Scott?”

She narrowed her eyes and said, “She has been here?”

Damian walked towards the river and continued to speak, “Alright well she’s not really the great Frances, she’s more like the evil queen Sahara.”

Evangeline followed him to the river and said, “My stepsister is the one responsible for this madness?”

He nodded his head and said, “Did you never question her hatred for you and the envy she had for Mathias’ love?”

She widened her eyes as it all made perfect sense. “We created this mad world didn’t we?”

He nodded his head and said, “Very good, you catch on quick. Unfortunately, because she has destroyed our world, you have made us all suffer along with yourselves. It is up to you to free yourself from this mad world and free us from our curse.”

Before either said another word, the water began to move in large tide waves. There was a big splash that came from the water and there they were. Marina and Pearl lifted their bodies out of the water and smiled at the sight of Evangeline.

Marina said in a loud and cheerful tone, “You have come to save us!”

Evangeline knelt down alongside of the river bank and smiled, "Marina, Pearl! Where is Venus and Melody?"

The mermaids exchanged a look with one another and this time, it was Pearl that spoke. "They are no longer with us for the evil queen has taken their lives." They bowed their heads for a brief moment and looked back at Evangeline. "Are you aware that there is a goblin standing next to you?"

Evangeline looked down at Damian and laughed, "Yes, I am. He is on a quest with me and my other friends. We are out to look for the long lost prince."

Damian shook his head and whispered, "What's wrong with being a goblin?"

Evangeline nudged him on the arm and whispered, "Nothing, you are perfect as you are."

Marina spoke this time, "We would gladly join your quest but as you can see, we are unable to travel on land with our fins." The mermaids frowned in disappointment and felt like useless creatures.

Evangeline whispered, "I wonder..." She began to slowly walk in the water and watched as the water changed from its beautiful blue into black as night wherever she touched the water. The mermaids exchanged a look of terror and watched Evangeline approaching them. The water passed her waist and rested just beneath her breasts. She put her arms forward and smiled at them, "Let me touch your tails." They exchanged a look of curiosity with one another but swam closer to her so they were just in arms reach. Damian stood on the land and watched what she was doing.

Evangeline gently placed the palm of her hand on either one of their tails and closed her eyes. A smile crossed her face as she opened her eyes. She tightly held their fins and turned them in circles as the water surrounded them. Damian wondered what was happening because he was unable to look over the giant water tides. Felicia and Bonzi came through the trees and froze as they watched the water tides standing over six feet high. Felicia glanced down at the dead beast and grabbed hold of Bonzi's arms in fear. Within seconds, the water calmed down and went back to its natural level.

Everyone's jaws dropped as they watched Evangeline, Pearl, and Marina walk out of the water together. Bonzi recognized the mermaids face's and said, "That is impossible!"

Evangeline smiled and glanced at the two women. "Nothing is impossible and this world has proven that to me."

The two ladies danced around the others in excitement and hugged Evangeline, "Thank you, thank you! You have given us our legs back and therefore we will bow down before you as you are our leader." The two ladies bent down on their knees and bowed before her.

"Please stand up, I only experimented and it just so happened that I was able to give you your legs back."

Everyone turned to stare at Evangeline and Felicia asked, "How were you able to do that, Evangeline?"

She stared at Damian as she answered, "Someone told me that I had inner powers and that I just needed to discover how to use them. I saw the opportunity to test that theory and concentrated on what I longed for and that was to have Marina and Pearl's help on our quest."

Bonzi jumped up in excitement and said, "Why don't you just wish for Prince Mathias then?"

She tilted her head from side to side as she thought about it for a moment and said, "I always wish for Mathias but that is the one wish that doesn't want to be granted. It is something we must find, not wish for."

Damian saw sadness in her eyes for the first time since she arrived in Somnia Viveret and it strangely made him feel sad, too. Damian stormed past everyone and began his journey. "Let's not waste any more time than we already have."

She nodded her head in agreement and said, “He’s right. We must go now before the rest of her soldiers find us.”

Chapter 22

Damian's Pendant

Days passed and the crew was getting exhausted from traveling the long distance through the forest. It was too quiet today and it made Evangeline cautious that perhaps something or someone was following them. On some days, she felt as if she was being watched and others, nothing.

She sighed in relief that they finally reached the mountain. "I think that we should tie a rope around our waists so if one of us falls, we can catch them. I don't want to lose anyone; I've grown fond of you all."

There was no rope around them so Felicia took a bundle of long grass and tied it together to form a long rope that everyone could tie around themselves. They began their long journey up the mountain.

It took them nearly three days to make it to the mountain top and the entire journey there, they didn't run into any other creature that could join their pack. Evangeline was disappointed that they had not accomplished anything and just wasted their time. They decided to spend the night up in the mountains for they were all exhausted and could not walk anymore. That evening, they made a fire and sat around it while they cooked the two squirrels that they had caught earlier that day. Evangeline glanced across the fire and noticed Damian had been staring at her for a while. He turned to face the view as she glanced at him.

Evangeline smiled and walked over to where he sat. "I'm sorry that this quest was a waste of everyone's time."

He kept his eyes locked on the view before him and said, "Why are you apologizing when it was me who suggested we climb the mountain?"

She looked at the view and said, "I could have said no and it was my idea to drag all the others in on it." They looked around the fire and noticed that everyone else had fallen asleep. "Damian, why don't you ever smile?" She had her full attention on him and waited patiently for him to answer.

He stared at her for a while before he spoke, "I don't deserve to be happy and I'm not even sure I know how to."

Evangeline grabbed hold of his hand and asked, "How can you say that? Everyone should be happy even if the world is ending. Look at me. I lost my husband and I still manage to put a smile upon my sad face."

Damian looked down at their hands and removed his from hers. "You should not fake your happiness."

"I do not fake it, you are the greatest friend I could ever ask for and you give me plenty of reasons to smile. I just wonder why it is that I cannot make you smile in return."

He looked away from her and said, "I told you, I do not know how."

Evangeline giggled as she had a brilliant idea. "Come on, then! We will practice." A big smile crossed her face and he looked at her as if she was insane.

"You are a remarkable individual but you are also very stupid. One simply cannot practice smiling."

Evangeline laughed at him and said, "Of course you can. I will help you!"

Damian shifted his body to face her and waited for her to do something drastically stupid. Evangeline began to make goofy faces but he did not budge. She tried to tell him jokes that she heard back home but he did not find humour in them.

"Ugh, you give me no choice, mister."

He narrowed his eyes at her as she placed a hand on either side of his face. His face burned in heat as he wondered what she was doing, no one had ever touched him before because they thought he was disgusting and ugly. On either end of his lips, she pushed it up to form a smile on his face.

She said, "There, now you are smiling. Not exactly what I had hoped for, but it will do."

He stared at her and said, "I cannot get over how beautiful your eyes are."

Evangeline dropped her hands in her lap and blushed at his compliment.

"I don't mean to flatter you but there is just something about your eyes that puts me in a trance. I don't know what happy feels like but that's where you take me when you look at me."

Evangeline looked away as she wanted to avoid the topic. She had grown fond of Damian but he was only her friend and she did not want to give him the wrong impression. She wanted to change the topic and noticed the pendant that hung from his neck.

She traced it with her finger and said, "This is a beautiful pendant. Where did you get this?"

He looked down at it and said, "I—I'm not entirely sure. I woke up one morning and it was around my neck."

She looked at him suspiciously and said, "Don't you wonder how it appeared around your neck?"

He shrugged his shoulders, "Sometimes I wonder and sometimes I feel like I already know."

"And what is it that you know?"

He held it tightly in the palm of his hand and said, "I just know that it defines who I am."

She threw her head back and began to laugh. “Alright, Damian, you are definitely defined as a circle. A circle of misery.”

He glanced up at her and nodded. “Perhaps that is true.”

They said goodnight to one another and fell asleep with the fire still burning.

When Evangeline woke up the following morning, she noticed that Damian was gone. She felt the spot where he had slept and found his pendant lying on the ground. She picked it up and tied it around her neck.

Within seconds, she rushed over to wake up the others. “Hurry! Get up! We need to leave now! Damian is gone and we must find him before they take his life!” Evangeline was angry and sad that they had taken her best friend. The crew followed the footprints down the mountain and through the trees. They knew they were close because they could hear sounds of laughter and growling of the beasts.

Evangeline put her finger to her lips as she hushed her crew. The sounds of the beasts became louder and louder and soon they became visible. Instead of just the one man she took down a few days ago, there were twenty more.

Evangeline gasped as she saw one of the creatures carrying Damian over their shoulder. Bonzi whispered to her, “Why would they take the goblin as opposed to you?”

Evangeline glanced up at him and said, “Perhaps he is of value to them, that or they like goblin.” They followed them for hours until the beasts finally stopped for the night. Evangeline gathered her crew in a huddle and whispered, “We need to gather sticks and sharpen them so we may kill them.”

Felicia looked at her in horror and said, “But, Evangeline, only you can kill them. They are shielded, remember?”

She looked over her shoulder at where they lay and said, “Then I will un-shield them and when I do, you must strike them in the face and do not miss because they can crush you in the palm of their hands."

The five of them began to gather sticks and sharpened them for the attack.

Evangeline counted down from three with her fingers and when she hit zero, they all ran towards the campsite and speared them in the head. They woke up when they heard the sounds of armor smashing together. The creatures began to fight back and had Evangeline's team out-numbered. Evangeline rushed over to Damian and untied him. He jumped up, grabbed hold of a spear, jumped onto a beast, and speared him directly in the face. He looked down at Evangeline and knew that she had un-shielded the creatures and smiled at her.

He raised the spear above his head and screamed, "Gone with the witch!"

Evangeline blinked her eyes as she realized that Damian had just smiled at her. She raised her spear along with the rest of her crew and they all shouted, "Gone with the witch!"

One by one, the beasts were taken down until there were none left. They were panting from the excitement and from being exhausted.

"No!" Pearl screamed a loud cry and threw her body on top of Marina. Everyone ran towards Pearl and noticed Marina's ocean blue eyes were black as night. "She's gone. They killed her," Pearl cried as she lifted herself off of Marina's body.

Evangeline knelt down beside her and stared at her in disbelief. "I thought we had everything under control..."

A tear rolled down the side of Evangeline's face as she knew what she had to do. She slid her hands underneath Marina's body and lifted her off the ground. Evangeline's powers had given her extreme strength and therefore she was able to hold Marina in her arms. She held her out before everyone and closed her eyes. She mumbled beneath her breath and then blew at Marina's body. Everyone watched as her body turned into ashes and floated away with the wind.

Evangeline whispered, "Rest in peace, Marina."

It was a sad walk through the forest as everyone was still grieving over Marina's death. They decided to make their way back to the destroyed land and see if perhaps Mathias was at the palace the entire time. They stopped for the night and hid in a dark cave that they found hidden behind a large bush.

The next morning, everyone was in a better mood as they did their fair share of grieving.

Damian walked alongside of Evangeline and said, "I wanted to thank you for saving me."

Evangeline smiled and said, "I saw you. You smiled."

He looked straight ahead and said, "No one will believe you."

Evangeline's smile vanished and she suddenly became very serious. "I and the others were talking and we wondered why they took you as opposed to me. I thought that I was the threat."

He narrowed his eyes as he thought about it. "I—I don't know." Damian had a puzzled look on his face as he tried to think of reasons why they would want him over her. He looked up at Evangeline and said, "Hey, you're wearing my pendant." Evangeline looked down at the pendant and took it off. She handed it to him and shocked his hand as she gave it to him. He stared up at her with his hand still out and said, "How come you do not wear your cameo?"

Evangeline stopped walking and stared down at him, "I beg your pardon?"

He glanced down at his circular pendant and said, "The cameo that once belonged to Princess Amelia. How come you do not wear it?"

She eyed him suspiciously and asked, "How do you know about that?"

He looked away as he was confused. "I don't know."

She grabbed him by his shoulders and looked into his hazel eyes, "Damian, how do you know about my cameo?"

He smirked at her and said, "You told me when you were sleeping. You sleep talk."

She pulled her eyebrows together in a frown and crossed her arms over her chest. "Alright, that's it. I demand you to tell me about your previous life before Sahara turned you into a goblin. I'm sure you were a man before just like Felicia was a woman and Bonzi was a boy."

He nodded his head and said, "Alright, but I don't see what you're getting at." Evangeline rolled her eyes and said, "Just tell me what happened, Damian."

"It is a blur to me now, but I was very well known and liked by many. I fell in love with this beautiful woman but then she disappeared. My world turned black and I became a miserable man. When Sahara took over, I became this miserable goblin." Evangeline stared at him as she waited for him to continue. "That's all I remember."

Evangeline smirked at him and said, "That cannot possibly be all you remember."

He thought hard on it for a moment before he spoke again. "She saved my life when I was left alone to die. She became my hero as I became hers. We loved each other like no man has ever loved another. Our life together was perfect, like a fairy tale, you could say. When Sahara took over, we were separated and I was told she was murdered. I wanted to die in that moment I heard those words but when I tried to hang myself, I noticed someone else had beat me to it. My mother had hung herself from the King's palace wall. I stared up at her as she taped a note to her dress. The note read: *You killed me without even touching me*. I was in such shock that I could not even cry. All the tears that I had, I had shed them for my wife when I heard she was dead. Instead I stared at my mother's hanging body and wished that it was me up there instead of her. I wondered why she did it because I wasn't aware that she hated her life so much. That was when I wondered off into the wilderness and became this disgusting creature that everyone walks away from. Then when I met you, I was able to joke around with you about my ugly appearance. I get mesmerised by your glamorous eyes and my cheeks burn whenever you come near me. I know it must sound terrible because I am a goblin, but you showed me how to smile again. I cannot help but wish that I was the man you married but instead he is lost somewhere in Somnia Viveret."

Evangeline stared at him in disbelief and said, "Your life is similar to someone that I knew back in Knaresborough."

Damian looked at her and said, "Well our worlds are connected. Perhaps you can figure out the puzzle." They walked for miles on end without saying a word to one another. Evangeline retold his story over and over in her head and suddenly, she stopped walking.

A smile crossed her face as the crew stood around her and eyed her in wonder and curiosity. "Damian, you need to find out what that pendant means because I think that is how we can find Mathias. You share a bond with him, I can feel it. I think the pendant you wear around your neck will lead us to him."

He looked down at his pendant and removed it from his neck. He stared at the pendant as it whispered spells to him in Latin. He was hypnotized by the spells and began to twitch.

Evangeline shook his body and said, "What? Why are you twitching like that?"

Everyone watched Damian as he stared at the pendant and only he was able to hear the Latin spells that Sahara had cast. Evangeline tried to grab hold of the pendant but he would not let go. Damian stopped twitching and soon the Latin spells stopped; Evangeline's touch had summoned the evil away. Damian looked up at her and smiled as he opened his hand with the pendant laying flat on the palm of his hand. He took his other hand and hovered it over the pendant as it began to shift into an object. Evangeline and the others watched as the pendant's circle turned into the Prince's crown. Their jaws dropped as they discovered that Damian carried the Prince's crown the entire time and that was why the beasts wanted him.

Evangeline said in a soft voice, “Do you realize what this means? As soon as the prince sees his crown, he will realize who he is and it will make our search so much simpler.”

Damian frowned at her as he placed the crown upon his green head. “It disappoints me that you still do not realize that I would never leave your side no matter what the circumstances may be.” In that moment, Damian placed his hand on her cheek. His hand changed back to its normal human form and followed down the rest of his body. He leaned in closer and kissed Evangeline softly on her lips. Her eyes remained open the entire time as she watched her best friend, the goblin, change into her lover, Prince Mathias.

Mathias kept his hand on her waist as he stared into her green eyes.

She stared at him in disbelief as she thought about all the obvious signs. “I knew something was up when you started to flatter me and when you were unable to tell me about your past life.”

He smiled at her as she jumped into his arms with joy. She wrapped her arms around him tightly and began to kiss him passionately. When she released her grip they looked at their pack and saw that they had bowed down before them.

Mathias gestured his hand for them to stand up and said, “My friends, please stand on your feet.”

Bonzi looked up at them and asked, “What will happen now?”

Mathias glanced in the direction of the palace and said, “Now, we form an army.”

Chapter 23

Preparation

Now that they had discovered who Mathias was, it made it easier to find more creatures that would help them fight the evil queen and her disciples. They walked into the deeper ends of the forest and one by one, creatures came out of hiding and bowed down before the prince. Evangeline looked around at all the different kinds of creatures and wondered how they had missed them all.

Bonzi nudged her on the arm and said, "They are very good at hiding, are they not?"

She nodded her head as there must have been hundreds of different creatures who showed themselves to the prince. They continued to walk through the trees as the people of Somnia Viveret followed after them. It took them nearly an entire day to gather everyone they could find. When they figured they had everyone, Mathias climbed onto a large rock and raised his arms to get everyone's attention. The crowd was instantly quiet and gave him their full attention.

"I have a huge request to ask from all of you and I will not hold it against you if you back down." The creatures looked at one another as they exchanged looks of curiosity. "The evil witch needs to be taken down and I cannot do it myself therefore I am asking kindly for your help. I believe that if we work together, we can take her down and destroy her. With us, we have the greatest weapon of all!" He glanced down at Evangeline and pointed at her. "Evangeline."

The creatures began to whisper amongst each other, "Is that the great Evangeline?"

"She cannot save us, she is only one girl."

"Be silent!" Mathias grabbed Evangeline's hand and had her standing at his side. "Evangeline is her sister and she is the only one who can break her spells. Without her, we cannot even touch Sahara or her evil disciples. Her death would be our end."

Someone from the crowd yelled, "If she is her sister, then she will betray us."

Evangeline took a step forward and said, "I would never betray the prince and his people. I was brought into this world to serve as your hero and I will go through with that. If I fail, then I will be lost in your world forever. I put my life in the hands of the people."

Mathias raised his hand once again to silence the crowd and said, "Now, who will join our army?"

The creatures looked at one another as no one stepped forward to volunteer.

Mathias nodded his head at them in disappointment and stepped down from the stone. "Come on, Evangeline. It looks like we will fight this battle ourselves."

They began to walk away from the creatures until they heard a voice. "I volunteer."

Mathias looked at his beautiful bride and then looked over his shoulder at the creature. He smiled in the sight of the little munchkin. The munchkin flashed a big smile at them as the creatures backed away from him. The munchkin raised his arms above his head and began to spin in circles extremely fast. As he span in circles his body grew bigger and bigger until he finally stood still. Evangeline looked up past the trees and down to his extremely large feet.

"I will crush the queen's army with one step!"

The crowd began to cheer loudly and one by one, they stood forward and revealed their inner beast. Prince Mathias began to laugh as he watched Evangeline staring at the creatures.

She whispered, "This is incredible!"

He stared into her beautiful eyes and whispered, "I will always love you."

Evangeline stared at him as if they were the only ones in the world. "Don't speak as if we will fail. Speak with motivation and courage because that bitch is going down."

Mathias smiled and fought back his laughter as he leaned in and kissed her. That evening, they spent the night in the woods where they could hide and not be easily seen. Tomorrow, they would begin the preparation for the battle of the century.

Mathias and Evangeline spent the night in a dark cave behind the waterfall. They lay down beside each other as they stared into one another's eyes.

Evangeline smiled and asked, "How did you know you were Mathias? Or did you know all along?"

Mathias lay on his back as he stared at the dark roof of the cave. "When you made me smile, that is when I knew."

She smiled and said, "She turned you into a miserable goblin and only true happiness could break the spell."

Mathias turned to face her and grabbed hold of her hand, "Exactly." Mathias leaned in closer to her and began to kiss her. He ran his fingers through her luscious red hair and down her back. They pressed their bodies together as they kissed one another like it was their last kiss. They made love that night and held one another as they feared what would come in the next few days.

Everyone woke before sunrise and began to gather large sticks and sharpened them into spears and arrows. The creatures practiced shooting with a bow and arrow and throwing spears. For amateurs they weren't all that terrible and their aim was right on. Evangeline practiced shooting apples from a tree with her bow and arrow.

Mathias touched her softly on her back and said, "You have incredible aim, Evangeline."

She turned to face him and said, "I fear that they will have greater weapons than us and take us down before we reach the gates."

He pulled her to the side of a tree and whispered, "Now who is the one that speaks of failure? You possess a great power; you just need to learn how to use it properly."

The creatures spent the entire day preparing for the battle and felt an adrenaline rush kick in.

Bonzi jumped up with joy and screamed, "Let's kill some beasts!"

Evangeline laughed at his excitement but could not help but think that everyone was getting too worked up about it. She whispered to Mathias, "I fear that they will be disappointed if it doesn't go as they think it will."

He looked around at all the creatures and understood exactly what she was referring to.

Bonzi walked towards where they sat and said, "I think I will miss being a leprechaun."

Evangeline leaned in towards him and asked, "What kind of life did you live before?"

Bonzi looked between Mathias and Evangeline before he began to speak. "I'm only a twelve-year-old boy beneath this leprechaun. I sometimes think the reason I became a leprechaun is because I was very crafty and leprechauns are usually alone. All my life, I fended for myself and lived in the sewers or in the orphanage. My mother and father were murdered by Sahara's father, Lance, just before Mathias murdered him. My father was working for Lance but when he discovered what sort of evil he was planning, he wanted to back out. Lance wouldn't allow it so my father tried to run away with me and my mother. We almost made it when Lance's guards caught up to us. They put us in chains and threw us in the back of their carriage as they brought us back to Lance. He chained my parents to the palace wall and used them as a target for his men to practice their shooting. My parents were shot with arrows nearly fifty times before their hearts finally failed. I hid under the wagon and watched my parents get slaughtered. Just before my mother's heart failed, she lifted her arm and whispered, 'Run.' I began to sob but I did as she said. Lance and his guards were too busy murdering my parents to notice that I escaped. They never bothered to search for me and I always wanted to attack him when he was sleeping but I couldn't find the nerve to. When I found out that Mathias had killed him, I felt slightly irritated. I felt like it was my mess to clean up and I should have been the one who watched him die. I got over it though because in the end, he got what he deserved. When I thought it was finally all over, I found out that he had a daughter. The worst part was that his daughter was a witch and she would do worse things than he ever did. For a few years, her attacks were kept to a minimum until a while ago when she turned Somnia Viveret into hell. She's the devil."

Evangeline slid her fingers through Mathias' and held his hand. "I think it's about time that we put an end to her cruelty. She has harmed too many already."

Mathias stood up and said, "Tomorrow we will attack."

Bonzi closed his eyes and said, "Finally. I was starting to think that we were never going to kill her."

Evangeline smiled and tapped him gently on the arm. "See you at dawn."

Chapter 24

Battlefield

"We need to make the platform at least six feet long and make sure that it is sturdy."

The creatures were building a platform so they could get over the broken bridge and get into the palace. The giant munchkin carried it over his shoulder as they began their march towards the palace. They exited the forest and began to walk on the dead grounds of Somnia Viveret. Far in the distance, they could spot the old palace.

They began to walk past the withered trees when suddenly, Evangeline stopped walking. Everyone stopped and watched as Evangeline walked towards the withered tree. She took something from the tree and walked towards Mathias.

He looked down and in the palm of her hands was Sparkle. "You must destroy her before she destroys you."

Sparkle fought for her last few breaths of life. She levitated off Evangeline's hand and was surrounded by a white fog. The fog grew bigger and bigger until it finally cleared. Sparkle was no longer a fairy; she was a grown woman. Her head was bent down as her long blonde hair hung before her face. She wore a white lace gown and had her arms crossed over her chest. Everyone stared at her in amazement as the beautiful woman slowly lifted her head.

Evangeline's jaw dropped as she took a step forward. "Caroline?"

Mathias' eyes became moist as he said, "Mother?"

Caroline smiled and said, "You are trapped in a world in between heaven and hell. I lived a sad life on earth and lived as a Queen in Somnia Viveret. It is sad to go but I must live my last life as an angel." She reached her hand out towards her son but as he went to grab it, she became a thick white fog and vanished.

"Everyone I know is trapped in Somnia Viveret." Mathias' smile turned into a straight line as he charged forward and screamed, "Down with the witch!"

The creatures all screamed and began to charge towards the palace. The grounds shook as they stomped their feet against the cracked grounds. The ground began to part as creatures fell into the ground one by one. Evangeline stopped running as she looked back at the cracking ground. She leaned over the edge and reached down to help Pearl from falling into the hot lava. Evangeline pulled her out but could not help but feel like she could have done more to save the others.

"Thank you, thank you."

Evangeline looked ahead as she watched the creatures being killed while her men struck them with arrows. Evangeline felt anger rise within her and took an arrow from her back. She placed it into the bow and shot it towards the palace. As it was midair its sharpened end set on fire and struck a beast right in the face. Evangeline raised her bow above her head and began to charge towards the palace.

"Quick, place the board down!"

Mathias and the giant munchkin put the board onto the bridge and crossed over to the gates. A hundred little fairies flew to the top of the gate and began to pull as the giant pulled from the sides. The beasts from the other side began to throw large rocks over the gates which crushed some of the creatures. It was a struggle, but with the help of many, the gates opened. On the other side of the gate stood hundreds of soldiers but there was no sign of Sahara. They charged into the palace and began to attack the beasts. It was a gory fight and many soldiers and creatures were killed in the process. Evangeline kept Bonzi in eyes' reach; he was only a boy and didn't want anything to happen to him.

She screamed at him, "Bonzi, behind you!" Bonzi turned around and speared the beast in the face.

When the beast hit the ground he ran towards Evangeline. "Come on, let's find the witch."

Evangeline and Bonzi dodged through the crowd of soldiers towards the palace doors. She shut the doors behind them. The palace was quiet. The only sounds they heard were from the other side of the doors. Evangeline glanced around at the beautiful palace and yelled, "Show yourself!" Evangeline and Bonzi began to wonder around the palace as they searched for the evil queen.

There was a loud echo of laughter that fled through the palace.

Bonzi looked at Evangeline in horror as they looked around but saw no trace of the evil queen.

Evangeline and Bonzi jumped as they heard the palace door slam closed. "It's just me."

They sighed in relief at the sound of Mathias' voice. They continued to walk slowly through the palace when suddenly, there was a loud thump on the roof. There was another loud echo of her evil laughter that filled the room.

They looked up as the roof began to crack, dropping large pieces of the roof on the ground. One final stomp and the huge dragon appeared before them.

"Ah, so we meet again." Draco pushed Bonzi and Mathias out of the way, throwing them a few feet back.

Evangeline stood in front of Draco as she stared up at him. He opened his mouth as he blew fire at her. The fire was inches from her face before she blocked it with the blink of an eye. He continued to breathe fire but stared at her in disbelief. She bobbed her head and smiled as the fire blew at him rather than her. Draco stumbled over his feet as he waved his arms in front of his face to cool down. Evangeline glanced up at the red curtains and grabbed hold of one as she swung from it like a man swinging from a vine. She swung towards Draco and landed on his head. She pulled out her dagger from beneath her dress and stabbed him multiple times in the head until he finally stopped moving. She slid off of his body as her hands were covered in dragon's blood.

Evangeline looked up as she saw Mathias wrap his arms around Bonzi's throat. He looked up as Evangeline watched him in horror. Mathias smiled as he cracked Bonzi's neck.

Evangeline screamed, "No!" Evangeline plopped down onto her knees as she stared at him in disbelief. He began to laugh in the tone that had echoed in the room earlier.

"You foolish girl! You killed my dragon so I killed your leprechaun. Fair is fair. Killing you will be so easy.... I was hoping for a little bit of a challenge." It was not Mathias that stood before her.

It was Sahara.

She slowly walked closer to Evangeline and with each step she took, she returned to her normal form. Her hair turned black as night and hung to the floor, her eyes red as flames, and skin white as snow. She wore a forest green dress that touched the ground.

Evangeline was flaming with anger and smashed her fist against the concrete ground. The palace began to shake as Sahara went flying into the wall.

She looked up from the ground and said, "That is impossible! You do not stand a chance against my powers."

They walked closer to one another and circled the room. "I do if I am of the same blood as you."

Sahara looked at her in frustration and pushed Evangeline to the far wall with her powers. The wall cracked as she hit it but she got up with only a single scratch on her forearm.

Sahara stared at her in disbelief and smiled as she said, "Prepare to die, human."

The two witches fought one another and destroyed the palace in the process. Everyone stopped fighting as they watched the palace fall to the ground. Sahara pushed her way through the stones and began to approach the battlefield. She said, "Your hero is dead. You will all suffer for trying to defeat your queen!" She raised her hands above her head as the skies turned black. Pearl gasped as she saw a stone moving behind Sahara and saw Evangeline coming through. Sahara continued to cast her spell as Evangeline quietly approached her. She took her dagger from behind her back and stabbed Sahara through her heart. Sahara's jaw fell open and her arms dropped to her sides. She looked down as the dagger was piercing through her heart. She glanced up as the entire city was watching her. She fell down onto her knees and watched as the creatures of Somnia Viveret were surrounded by a giant grey fog. As the fog began to pass, the creatures were gone. They were replaced by their normal form: human. Sahara fell on her face as her body lay on the stones of the palace to rot.

Evangeline raised her arm in the air and said, "The evil queen is dead!" Evangeline walked past her dead body and towards her prince. They looked around at the destroyed city and at the people of Somnia Viveret. "It looks like you will have to reconstruct your palace."

Mathias giggled and picked Evangeline up into his arms. "I love you, Evangeline."

She blushed and said, "As I love you, Mathias." They leaned in and kissed one another.

Mathias glared up at her and flashed a big grin. She smiled back at him but her smile vanished just as quickly as it appeared when she saw

Mathias' eyes change from hazel to red. "Ha ha ha, you didn't think killing me would be that easy did you?" Sahara grabbed Evangeline's dagger and pressed it through her chest. She dropped Evangeline onto the concrete ground.

Evangeline placed her hands over the dagger and looked up at Sahara in disbelief. "Who did I murder then?" Evangeline glanced over her should as she saw Prince Mathias' dead body lying on the ground. "No!" Tears began to stream down her cheeks as she realized that she had just murdered her husband. Evangeline pulled the dagger from her chest and stood up as her blood spilled all over the ground.

Evangeline took deep breaths and closed her eyes. The people of Somnia Viveret watched in shock as they realized that Mathias had been murdered. Evangeline opened her eyes as she smiled at Sahara. "I've had enough of your magic, dear sister. Fight me like a woman and pick up that sword."

Sahara laughed at her and kicked the sword up into the air and caught it. "Sword or wand, you cannot defeat me."

Evangeline pulled a gold sword out from beneath a stone. "Watch me."

Evangeline and Sahara walked in circles as they waited for the perfect moment to strike. Evangeline took her sword and stabbed it into the ground of Somnia Viveret and looked up at Sahara through sad eyes. A wave of power swept through the land as the land began to heal itself. The cracked land filled the broken gaps. The dead ground became moist with soil and grew fresh grass. The withered trees returned to their natural colour and bloomed with flowers and leaves. Sahara glanced around at the people of Somnia Viveret only to notice that they all looked like her father, Lance.

Sahara dropped her sword to her side as she looked around in fear.

"You fear him, don't you?"

Sahara remained silent and tried to hide her horror.

"He is the reason why you did all of this, is it not?"

She shook her head and said, "Shut up."

"You just wanted to bring him back from the dead, is that not true?" Evangeline walked into the crowd of people and stood next to Pearl. "Mathias is dead because of you and so I must kill your father, again."

Sahara looked around the crowd of people as she searched the crowd for her father. Evangeline took her sword and stabbed Pearl in her heart. She fell onto her knees and screamed in pain. "Lance was never dead; he helped you find me. He took possession of the most innocent and beautiful creature in Somnia Viveret, Pearl, and played the role of a scared human girl." Sahara ran towards her dying father's side and said, "I'm sorry I have failed you, Father. Please forgive me." Sahara held her dead father's body in her arms like she had done once many years ago. His body turned into black ashes and Sahara blew them into the air.

Sahara stood up and began to approach Evangeline. She dragged the sword on the ground and slowly walked towards her. "Everything is always Evangeline this, Evangeline that; whatever happened to Frances?"

A hand from behind her grabbed her by the hair and held a sword to her throat, "I am Frances and I want my life back." Frances cut Sahara's throat with her dagger and let Sahara's body fall to the ground. She put her foot on her head and stomped on it as it turned to ash and sank into the ground.

Frances walked towards Evangeline and said, "Ever since I read your journal back at Shire Dale Academy, she began to use my body as a host to make her even more powerful. I constantly had an urge to kill you because of her hatred for you. I hated you because you married the man I loved. I feel like a weight has been taken off my shoulders and I owe it all to you, Evangeline. Thank you." Frances wrapped her arms around Evangeline and hugged her tightly.

Evangeline stared at Frances for a moment and asked, "She used your body as a host?"

Frances nodded her head and said, "Yes. I went into a deep sleep and when I had finally woken up, I didn't feel the same. My father treated me like royalty but also feared me. I asked him why he was acting so strangely and he simply said, 'I'm following my orders.' I eyed him suspiciously but before I was able to say more, he walked away from me. I hurried after him but by the time I reached the front door, he had already made his way back to the docks. I turned around and glanced around the empty house and that was when I heard an echo. She said, 'Kill her.' I was confused and most of all terrified as I wondered where this voice was coming from. She repeated, 'Kill her!' My body was shaking in fear and I asked, 'Who are you?' A loud laughter echoed through the house and suddenly, the woman was serious and said, 'I am you.' I didn't understand what she was talking about until I suddenly felt different."

"How did you feel different?" Evangeline waited patiently for Frances to continue.

Frances tried to find the proper words and continued, "It's difficult to explain. All I knew was that I wanted you dead."

Evangeline didn't understand why Sahara wanted her dead so desperately and asked, "Why did she want me dead?"

"You posed as a threat to her and because I am your sister she felt that we would have a connection and that our powers would be similar. Turns out that I was never granted any powers, instead, Sahara granted me limited abilities."

"But I don't understand why I posed such a great threat to her."

Frances looked at the destroyed palace as she spoke, "You have the dark witch's powers."

Evangeline was confused and tried to grasp all the information. "How do you know so much?"

Frances laughed and said, "She lived in my body for weeks. I grew to understand her life as she understood mine."

Evangeline giggled shyly as she recalled Frances' saying that. "Who is the dark witch?"

Frances sighed as she realized that this would be a long conversation. "Sahara's mother." There was a moment of silence as the girls glanced around at the people of Somnia Viveret. "She used to be known as the white sorceress of purity and goodwill. Her name was Aisling. She was well-liked by the people but she kept her distance from the city and lived in the wilderness along with the creatures. She was tricked into marrying Lance when he casted a spell on her. She was not aware that he was the dark wizard and all he wanted was to reproduce a child with a powerful sorceress. Their child would be the end to this fairy tale and the leader of the dark world in which he was creating an army for.

"Aisling discovered the horrible truth when she spotted her daughter drenched in human blood. She was shocked and looked around the scene when she saw her husband standing just a couple feet away. She took a few steps towards them when she realized that Lance was not who he claimed to be. A huge grin crossed Lance's face as he looked at Aisling and back at their daughter. He walked over to his daughter and knelt down beside her and asked, 'Sahara, can you bring this to your mother?' Sahara looked into her father's black eyes and smiled as her eyes flashed red and then back to its original shade of green. Aisling tried looking at what Sahara held in her tiny hands but Sahara covered the object between the palms of her hands. When she approached her mother, Aisling knelt down and looked into her daughter's green eyes. Sahara smiled innocently at her mother and said, 'Father and I made you a special present.' Aisling smiled at her little girl and would question Lance later about his lies. Sahara opened her small hands as a floating crystal ball was levitating an inch off the palm of her hands. The crystal was glowing shades of blue and purple; it was beautiful, but what was its purpose? Aisling smiled as Sahara extended her arms towards her mother. Aisling stared at the crystal for a brief moment before she picked it up into her hands. She stood up straight and noticed that the ball suddenly was filled with black fog. She looked up at Lance with fear in her eyes but just as the crystal had turned foggy, so had the scene around her. Her body felt heavy as gravity was pulling her down. She fell to her knees with the crystal still in her hands. Lance was now standing only inches away from her as he spoke, 'You are no longer of value to me.' The crystal drained Aisling of her powers and made her weak. She took the crystal from her hands and handed it back to his daughter. 'Place it in a safe spot and reclaim it when you need it.' He returned his attention on Aisling, but she was no longer lying on the ground. Instead she stood before him with her head bent down, her dress was now black, and her hair fell before her face. 'I am the most powerful sorceress that Somnia Viveret has ever had. How dare you try to defeat me.' Lance laughed at her and said, 'As I am the most powerful wizard. You can't possibly think that I didn't know you had a dark side underneath all that good, did you?' Aisling raised her head and stared at him with her black eyes. 'We will dispose of your goodwill and use your black magic.' Aisling extended her arm but just before she struck him with her powers, Lance lifted Sahara in front of himself. She struck her child rather than her dishonest husband. To her surprise, her powers did not affect Sahara. Instead, Aisling was unable to stop as she realized that Sahara was stealing her dark powers.

"Aisling fell to ground once again because she had been completely drained of her powers. A tear rolled down the side of her cheek as she knew that she could not harm her own child. Lance said to Sahara, 'Try out your new powers like you did to that man earlier.' Sahara nodded at her father and knelt down beside her mother. Aisling glanced up at her little girl and reached out to her. Sahara grabbed hold of her mother's hands and clenched them tightly. With enough force and the use of her magic, she murdered her mother."

Evangeline asked, "What happened to the crystal ball with her good powers?"

Frances stared at Evangeline and said, "Shortly after Aisling was murdered, Lance stored it in our world. It was our mother that received the crystal. She didn't personally receive it; it was placed in her womb so that her child would carry it with them until it would be needed in Somnia Viveret. Little did they know that Cecilia conceived two daughters as opposed the one that they predicted. It was supposed to be my powers but apparently, it thought differently and left it for you. Therefore you carried the rarest power of all and she wanted it back. In order to do this, she needed to murder you and cut open your chest. It is implanted in your heart but you cannot notice it unless you know that it is there."

Evangeline sat on the cold ground as she absorbed all the information.

Frances knelt beside her and said, "My time is up, dear sister." Evangeline glanced up as Frances continued to speak. "It's a pity that you will never wake up."

Frances' body slowly began to fade away and soon she was gone.

Chapter 25

Sweet Dreams

"Henry, Dr. Walter is here to see Evangeline."

Henry hardly slept in the last year as he was constantly stressed about his daughter and on some nights, he didn't sleep at all. "Let him in." Henry sat on a chair next to Evangeline's bed and held her hand in his.

"What is the emergency, Mr. Beckem?"

Henry had bags under his eyes from lack of sleep and looked like complete crap. He removed her covers and revealed the blood stain on her chest. "I came to check up on her and noticed she was bleeding. I lifted her shirt but there was no scar. Nothing. Just blood."

Dr. Walter walked towards Evangeline and lifted her shirt and began to feel her stomach and chest for any signs of a wound. He put his fingers on her neck as he searched for her pulse. He sighed and removed his glasses from his nose. "Henry you cannot keep on hurting yourself like this."

He stared at his daughter and said, "I don't know what you are talking about."

Dr. Walter pointed at Evangeline and said, "This! She has been asleep for a year and her body is beginning to reject the nutrients that

that we are injecting into her blood stream. Her body is eventually going to fail and die."

Henry stood up from his chair and looked Dr. Walter in the eyes. "If this was your child, would you let her die?"

He glanced down at her and said, "As a matter of fact, I would. I would not be able to bear seeing her suffer as she is right now. Look at her, Henry. You can see her bones. That's how thin she is."

Henry buried his face in her bed sheets and began to sob. "I know that she is suffering but you told me she was dreaming."

Dr. Walter looked at Evangeline's face and saw sweat forming on her forehead. "She is dreaming but it looks as if she cannot wake from this dream. Either she is choosing not to or she can't."

Henry held her hand in his and said, "If it is a dream then she will wake up. She has to wake up."

Dr. Walter walked out of the bedroom and closed the door behind him. Steven waited on the other side of the door. "What's going on, Doctor?"

Dr. Walter crossed his arms across his chest and said, "Evangeline needs to rest in peace but Henry is not allowing her to."

Steven sighed and stared at the door, "It is hard to give your child up like that but if it is what's best for the girl, then so be it."

Steven grabbed Dr. Walter by the arm and directed him towards the sitting room for more privacy. "I will try to get Henry out of the house and when I do, I give you permission to let her rest in peace."

Dr. Walter nodded his head and said, "It is not that I want her life to end, but she has been in a coma for a year and she shows no signs of waking up."

Steven nodded his head to notify him that he understood. "It disappoints me that I was never able to meet my granddaughter."

Days passed but Steven was unable to get Henry to leave Evangeline's side. That evening, Henry heard a loud bang on the front door. He ran down the stairs before the loud bang woke anyone up. Henry froze as he stared at Lawrence Scott. He walked outside of the house and closed the door behind him.

Lawrence smirked at him and said, “Ah, Mr. Welsh. So there you are. I have spent the last year of my life searching for you and it appears I walked right pass you.” Henry looked over Lawrence’s shoulder and saw a crew of ten other men waiting for him. “I must say, you look terrible!”

He bowed his head and kicked a rock, “My daughter has been in a coma for the last year and they want to let her die.”

Lawrence searched Henry’s face for lies but only found sadness. “It seems as if serving in my family’s army would only do you good; at this point, you are just waiting for death, is that not true?”

He looked up at him and said, “I long for death to take my life so I don’t have to watch my daughter suffer anymore.”

“It’s strange that you say she’s in a coma because a while back, my daughter experienced a similar case such as yours. Frances woke up a month ago and when she woke up she cried out your daughter’s name. Her eyes were filled with tears and she continuously repeated, ‘She’s stuck in the world of unconsciousness forever.’ I asked her what she was talking about and she told me where you were staying so we returned to Scotland. Like you, I would do anything for my child. She told me that Evangeline was in danger here and that I had to bring her back to Knaresborough where she would be safe.” Henry stared at Lawrence and for the first time in his life, he liked Lawrence.

“I need to get my daughter out of here. I heard them talking the other day and they’ve been trying to get me to leave the house so that they may have the opportunity to put her to sleep for good.”

Lawrence walked past Henry and opened the door. “I do not like you, Henry, and your daughter has given me a hard time. The only reason I am doing this is because my daughter asked me to. She wants her sister home.” Lawrence followed Henry up the stairs to Evangeline’s bedroom. He looked at her and noticed the tube that was down her throat, "Doctors think very much alike, huh? They did this to Frances as well when she was asleep."

The men lifted Evangeline off the bed and carefully carried her down the stairs. Outside of the house waited his crew. They placed Evangeline on the back of a carriage along with some of her belongings and more sugar water to help her survive.

They loaded onto Lawrence's ship and set sail before the sun set. Henry remained at Evangeline's side the entire time they were on the ship. The ship ride was long and bumpy. The tides were very big and they came across a terrible thunderstorm. What should have been a three day ship ride ended up taking five days on account of the terrible weather.

The ship docked at sunset and by then water had calmed down and no waves were in sight for miles. They placed Evangeline onto a stretcher and onto a carriage as they brought her back to Lawrence's house. When they arrived, Frances waited on the front steps of the house.

"Evangeline!" She screamed her name and ran up to her. "She can't wake up; she's trapped in a world between."

Henry looked up into Frances' brown eyes and asked, "What do you mean, she's trapped?"

The men continued to carry her into the house as Henry and Frances fell behind to talk. "When we fought the battle to save their world, the evil witch stabbed Evangeline in the chest…"

Henry interrupted her and whispered, "That explains the bleeding…"

Frances nodded her head and continued, "In Somnia Viveret, she was gifted with powers and therefore she didn't die from her wound. Instead, if she did wake up she would have died due to her wound. Therefore she is living in Somnia Viveret because there, she still has a life to live. Here she would just become buried in the ground."

They walked into the house together and Henry tried to play it out in his head for it to make sense. "If we let her die, would she die in their world?"

Frances stared at the stretcher as the men carried it into one of the guest bedrooms. "Then it will be as if she never existed."

The men placed Evangeline onto the bed and had Dr. Baker slowly pour a sugar water concoction down her throat through the tube that the previous doctor had used. "She's in good hands with us, Mr. Welsh. We would never try to take her life away from her. She is part of Knaresborough and we respect one's family." Dr. Baker left Henry and Frances in the room to talk.

"What do you suggest I do?"

"Just keep her breathing and she will live her life in the fairy land."

He ran his finger over her tiny wrist and said, "Won't her body fail her?"

She shook her head and said, "No, Dr. Baker is very good at what she does."

There was a soft knock on the door and Frances walked towards it and opened it.

"Hello, Mr. Welsh."

Henry walked closer and shook his hand firmly, "Mathias! Where have you been off to this past year?"

"Lawrence left me in Rome where I helped construct different models of your steamship. As soon as I earned enough money, I traveled back to Knaresborough to find Evangeline. When I arrived, she was gone so I went to your house and you were gone, too. I went to the docks and the ship was also gone. I worked for Lawrence again as he promised me that I would see her again and then I fell into this deep sleep and there she was, beautiful as ever."

Henry narrowed his eyes and said, "Was everyone dreaming besides me?"

Mathias giggled a sad laugh, "It was an extraordinary world but when I was murdered, I woke up. I tried to fall back asleep because I knew that she was in danger but I couldn't. I died in that world just like she died in ours." Mathias glanced over Henry's shoulder and saw her lying on the bed. "May I see my wife?" Henry moved out of the way as Mathias walked towards her.

He stood over her body and stared at her with sad eyes. He fell to his knees and held her hand against his cheek. Tears began to stream down his cheek as he kissed her hand. He whispered, "I will never love another like I loved you. I step out onto the streets and only see darkness. When you were at my side, the world lit up like a million stars in a dark night's sky."

Frances leaned against the wall as she listened to Mathias speaking to his wife. She knew it was an invasion of privacy and that she should probably leave but Mathias had asked her to stay and witness the love that she had tried to separate years ago.

Mathias lay down beside Evangeline and stroked her long red hair. "Always remember that I will never stop loving you. Sweet dreams, Evangeline."

What would you do if you couldn't wake up?

Epilogue

Dear Journal,

A year has passed since we killed the evil queen and it feels like it has been an eternity. I understand now what Damian meant about the time difference between Somnia Viveret and my previous world. If four years passed in my previous world and only three weeks had passed here, then they have lived seventy years of their lives whereas I have only lived one year. After the battle was over, the people crowned me as their queen due to the fact that I was married to the prince. It only made sense at the time. As much as I have enjoyed living in this world, I have missed life on earth. I lived a hard life there but I worked hard to be where I was and to see it all go to waste like it did is such a shame. Sometimes when I go to sleep at night, I try to sleep in as long as I can in hope of waking up at home in my bed next to my husband. There have been multiple times where I thought that I felt his touch on my arm or upon my soft lips. Some days, I blame myself for murdering him in this world and other days, I thank myself. I blame myself because I have to live my life without him. I thank myself because he was able to live a normal life. I cannot image how terrible my body must look in their world.

All the creatures turned back into their human form after Frances slit Sahara's throat. It was interesting to see them as their normal selves but I also miss them as creatures. I dug Bonzi out from underneath the collapsed palace. He, too, changed back into his human form. He was so young, it saddened me that the evil witch murdered him. His eyes were blue as the sky, short honey brown hair, and such a delicate baby face. He was so full of life and easy to fall in love with. I shed tears for him on his funeral day.

Some days, I wandered off from the palace so I may take adventures of my own and paint pictures of memories that I had long before. I am sitting on top of the mountain where Damian first showed me his pendant. Someone will find my journal back in my previous life and they will think that I was mad. Then they will go to my room and see that I am still in a deep sleep. I am waiting for the day that someone lets me die. I feel as if my life is set on pause and I'm waiting for someone to turn it off. People will say, "There goes the broken-hearted queen." Therefore if anyone is reading my journal right now, please kill me.

Sincerely,
Queen Evangeline

About the Author

Dorothea Sawatzky is a freelance writer and a poet who is pursuing her career in English Literature. She was born in Paraguay and immigrated to Winnipeg, Manitoba, at the age six and fell in love with English Literature. She wrote short stories, poems, and her first novella *Lily Of The Valley* and also *Canvas of Dreams*.

"There are reasons for everything in life;
to write is to create a world that is worth living in."